“Read this book i[illegible] by former *GQ* edit[illegible] with the spawn of the global financial elite, we're going to assume that the partying happened, the drug-dealing arrest did not, and the casual sex with wanton rich girls was absolutely 100 percent, down-to-the-last-detail true.”

—*GQ*

“*Down the Shore* is a look at how we screw up, try to redeem ourselves, and inevitably screw up again. . . . For a debut novelist, Parish shows a knack for balancing things, pacing his story, and painting a picture that makes *Down the Shore* one of the year's best debut novels, as well as the type of book that, based on that cover alone, just calls out to be read during the summer.”

—Jason Diamond, *Flavorwire*

“Compelling . . . Parish deftly lets the issues of identity, culpability, and class ripple around his characters. . . . Invigorating . . . *Down the Shore* reads like a long, fast rolling wave, expertly and purposefully ridden right to its gentle, subsiding end.”

—*New Jersey Monthly*

“A stunning debut . . . A fast-paced novel . . . A beautifully layered, beautifully written work . . . Scene after scene, expositions create complex characters and capture the details of the excess of the years right after the turn of this century while also carrying out timeless and compelling themes of friendship, family, and self-discovery. . . . As I was reading, I couldn't help but compare this novel to classic coming-of-age books like *A Separate Peace* (1959) and *The Outsiders* (1967), undoubtedly still on the reading list at schools like Lawrenceville. *Down the Shore* is awash in all the literary qualities of those classics, but captures contemporary culture, making those great works seem dusty and quaint. Parish deftly shows the wonders of the big, wide world of opportunity in which today's privileged young adults live—but also the challenges of having too much too soon, before you have time to know who you really are.”

—*Fort Worth Star-Telegram*

"Tom, a Jersey Shore boy who derailed his scholarship to the Ivy League with a drug bust, and Clare, the son of a very wealthy but disgraced financier, become friends and enroll at St. Andrews University in Scotland. Tom has both brains and ambition but the two fall in with a crowd so wild it could sink anyone's future. Can he save himself twice?"

—*New York Daily News*

"Recalls summer in all its glory . . . [Parish's] knack for imagery results in a compelling debut as memorable as the bygone summer excursions its title recalls."

—Departures.com

"Few novels have shown us inside the lives of disgraced financial titans as brilliantly as *Down the Shore* does. Stan Parish's mesmerizing novel belongs in the grand tradition of the outsider who makes himself indispensable to the ruling class, learns all their secrets, and then passes himself off as one of them—as if Patricia Highsmith's Ripley had a son he left behind in New Jersey."

—Alexander Chee, author of *Edinburgh*

"Mr. Parish's deft prose and irresistible characters lead us down a path between the American Dream and its waking nightmare."

—MRPorter.com

"*Down the Shore* is both a classic campus novel and an entirely fresh, fast-paced story of modern wealth and excess. I couldn't put it down."

—Cristina Alger, author of *The Darlings*

"Written by a *GQ* alum, this book has a little bit of everything. Prep schools, status, surfing, outrageous parties, sex, drugs, and other aspects of the privileged life make for a hell of a tale that's part *The Wolf of Wall Street*, part *The OC*."

—Brash.com

"This smoothly written coming-of-age debut by former *GQ* editor Parish is filled with dynamic but flawed young characters. . . . Parish shows promise as a storyteller, moving the plot along at a good clip."

—*Publishers Weekly*

"An energized, ambitious tale of youthful excess and desire, studded with secrets and deceptions."

—Michael Hainey, author of *After Visiting Friends*

"The partying is intense in this first novel, a look at America's bright young things under a cloud or two." —*Kirkus Reviews*

"It is the exceptional coming-of-age novel that shows us the truth not only about its hero's maturation, but about the singular age into which he is maturing. *Down the Shore* is an intimate portrait of a young man, and a sweeping story of the daunting age of global finance. Stan Parish's debut is raw, elegant, incisive, and above all, wise."

—Matthew Sharpe, author of *You Were Wrong* and *Jamestown*

"A globe-trotting, cocaine- and alcohol-saturated debut novel about wealth, excess, debauchery, and the dream of living the good life. . . . Ambitious . . . For fans of coming-of-age novels." —*Library Journal*

"In *Down the Shore*, Stan Parish has written a fast-paced tale of drugs, crime, and surfing, which also manages to be a tender and perceptive novel about class, family, and the tension between ambition and honor."

—Alexander Maksik, author of *You Deserve Nothing* and *A Marker to Measure Drift*

PENGUIN BOOKS

DOWN THE SHORE

Stan Parish was born in Texas and grew up in California and New Jersey. His writing has appeared in *GQ, Esquire, Departures, New Jersey Monthly,* the *New York Times,* and the *New York Times Magazine.* He lives in New Jersey and New York.

DOWN THE SHORE

A NOVEL

STAN PARISH

PENGUIN BOOKS

PENGUIN BOOKS
Published by the Penguin Group
Penguin Group (USA) LLC
375 Hudson Street
New York, New York 10014

USA | Canada | UK | Ireland | Australia | New Zealand | India | South Africa | China
penguin.com
A Penguin Random House Company

First published in the United States of America by Viking Penguin,
a member of Penguin Group (USA) LLC, 2014
Published in Penguin Books 2015

THE LIBRARY OF CONGRESS HAS CATALOGED THE HARDCOVER EDITION AS FOLLOWS
Parish, Stan.
Down the shore : a novel / Stan Parish.
p. cm.
ISBN 978-0-670-01642-6 (hc.)
ISBN 978-0-14-312733-8 (pbk.)
1. Male college students—Fiction. 2. Ambition—Fiction. 3. New Jersey—Fiction.
4. Scotland—Fiction. 5. Psychological fiction. I. Title.
PS3616.A74314D69 2014
813'.6—dc23 2013047844

Printed in the United States of America
1 3 5 7 9 10 8 6 4 2

For Herman Stanley Parish III and
Rosemary Jacqueline Cilenti Parish

PART I

2003

The birthday girl kicked off her heels and boosted herself onto a barstool to propose a toast. Courtney swayed as she stood up, digging her toes into the cracked vinyl of the cushion, bare arms outstretched. There was no fear in her expression once she'd found her balance—four years of extracurricular opera had taught her how to hold a crowd. Her dress, a loose white sheath, was opalescent in the thin light from the neon signs. It was just after 2:00 a.m. on Memorial Day, the Monday of a three-day weekend. The bar's AC was either dead or overpowered by a cloud of body heat, and the air inside the long room felt like something you could swim through. I peeled off the top half of my tux as Courtney raised her glass and called for silence. She reminded us that we had nothing to do today, tomorrow, whatever this was. A cheer went up from the crowd, and I whistled through my teeth even though I had the sense, with exams looming, that we were all on borrowed time.

The bar was packed with high school kids in formal wear, most of us from the Lawrenceville School in New Jersey, sixty miles southwest of Manhattan. Courtney's official eighteenth birthday party, dry and closely chaperoned, had been thrown by her parents at the Plaza Hotel. This was the after party: Kildare's Irish Pub, six blocks south of the Plaza, and not particular about the age of its patrons. We looked less young all dressed up, but we did not look old enough. A knot of regulars had holed up by the bar's blacked-out front window, nursing Harp and Cutty Sark, keeping to themselves.

I was waiting on an ice water, thinking through the drive back to New Jersey, when I saw a girl sitting alone at a table by a blinking arcade game. She was sketching in a notebook with a pencil, her eyes flitting from the page to the crowd. She discovered something unpleasant in her mouth just then—a strand of hair, a fleck of loose tobacco—and spent the next few seconds trying to extract it, pinching the tip of her tongue, going slightly cross-eyed as she stared down at her fingertips, spitting as gently and politely as she could. She looked like a courtesy invite who had run out of conversation, but that probably had more to do with my feelings than any signals she was giving off. She swept her brown hair back to reveal an earring in her right ear, something long and delicate and gold, but nothing in her left. I left my water on the bar and walked toward her. She saw me coming and snapped her notebook shut.

"Hi," I said.

A tight smile, nothing else.

"What were you drawing?"

"Boys in jackets."

"You don't go to Lawrenceville."

"No," she said. "I don't."

She was fingering the elastic strap that held her notebook closed, anxious to get back to work. Up close, her earring looked like wind chimes.

"Did you lose the other one?" I asked, tapping my earlobe.

"Yeah," she said. "Three years ago."

"How do you know the birthday girl?"

"I'm Courtney's cousin."

"I'm in her class. At Lawrenceville. Can I get you a drink?"

"I'm fine," she said, "but thank you."

"Where do you go to school?"

"Far away."

"I'm Tom."

We shook hands, awkwardly. She didn't give her name, but she did turn my hand over as I was about to take it back.

"You have nice hands," she said, as if considering them for her sketch. She caught herself then, realizing she had given me an in, but she was saved by some commotion from across the room. I turned to find a crush of people at the men's room door.

"What's that?" I asked.

"I don't know," she said, pulling her hair back into a ponytail, a hair tie between her teeth. "You'll have to go see."

I nodded and smiled, dismissed. But just before I'd turned completely, she looked up from her book and smiled back, thanking me, I guessed, for leaving right on cue.

By the time I shouldered through the crowd, two boys were struggling through the narrow door, propping up a girl who had been sick before she passed out in the stall. A freshman from some other boarding school, she had been throwing herself at someone from my class at Lawrenceville all night. I had seen her in the men's room at the Plaza, where a plastic surgeon's son was holding court with a film canister of Molly, powdered and ostensibly pure Ecstasy, shipped in from Oahu, which he was doling out with the wet end of his little finger. I saw the girl again, later, standing on the dance floor, running her bottom lip between her teeth so that it seemed to come out fuller every time. Then she was making out with my classmate in a back corner of Kildare's, and now she was too far gone to stand.

A bartender hopped the bar. He hoisted the girl into his arms, shaking his head at her, at all of us. His forearms were wiry under blurred tattoos as she squirmed against him.

"She with you?" the bartender asked one of the boys, who shook his head. "Who's she with?" he called out over the heads of the people who were inching backward, distancing themselves.

The answer to his question was standing by the bar: Clare Savage, tall, lean, nationally ranked in squash, and almost as blond as the very blond girl. A senior at Lawrenceville, like me. Our relationship had been mostly transactional; he smoked more pot than you might think to look at him, and I had been his regular supplier. Clare and I had both been day students at Lawrenceville, but there was a rumor that he had just become a boarder and moved into a dorm, which was unheard of this late in the year. I knew more about his father, a famous money manager, than I did about Clare, who was inching backward now, along with everyone else.

"She's with him," I said, pointing. "Clare, give this guy a hand?"

"Yeah, sure," Clare said, looking anything but sure as he took stock of all the eyes trained on him.

"She your date?" the bartender asked.

"I guess so," Clare said.

"Good for you."

He dumped the girl on Clare, who held out his arms to catch her, and eased her onto her feet with an arm around her back.

"What should I do with her?" Clare asked.

"Get her the fuck out of my bar, for starters."

The bartender opened the door and jerked his head toward the traffic on Third Avenue. Clare stared at him in disbelief, unused to taking orders from the help. As the bartender turned his back, I recalled my mother telling me to look out for a particularly wasted woman at a party we were catering to make sure that whoever took her home seemed like a Good Samaritan and not a sex offender. I had wanted to stick Clare with this mess, but I had overstepped, which made the girl my problem too. Clare was trying to coax and carry her through the door when I came up behind him.

"Here," I said, "put your arm under hers, like this. I've got her. Ready?"

She was limp but light. We eased her down onto the warm sidewalk outside and propped her up against Kildare's. Her eyes fell open and she seemed to register Clare's face before she slipped away again.

"She'll be fine," I said. "Does she live in the city?"

"She lives in Jersey. In Far Hills, I think. Fuck, I barely know this girl. How did she get like this?"

"Molly," I said.

"Molly McPherson?"

"The other Molly. Molly from Hawaii."

"Oh, right," Clare said. "Jesus. What do we do now?"

"Just wait here. My car's down the street. Far Hills is pretty close."

"Are you sure?"

"I'm sure. Stay put."

I wasn't sure. I checked my watch as I drove west on Forty-third Street and wondered if I should forget this, hit the road, and tell Clare when I saw him back at school that something had come up. It was almost 3:00 a.m., and I had a strong urge to take the Holland Tunnel and fly over the marshland on the southbound turnpike with the wind beating through my open windows. I kept looking at my hands on the steering wheel, thinking about what the girl in Kildare's had said. The last knuckle on my right ring finger was bent and fat, the result of a wipeout on a head-high wave, a collision with a sandbar. My hands had always looked weak to me. I hit a yellow light on Lexington, which made for an easy left in the direction of the bar.

Clare was squatting next to his new friend when I pulled up to the curb. He gave me a wave and then turned his attention to the girl, who had come to again while I was gone. My hazard lights turned her pale skin orange as Clare helped her into the backseat of my Explorer where she stretched out and closed her eyes. He had rescued her white leather clutch somehow, and we found her address on the New Jersey learner's permit folded up inside. Her full name was Paige Alexandra Baldwin; she lived in Ridgewood, not Far Hills. I drove south and took Forty-second to the West Side.

"Thanks for doing this," Clare said. "I'd be fucked if you had taken off."

That was generous, and I wondered why he wasn't pissed at me for calling him out back at the bar. He seemed uncomfortable and unsure of himself in a way I hadn't seen at Lawrenceville. Something else was on his mind. We were in the Lincoln Tunnel, the reflections of the overhead lights sliding rhythmically across the finish of the hood, when Clare reclined his seat a few degrees and tossed his cummerbund onto the dashboard. Make yourself at home, I thought. He was staring up at the tile ceiling, his eyes skipping slightly in their sockets, fixing on each light for a split second as it passed.

"How do you know her?" I asked.

"I don't. I wasn't kidding about that. She walked up to me at the Plaza and asked me for a cigarette."

No approach required. Good for him.

We stopped for gas outside Fort Lee. In the Speedy Mart, I took a map off a rack and spread it out to find her street. Clare was leaning on the counter, his black and white clothes framed by boxes of candy, packs of cigarettes, rolls of scratch-off Lotto tickets, his blond hair already bleached by the sun. He had draped his jacket over Paige, and I could see now that he was all long muscle after years of pulling in sails hand over hand and countless hours on the squash court. A body built in recreation. The cashier was ringing up the gas and a bag of Skittles that Clare had plucked from the candy rack. I was trying to remember who had told me that a sweet tooth is a sign of weakness.

"You smoke, right?" he called to me. "Camel Lights?"

I nodded.

"And a carton of Camel Lights, please," he said to the cashier.

The cashier scrutinized his license, and Clare tossed me the carton, which I caught with the open map.

"Thanks," I said. "You didn't have to do that. Here's her street. I'm not that good with maps."

Clare tore into the Skittles with his teeth and tipped the bag into his mouth, chewing slowly as he scanned the tangle of rivers and roads. He looked up at me and nodded to say that he could get us there.

As we pulled out of the gas station, I thought back to the last time Clare and I had occupied the front seat of a car. Most of the people I sold to at Lawrenceville seemed to get off on the ritual buys, the overly clandestine meetings, the inane questions about quality and provenance. And most of them understood that waiting was part of the game. But then one day I showed up an hour late to meet Clare, who stared straight ahead when I collapsed into the passenger seat of his black Saab, parked behind the pizza joint across the street from campus. I apologized and asked how he was doing.

"What took so long?" he said.

I had been glancing at my watch so often that I could have answered with the precision of a ship's log: eleven minutes on the road from Lawrenceville to the brick blocks of low-income housing behind Mercer Mall once I realized that I was a quarter ounce short. This was in the two days between winter trimester finals and

Christmas break, when demand always outstripped supply. I spent four minutes ringing the buzzer of number 147 before the door buzzed back and I shot across the living room, past Eduardo's grandmother, installed like a gargoyle at one end of the sofa, a bath towel draped over her knees as a blanket. Fourteen minutes up in Eduardo's room after he held up an Xbox controller in greeting and insisted that I play some Grand Theft Auto III with him, because I only called him in emergencies and he knew that I was scrambling. Twenty minutes back to campus, the traffic thickening as cars coursed out of the office parks that lined Route 1. I had been shuttling between two worlds, which takes time. I let Clare's question hang between us, overcharged him, and went home.

A winding county road ran past darkened strip malls and sprawling public schools once we were off the highway. Clare was staring out at nothing, giving me occasional directions in a voice that sounded either bored or tired.

"You're not worried about this?" I asked him. "You don't think they'll be pissed?"

Clare shook his head. He was the clean-cut kid you'd want to bring your daughter home if she got sick in the city. There was nothing for him to be afraid of. I turned to look at Paige, hoping for additional assurances, but Paige had left the building.

"Take the next left," Clare said. "No, wait, it's this one. Turn here."

A new development, with massive houses stacked on both sides of an unlined street. The first one we passed looked like an Italian villa with adolescent trees scattered across the lawn. The granite curbs that lined the road were high and clean.

"What should we tell these people?" I asked.

"I don't know," Clare said. "We can't leave her on the lawn, though. This is it. This one on the right."

The house had a soaring brick façade. I stepped out of the car while Clare tucked in his shirt and smoothed his hair. His movements were sharper now, but he seemed relaxed and purposeful as he rolled his sleeves back down his forearms and dug through his pockets for a pair of silver cuff links. I stared up at the floodlights trained on us as we walked the flagstone path to the front door. Gnats formed a haze around the fixtures, swarming, crashing into the glass. Clare rang the bell.

A flash of light from an upstairs window, and then a long pause broken by a deadbolt's heavy click, and the scream of new hinges as the door swung open. The man behind it wore pleated suit pants, a wrinkled undershirt, and salt-stained boat shoes that seemed to be on the verge of exploding as the weight of his body strained the stitching and squashed the rubber soles against the marble floor. He looked wide awake, ready to take on both of us, if that was what it came to. This was exactly what I had been afraid of.

"Can I help you?" he asked, one hand on the doorknob, the other half clenched at his side.

"Hi, Mr. Baldwin," Clare said. "Clare Savage. Sorry to wake you up like this, but Paige got a little sick at this thing in the city and we wanted to make sure she got home."

"It's Mr. Quinn, actually. I'm her stepdad." Then: "Clare Savage? Are you Michael's son?"

There was a ripple in Clare's clothes as his entire body tensed. The shock of Mr. Quinn's recognition reminded me of the way lightning was described in my sixth-grade science textbook: a bright upstroke that changes the temperature around it.

"Tom Alison," I said, offering my hand, which Mr. Quinn shook without looking at me.

"Where's Paige?" he asked, coming back into himself, remembering his duties as a guardian. "In the car?"

"In the back," I said. "Asleep."

"You drove?"

"Yes, sir."

"Well, at least you made it. Let's get her inside."

I hung back as we headed for my car, trying to get Clare's attention and to understand why this man was interested in anything besides his semiconscious stepdaughter. Mr. Quinn took Paige in his arms and crossed the lawn with her head against his chest, one high-heeled shoe swinging from her foot by the strap across her toes. Paige stirred and her stepfather whispered something to her as he turned and paused for me to get the door. He raised a finger on the hand under her knees, and mouthed "wait here" before he climbed the stairs.

"Clare," I said, when Mr. Quinn was out of earshot.

Clare was watching the place where he had disappeared.

"Hey, do you two know each other?"

"Do you know who he is?" Clare asked.

"He's her stepdad. He said that."

"We have to leave."

Clare took a step toward the door, just as Mr. Quinn appeared on the landing above us.

"I have beds for you two," he said, as he descended. "I appreciate you bringing her home, but I don't want you back on the road tonight. Sleep it off, take off in the morning. Can I get you some water?"

I looked at Clare, whose eyes were flitting between my face and the door as if he were contemplating a twenty-five-yard dash for the car.

"I'm fine," I said.

"OK," Mr. Quinn said, as he shot the deadbolt back into place. "Follow me."

I glanced over my shoulder to make sure Clare was still with us as we started up the stairs. Our room for the evening was halfway down the hall. Mr. Quinn waved us inside.

"You boys need anything else?"

"Thanks," I said. "We're good."

He said goodnight and closed the door. There were two beds against the far wall, both covered in madras pillows. Clare sat down on a window seat as if someone had kicked out his knees.

"Clare, what the fuck is going on?"

Clare stood up and cased the room, looking for a way out. It was a sheer drop from all the windows, and what might have been another exit led only to an empty closet. There was a crisp knock on the thinnest panel of the door.

"Come in," I said.

Mr. Quinn did not come in. He stood in the hall, and shook a big watch down his wrist.

"Let's talk," he said to Clare.

Clare followed him down the hallway and the stairs. Suddenly I could hear them again, and I realized that they were on the deck behind the house, just below the guest room. I slid the window open very gently so that the only thing between us was a screen. Clare sat on the edge of a lounge chair facing the yard, Mr. Quinn in a rocker beside him.

"He left Lehman way before I did," Mr. Quinn was saying. "We know a lot of the same people, which is how I heard."

Clare said nothing. Mr. Quinn dug into his pocket, produced a soft pack of Marlboro Lights, and shook one loose. He offered it to Clare, who shook his head.

"You doing OK?" he asked, his teeth clamped down on the filter. "You're not going to get sick on me, right?"

"I'm fine," Clare said.

"Look, I'm sorry for what your family's going through. I wasn't trying to embarrass you. You look a hell of a lot like your dad."

"I know," Clare said.

A door opened down the hall, and I planted my ass on the bed, pretending to untie my shoe. Someone took the stairs very slowly, listening, assessing. I went back to the window in time to hear Mr. Quinn say: "Who knows how these things start. It's funny, we used to give him shit about that French passport he got through your mom. I'm sure he's having the last laugh, wherever he is. So where are you—"

A door opened behind them, and Mr. Quinn flicked his cigarette into the yard as Paige's mother stepped onto the deck, cinching her robe around her body.

"Alan, who's in the guest room? Do you know what time it is? What the hell is going on?"

"Go back to bed," Mr. Quinn said. "Everything's fine. You remember Clare Savage, Michael's son. Paige got sick in New York and he brought her home. Him and his friend. They're spending the night."

Mrs. Baldwin stared at Clare in naked shock, and then looked back at her husband.

"It's OK," Mr. Quinn said to her. "We're talking. I'll be up soon."

"Is Paige all right? What happened?"

"She got a little carried away. She's fine. She told me she left without saying her good-byes when I put her to bed. Go back to sleep, I'll be right up."

"Sorry, hi," Mrs. Baldwin said to Clare, offering her hand. "Nice to see you. Thank you for bringing Paige home." She turned back to her husband. "It's four o'clock in the morning," she said, and walked away.

"She's a handful," Mr. Quinn said, lighting another cigarette.

"Paige, not Lydia. She's a sweetheart when she wants to be, but you have to watch her every minute. How do you two know each other?"

"We don't," Clare said. "I just met her tonight."

"Hell of a first date. You're a senior, right? Following your dad to Yale?"

"I was on the wait list, but he managed some of their endowment. That probably won't help."

Mr. Quinn took a long breath.

"You'll be fine, OK? You're what, seventeen? Eighteen? I know this looks like the end of everything, but it's not. Not even for your dad. Look, I've got a car coming in two hours, but tell Michael I say hello if you talk to him."

"I will," Clare said, as Mr. Quinn stood up.

I kicked off my shoes and pulled my shirt over my head while someone shut the door to the deck. When Clare came in, he stood in the middle of the room in the darkness before he undressed. I was in bed by then, facing the wall, feigning sleep. Clare shut the window and pulled back the sheets. They were soft and clean, and I imagined I'd have all kinds of pleasant dreams between them, but nothing came after I drifted off.

It was bright as hell when I woke up, a hot rectangle of sunlight draped over my legs. Clare was sitting on the bed across from mine, already dressed.

"Hey," he said. "You're up."

I wondered how long he'd been awake, trapped up here in the air-conditioning, afraid to show his face downstairs. The front door slammed, an engine started in the driveway. Clare walked to the window and stared out at the yard while I stepped into my pants and pulled on my jacket. This was the most mileage I'd ever gotten out of a tuxedo rental. Clare's tux looked like something he owned.

Judging by the boxes and the sparseness of the built-in bookshelves, the Quinn-Baldwin family hadn't lived here long. We walked softly on the ground floor, through the entryway and empty dining room, unsure what to expect. I had worked parties at dozens of new houses like this one with grandiose exteriors borrowed from another period and layouts with no imagination brought to bear, just a series of boxes to move through. A breakfast spread was laid out on the marble island in the kitchen. Between a plate of pastries and a bowl of sliced fruit was a note from Mrs. Baldwin informing us that she was at the gym. The coffee she had made was bitter, burnt.

"Let's go before they get back," Clare said.

"Relax," I said. "I'm starving."

I wondered if Mrs. Baldwin had dragged Paige to the gym as punishment, which is what my mother would have done. Clare kept an eye on the front door and the foot of the stairs while I scarfed down some honeydew balls and half a corn muffin.

"Ready?" he asked as I brushed crumbs off my lapels.

We cut across the lawn, making for my car. The electronic lock chirped over the distant whine of a mower.

"So how long before you call her?" I asked as I backed down the driveway.

"Ha ha."

"Look," I said, punching the cigarette lighter into the dash and smacking a fresh pack of Camel Lights against my hand. "Even her stepdad says she's a full-time job. Sometimes the fucking you're getting ain't worth the fucking you're getting, as the saying goes."

"I've never heard that before," Clare said, laughing.

I'd never said that before; it was something that my mother's produce supplier used to say about sleeping with his ex-wife.

"So you heard us talking," Clare said.

"The window was open."

"The window was open, or you opened the window?"

"The window was open," I said. "Take it easy. You had no idea who her stepdad was?"

Clare shook his head and said: "Small world."

No, I thought, it's not. But after four years at Lawrenceville, I was used to everybody in this circle knowing everybody else.

"Are you on campus for the weekend?" I asked. "I heard you're a boarder now."

"I switched over a week ago. That's when my parents left. They gave me Harrison's room like two hours after they expelled him. The deans don't really know what to do with me."

The new music building was named for Clare's mother; I was pretty sure the deans would figure something out, but I didn't know what to do with him either. I had written him off after our Christmas break encounter, and now we were rolling through the suburbs of New Jersey on a sunny Monday morning with nowhere to be. Tuesday was our senior skip day, twenty-four hours of school-sanctioned rebellion. I searched for some tactful way to ask Clare how his father had gone from a man listed under "Angels" in Princeton symphony programs to a man on the run. Did Clare try to reconcile those versions of his father, or did this mess make him realize that he didn't really know the man at all? We probably had that in common. I didn't know three things about my dad.

My mother had a catering company in downtown Princeton. The first floor of our house held a commercial kitchen and a market that sold breakfast and coffee and ready-made meals. One night in January, a woman came in, bought dinner, and then asked for our trash, the empty packaging from the ingredients, to leave on the counter of her kitchen as if she had made the meal herself. She offered to pay for it. My mother told her that the garbage was out at the curb, but she was welcome to dig through it at no extra charge. I had been studying in a corner of the kitchen, which is what I had planned to do before Clare and I got sidetracked. My mother had a hard-ass catering captain she brought in for big jobs, and watching Clare drum his fingers on my dashboard reminded me of a line he used on lazy staff. "You know what you look like?" he would say, walking up on someone's third cigarette break. "You look like my money just standing around." It was actually the client's money, but people felt like they owed him something when they heard that, which got them back to work. You know what you look like? I thought, glancing sideways at Clare. You look like my AP econ score going down. Clare was staring out the window at a man and a boy who were pushing a mower into the bed of a dirty red pickup, a striped and shining lawn behind them. The lighter popped out of the dash and I passed it to Clare, who lit his cigarette and dug his buzzing phone out of his pocket. I glanced at the caller ID, which read: UNKNOWN. His father calling from some undisclosed location to check in?

"Hello? Yeah, hang on. He's right here. It's for you," Clare said, handing me the phone.

"What?"

"Some girl," he mouthed.

"This is Tom."

"Hi. It's Kelsey. We met last night before you ran out. I was drawing."

"Right," I said, trying to sound calm. "I remember you."

"Good thing you two are still together. Everyone had this nonworking number for you, an old pager or something. Did that girl get home safe?"

"She did," I said.

"Where are you now?"

"New Jersey, 287 South." We were passing signs for 202 and 206, roads that led back to Lawrenceville and Princeton.

"I wanted to invite you to a party. It's in Spring Lake, down the shore."

"I know Spring Lake."

"You do? It's the house on Howell and Ocean. You should come."

"Sure," I said. "Whose party is it?"

"This family I grew up with. It's less dressy than last night. Why don't you call me when you're closer."

"Who was that?" Clare asked as I hung up.

"This girl I met last night. There's a party in Spring Lake."

"Are we going?"

"If you're up for it. If not, I can drop you at the train."

"It's not a Lawrenceville thing, is it?"

I shook my head, and wondered if people at school had already heard about his dad, if I was the last to know. Clare seemed happy to steer clear of Lawrenceville, which was lucky for him because there was no train, and we were going to this party whether he wanted to or not. I had been thinking about Kelsey since I woke up, Monday-morning-quarterbacking our exchange in Kildare's. That she had managed to reach me seemed like a sign from whatever god was responsible for these things. Maybe our first interaction would become a joke between us as we lived out the rest of our lives together—the night she blew me off in New York.

"I need something else to wear," Clare said, sitting up, suddenly alert. "You have clothes with you, right?"

"Just these," I said.

"Find a store. We can't show up like this."

Just before we hit the parkway, I saw a sign for a strip mall that held a Ross Dress for Less, an Acme grocery store, and a restaurant called Cluck-U Chicken. Clare, who I had never known to smoke, lit another cigarette as we stepped into the thick heat radiating from the parking lot.

Inside the windowless clothing store, the metal racks and polished floors reflected the fluorescent light while the clothes seemed to take it in like water, saturated with color, heavy on their hangers. Clare was leafing through a rack of jeans.

"What size are you?"

"I don't know," I said, fitting my hands over my hip bones. "Thirty-two?" Clare's waist was smaller, but there were two pairs of size thirty-two jeans that contained some defect that neither of us could see. The coin pockets were flagged with orange "irregular" stickers, and the inside tags and leather patches had been sliced out with a razor blade.

"These work?" Clare asked. "They might be a little long."

"It's fine," I said. "We'll cuff them."

Clare folded the jeans over his arm and headed for a rack of white T-shirts.

"Medium?" he asked, holding up a three-pack.

I saw the basket of shower sandals before Clare did. He went right for it, considering my feet to judge their size and digging for two pairs in flat black. I took an inventory of the outfit in his arms: dark jeans, disposable footwear, T-shirts like blank paper. All new things.

Clare took a pair of aviators off the sunglasses rack and hung them from the collar of his shirt while we stood in line. He shook his head when I tried to give him cash, and passed a credit card to the cashier, who turned it over in her hand and then looked up at him. It was a black American Express, stamped out of titanium. I had read about the card, an invitation-only line of credit with an in-house concierge that could get you Kevin Costner's horse from *Dances with Wolves,* if that was what you wanted. Am Ex offered it to people who charged more than $250,000 a year on personal luxuries. It was baffling to me that his father's credit cards still worked after he had fled the country, that Clare still had access to money the way I had access to clean water. It reinforced my long-held suspicion that there were two very different sets of rules. His family's trouble should have laid them low, but here we were, on credit.

"Let's swing by the grocery story," Clare said, as he signed a screen.

The glass doors of the Acme sensed us, slid apart, and let out a cold breath as we walked inside. The space was small as New Jersey supermarkets go, a place from another era with low ceilings and harsh lights hanging down over the aisles. Clare was on a mission, and I lost him when I stopped to watch the action in a tank full of live lobsters. The store was packed and everyone was party shopping, filling carts with stacks of Solo cups and Firecracker Popsicles and cheap meat for the grill.

I found Clare unloading a basket in the express checkout lane. He counted everything he'd laid on the conveyor belt to make sure that the two sticks of deodorant, two-pack of toothbrushes, travel tube of toothpaste, and bottled water didn't put him over the twelve-item maximum. I hadn't thought of him as someone who obeyed posted limits. Clare swiped his card again and swept his purchases into the bag of clothes.

He tore into the T-shirts as we crossed the parking lot and tossed one to me. We changed in the front seats, and when we had both wrestled into chemically fresh clothes, Clare handed me a toothbrush and stepped out of the car. The sandals he had bought for me were on the dash, but I slipped my black lace-ups onto my bare feet and joined him on my front bumper. We brushed our teeth, spitting gobs of Crest onto the pavement. I had been too preoccupied the night before to notice that Clare and I both wore Rolex Submariners in stainless steel, designed to be used underwater. I imagined Clare picking his out on a whim at a St. Barts duty-free shop. Mine had shown up sometime before my fifteenth birthday. My mother produced it from her purse as she was digging for her wallet after dinner at my favorite restaurant. My birthday was two days away, but we were celebrating early because we had jobs lined up three days out.

"This came for you," she said.

If there had been a card, there wasn't one now. The watch itself, the mirror-polished casing and thick crystal, was heavy, but the bracelet and the clasp felt like something you could snap with your bare hands. The anticipation of loss was the first thing I felt when I slipped it on. It was the most expensive thing I owned by a long shot, a piece of another world. It was used, loose on my wrist, and if it was from my dad, as I assumed, then it was the only thing I had that he had touched. My mother made a crack about whether it was real or not as I snapped the clasp shut. The watch wound itself with the movement of your arm, which meant I never had to take it in for a new battery and have an expert poke around inside. I had a link removed from the bracelet at a jeweler in Quaker Bridge Mall, a place where they wouldn't know the difference between the real thing and a good fraud. A Rolex was like camouflage at Lawrenceville, and it was funny to watch people spot a watch like that and assume things about your life, the way I had just assumed something about Clare's. Who knew why he had $5,000 on his wrist.

Traffic was light on the Garden State Parkway, the twin southbound lanes walled in by trees in full bloom.

"You got in early to Columbia, right?" Clare said.

"Yeah, in December. They changed their mind after I got in trouble."

"They pulled your acceptance over that? Shit, I'm sorry. Where are you headed next year?"

"St. Andrews."

"The prep school? For a postgrad thing?"

"No. The university in Scotland."

"Really?" Clare said, turning in his seat to face me. "Is it hard to get into?"

"Not that hard. They like Americans because we have to pay tuition. The Brits basically go for free."

My mother had a small trust to help with my education, given to her by a man she dated when I was too young to remember, and St. Andrews was half the price of an American school, even after the exchange. When Columbia took back its offer of admission, the head of college counseling at Lawrenceville told me that I had two choices: a year off or a year in Scotland. Every American university asked you to check one box if you had been subject to serious disciplinary action, and another if you had ever been arrested or convicted of a crime. Check, check. Those questions were replaced on the St. Andrews application by a yes-or-no declaration asking whether you could pay in full.

"So what's the application deadline?" Clare asked.

"It's rolling. So whenever, until they fill the slots. I got in two months ago."

Clare's phone was ringing again.

"Hello? Yeah, hang on. It's for you again," he said.

"Hi, Kelsey."

"Did you blow me off? I thought you'd be here by now."

"We had to make a stop. We're close."

"It's 567 Ocean Avenue, right on the water. Ask for me. I'll be out back. Drive safe."

I knew the house on Howell and Ocean, which sat across from my favorite surf break in Spring Lake. Like most of the homes on Ocean Avenue, it was a busy mash-up of Dutch colonial and Victorian architecture, accessorized with turrets, balconies, and something that looked like a two-story gazebo attached to the north end. We took a space from a departing Mercedes and crossed a strip of bright green lawn. Someone inside was beating on a drum.

Two girls burst through the door as Clare and I hit the front steps, leaving it open for us as they raced across the grass. The drummer I had heard was perched on a piano bench with a djembe between his knees and his back to a white baby grand piano, the centerpiece of a two-story sun-drenched living room. On the floor at his feet, two kids were trading blues licks on acoustic guitars. This was clearly someone's summer home, but it had none of the seaside kitsch I associated with even the biggest houses in the beach town where we lived when I was younger. Clare and I cut through the kitchen, where someone had arranged empty champagne bottles like bowling pins on a table made of steel and glass.

The door to the back deck swung open and a wave of noise washed in from the yard—hip-hop from a tinny stereo, a splash, a scream. We cut through a tipsy badminton game to the pool deck covered in people who paid us no mind as we walked among them. A well-dressed couple in their fifties were playing beer pong on a patio table with a couple less than half their age, and as we looked around, I realized there were at least a dozen adults here. Parents drinking alongside their underage children was something I had seen only at the poles of the economic spectrum—in the trailer parks of the Pine Barrens and places like this.

We found Kelsey smoking on one of the lounge chairs by the diving board, deep in conversation with an elegant blond woman in a lot of gold. The woman placed a hand on Kelsey's arm and leaned out of her chair to say something *sotto voce,* entering into some confidence with Kelsey, who seemed used to talking to adults like this. She waved to us without taking her eyes off the woman's face, and the woman, realizing that Kelsey had company, kissed her on the cheek and excused herself. Kelsey beckoned to us. She seemed much older than she had in Kildare's.

"Better late than never," she said, as we drew near.

It seemed to get dark all at once. Clare and I were leaning on the railing of a second-story balcony that faced the ocean. Behind us, in a guest bedroom not unlike the one where we had spent the night before, some girls were shooting Polaroid portraits of each other, littering the rug they sat on with their faces. Earlier, someone had handed me a Dixie cup of punch, which I took down like a shot before I heard that it was made with mushrooms.

"Don't freak out," a girl said when she registered my shock. She was wearing a bandana as a shirt. "Just go with it. It's already in you."

Forty minutes later I felt like someone had loosened my joints and rubbed something warm into my skin. I experienced no stark hallucinations, just colorful tracers as people came and went under the halogen lights out on the balcony, as if everyone was losing a little of themselves with every move. The ocean looked like it went on forever, but the ocean always looked that way to me. Clare had suggested that we come up here to get some air. I was lost in my head, trying to decide whether the effects of the punch were waxing or waning. I didn't do a lot of drugs at that point in my life. Down the block, someone was setting off fireworks, shaky little balls of light that looked like dandelions gone to seed once they exploded and began to fade.

"My dad was under investigation for insider trading," Clare said, out of nowhere. "And what they found while they were looking into that was worse. That's why he left. I don't think they're coming back."

"I'm sorry," I said, with questions mushrooming in my mind. I thought: What took so long?

"So, I want—" he said, as a girl came up behind us and threw an arm around his neck.

"I'm so fucked up," she said with a theatrical slur. "Scrape me off the floor. Take me home with you."

I didn't recognize her, but she must have been at Kildare's with us the night before. I wondered who had put her up to it as she ran back into the house. Clare smoothed his shirtfront, annoyed at the interruption.

"I want to go with you," he said. "To school. To Scotland."

I knew what he meant because it felt like we had been through this before. There were layers to the déjà vu—I remembered Clare asking me this, and I remembered it happening again and making a mental note of the repetition, as though this conversation had taken place three times. My mind turned to the pictures of St. Andrews on the school's Web site: majestic buildings perched on cliffs above the water, smiling students walking through the quad with books under their arms, an afternoon pub scene where everyone was leaning in and laughing. I tried to picture the two of us across the ocean, but I couldn't shake those images, so I added us to them. In my mind we were sitting in the pub just behind the people in focus; we were obscured by pillars on the quad; we were standing on a rock overlooking the water, invisible to the camera's eye. There was something comforting about the altered pictures in my head. They contained a familiar face, I realized. I wasn't there alone.

"Is that OK with you?" Clare asked. "If I come?"

The party had been lightly catered all day, but by the time we made our way downstairs, the first floor had been transformed into a food court by a late-night supper. The heat lamps at the carving stations cast an orange glow on the walls, crepes soaked in brandy simmered over blue flames. I tried to read the expressions of the servers, to imagine what was going through their minds. I knew what my mother would say after a gig like this.

The adults said their good-byes a little after 10:00 p.m. I caught a glimpse of the owners as they departed to a standing ovation from the drunk teenagers occupying their home. They were crashing at a nearby bed-and-breakfast, someone said, leaving the kids to their own devices for the night. Something or someone had spooked Clare. He kept glancing over his shoulder as we stood in line for steak sandwiches, repositioning, using me as a screen. The trouble his father was in had changed him and dissolved the unassailable quality I had seen in him at Lawrenceville. I remembered a line from my mom's favorite song by the Band: "And now the heart is filled with gold, as if it was a purse." Maybe that's what money did—filled you up and hardened you. I understood it in the negative now that I could see what was absent in Clare. I was staring at his profile when I realized that the man carving the meat was talking to me.

"You're Diane Alison's son, right?"

"Yeah," I said, blood rising to my cheeks.

"We used to work Princeton reunions together. I'm down in Manasquan now. You don't remember me?"

"No," I said. "Sorry."

"Night off, huh? What can I get you?"

"I'm OK," I said.

"Hey, if your mom needs help this year, tell her to call me. You sure you don't want something?"

"Thanks," I said. "I'm fine."

I found a half-full bottle of Sancerre on the kitchen counter, and tipped half of what was left into my mouth, the wine colder than I expected, like the mouth of a girl coming back to bed after a glass of water. Kelsey had texted Clare earlier to say that she was on the beach with friends. I floated around the house until I found her out on the gazebo-shaped balcony, sharing a cigarette with a boy in a Columbia Football sweatshirt, which stung a little. I stood a few feet from the door, trying to take the temperature of their conversation, shifting right and left so that my reflection in the glass blocked as little of her as possible. I was moving enough that she noticed me, and motioned for me to join them. The boy thanked her for the smoke and slipped inside as I went out.

"You know Spring Lake," she said.

"I surf here sometimes. There, actually. Right across the street."

"But you're not from here."

"I grew up on Long Beach Island."

"I was about to say you remind me of the boys I grew up with, but I guess that makes sense. I'm from Ocean City. My parents live two towns over now, in Avalon. I can't believe this moon."

It was almost full, its light bright enough to read by, the water underneath it glinting like mirror shards. It looked like someone had taken a bat to a disco ball, and I said that before I had a chance to stop myself. Kelsey laughed.

"You have kind of a poetic side, don't you?"

"No," I said, afraid that it would make me seem less serious to her. "I'm just high."

"We should find a place to crash unless you're driving back to Princeton, which I wouldn't advise based on those pupils."

I stared at her, wondering if this was the onset of auditory hallucinations, or if the thing I had been hoping for was now coming to pass.

"You're funny," she said.

"Funny how?"

"All starry-eyed. Are you seeing six of me right now?"

"I'm not that high," I said. "I bet I can find us a room."

We knocked on door after door, encountering disembodied voices that told us to fuck off, that the room was taken. The hall ended in double doors, and I watched Kelsey press her cheek against the wood to listen. She knocked and tried the handle.

"Locked," she said.

I waved her aside and dug out my wallet. With my palm pressed against the seam between the doors, I slid my Lawrenceville ID under the strike plate, feeling for the angled latch. My mother taught me how to pick a lock. There was a sharp snap and the doors broke open. We slipped inside and Kelsey shut us in while I felt along the wall until I found the lights.

It was the master bedroom, complete with a California king and a wall of windows obscured by heavy blinds. I ran my hand along the varnished surface of a long, low dresser, stopping at a brass ashtray filled with gold cuff links and foreign coins and collar stays. I had worried about leaving everything exactly as we found it, but the solidity and sparseness of the room made me think of a line from the Gettysburg Address, something about our poor power to add or detract. I wondered what the owner had done to acquire all this weight and space. And then I saw Kelsey in the mirror over the dresser, her image like a portrait framed by the double doors. I tried to decide what made her look at home here, but she reached behind her without looking, almost out of habit, and turned the light back off.

She was sitting Indian style in a crater in the comforter by the time my eyes adjusted to the darkness. I was lying on my side. The stiff denim on my shin was inches from the smooth curve of her knee, and I thought I could feel the heat from her skin, but that was my imagination. The house was nicely chilled.

"Are you an EMT or something?" she asked.

"No," I said. "Are you experiencing a shortness of breath?"

"You just seemed like you knew what you were doing with that girl."

"I've picked up drunk girls before."

"Think about what you just said."

"I mean I've helped them up," I said, laughing.

"That's a better story. It was nice of you to make sure she got home. Every girl should have someone like you around when she gets that fucked up."

Something tightened in my chest when I realized this was personal history disguised as praise, that she hadn't been that lucky once. She returned my stare, unblinking. The drugs I had taken were making sense to me in a different way now—a self-administered anesthetic for the invasive things that she was doing with her eyes.

"Where did that little adventure take you?"

"Ridgewood," I said. "That's where she's from."

"And you live in Princeton with your parents."

"With my mom. Who told you that?"

"My cousin. Do you have siblings?"

When I was nine or ten, my mother would sometimes use her sous chef as a babysitter. I would sit by the stove while he made stock and sauces and talked to me as if I were his age. One day after school he told me something I never forgot: Pay attention when a woman asks about your siblings. The desire to know about your brothers and sisters, he explained, signals a curiosity about how the genes that made you might express themselves in another manifestation of the self. He had long blond dreadlocks, and I remembered their earthy, oily smell mixed in with the smell of shallots over heat. It means she really wants to know you, he said, splashing wine into a pan, and it's because she's thinking about fucking you and, by extension, about having your kids. My mother used to call him Professor Horseshit. I was praying he was right.

"It's just me," I said.

"I didn't think you were an only child."

"Is that a good thing?"

"Yes," she said. "It is."

"So when was your eighteenth birthday party at the Plaza?"

"You can just ask me how old I am."

I laughed, and bit my lip. I knew that she was older. That wasn't why I'd asked.

"I'm older than you. And I didn't have an eighteenth birthday party in the city. My dad was a carpenter. He built this house, actually. So I didn't go to boarding school. I went to public school."

"Me too," I said. "Before this."

"Right," she said, her gaze drifting to the room around us. "So 'this' is pretty new for you too. I didn't grow up like this either."

That was what I had been wondering.

"You seem more relaxed than last night, but maybe that's the punch. Or maybe it's because I'm being nicer."

"It's OK," I said. "No big deal."

"That wasn't an apology, sweetheart. Do you like being a day student? My cousin keeps trying to board, but her parents want to keep an eye on her."

"It has its upsides."

"Right," she said. "I bet it does."

"What does that mean?"

"When I was asking for your number, the first thing everybody told me was that you weren't dealing anymore. Like there was no other reason I'd be looking for you. My cousin did the same thing."

"What else did she tell you?"

"She was complaining about how hard it is to get high with you being good."

"I'm sure she'll figure something out. Why were you drawing in the bar last night?"

"I make clothes," she said.

"Are you in school for that?"

"OK," Kelsey said, after a deep breath. "This might seem strange to you. Or maybe not. It seemed a little strange to me when I figured it out. You're going to St. Andrews, right? I go to St. Andrews."

"I can't tell if you're fucking with me," I said, finally. "This is crazy."

"Well, it's a very popular place to go these days, so it's not *that* crazy. But like I said, I was a little surprised. And no, I'm not fucking with you."

I wondered whether she was more surprised than she was letting on, if she attached any real significance to this discovery, even if it was only a tenth of the significance I felt now that what she had said was sinking in.

"Anyway," Kelsey said, "I make clothes and show them in the fashion show the school puts on. You'll be there next year. That's funny to think about. Everybody goes."

She had made the shirt she was wearing, and she pulled it over her head to show me the French seams on the sides. A tattoo of the outline of New Jersey ran down her rib cage just below her armpit, the eastern coast bordering on the gentle swell of her right breast. She was almost boyishly flat chested, with smooth shoulders and strong arms. Her shirt sleeves were bunched up around her wrists and the sheer white fabric was stretched between her hands when I leaned forward and kissed her. Her mouth was stale from cigarettes and waxy with a coat of lip gloss that tasted like mint candy. She pulled back after a split second and gave me a warm glare. I panicked, wondering if I had read this wrong, but then she closed her eyes and leaned in. Later, she described her skirt to me as she unzipped it and worked it down her legs. She seemed to be giving off more heat now, and there was a new smell in the air around her, something sweet and heavy. What she was wearing under the skirt was black and barely anything at all.

"Stand up," she said. "These pants are long on you. And so new."

I had been meaning to cuff them. I pulled my shirt over my head and stood on the bed while Kelsey circled me on her knees, tugging and cuffing the denim, fitting it to my body. I had broken out in a light sweat despite the chill of the house, and I remembered a middle school D.A.R.E. instructor telling our class that the chemical in mushrooms was a mild toxin. To fill the silence, I described how Clare and I had gone shopping and cleaned up.

"Just two guys stripping down in a parking lot," she said, pressing her mouth against my hip to tear away a loose thread with her teeth. "Welcome to New Jersey, right? There. That's how they should look."

"I hate to ruin it."

"You have to. We can't have denim bleeding on these nice white sheets."

"No condom?"

I shook my head.

"You high school boys," she said. "It's always amateur night, isn't it? I forgot what this was like."

"Wait," I said. "Hang on."

I stood up and walked to the dresser in my boxers. The first drawer I tried was all socks—black and stacked in pairs like firewood. I felt between them with my fingers, but there was nothing underneath. The drawer below was full of Lacoste polo shirts, in black and teal and lavender, dozens of them, the shirts near the bottom still wrapped in cellophane. I tried to imagine where this man spent his mental energy so that there was none left for things like getting dressed on weekends. It seemed like a sickness, but maybe that's what it took to build a second home that took a high school party to fill. I wondered if I had that in me.

"What are you doing?" Kelsey said. "Stop that. Come here."

I looked up at her. I thought: The difference between us is that she doesn't care what's in these drawers. Kelsey pulled me onto the bed by my wrist and pushed me hard enough that my head hit the wall of pillows stacked against the headboard.

"You're wasting your time," she said.

It occurred to me that I hadn't showered since the day before as she crawled backward down the length of my body, her hair trailing behind her like a wedding train, hiding her face.

I kept breaking the surface of sleep, as if the drugs had made me too buoyant to stay under very long. I decided, finally, that the problem was my unbrushed teeth, that they were signaling my mind to stay awake. In the cabinet under the bathroom sink, I found a package of toothbrushes between a case of razor blades and a half-gallon of mouthwash. I stole a pink one and bit through the plastic backing.

"Can I do that?"

I looked up to find Kelsey reflected in the mirror in front of me, naked, leaning on the bathroom door.

"There's a whole mess of them," I said, pointing to the cabinet, confused. "Lots of colors."

"No," she said, coming up behind me, sliding her right hand

across my stomach, and placing her left hand gently over mine. "Let me do that for you."

She fit her body against my back and loosened my grip on the brush.

"Can I?" she asked.

I dropped my hand, and made a wall of my front teeth. She started with gentle circles, and then switched to a back-and-forth motion, which seemed more difficult for her. I realized that she must be left-handed too. Her right hand held my hip to steady me, as if we were about to dance. The occasional click of hard plastic on enamel, the bruising my gums took when she slipped and punched them with the blunt end of the brush. She opened her mouth as a sign that I should open mine, and I held my breath as she worked her way back to my wisdom teeth. This required faith, and it was the first time I had really listened to my teeth being brushed, thanks to a heightened awareness that I recognized, finally, as fear. I was watching her in the mirror while she kept her eyes on the reflection of my mouth and the work she was doing. The bathroom lights were blinding, but her pupils looked like saucers. She hadn't let on that she was also high.

"Am I done?" she asked.

I nodded.

"Spit."

I followed her into the blackness of the bedroom, where we lay on the bed, side by side. The room smelled like her now, and I could hear her breathing getting faster. My eyes were taking a long time to adjust.

"OK," she said. "Come here before I change my mind."

"Where?"

She reached across my body for the hand farthest from her, and slipped underneath me as she rolled me over. I felt her take my dick in her hand and guide it to the exact midpoint of her spread legs. She sucked in a breath as I slid into her with so little friction that I was almost certain I had missed. She gasped a little, and I froze.

"No," she said.

I started to withdraw, but she caught me by the hips and pulled me all the way into her. I hadn't understood. I wanted to see her face, but my eyes still hadn't adjusted. I opened them wide as they would go, but even then there was nothing I could see.

I woke up to the sound of a siren from the street. Kelsey, sleeping on her stomach, looked like she was floating face down in calm waters, her hair spread out as if the creased white sheet was liquid, her breath rocking her body like waves. There was a shine to her shoulder where it met the sheet, a streak of sweat. I picked my watch up off the bedside table—4:50 a.m.—and closed my eyes again.

She was at the window when I woke up for good, flexing her calves by standing on her toes. As she steadied herself on the window frame, I saw daylight in a ripple at the edge of the blinds and wished that I had woken up sooner and stretched the night out with one more cycle of waking and sleeping here with her. She dressed quickly, and I was watching her clothes get reacquainted with her body when we heard someone playing the piano downstairs—a loud minor chord with a trickle of notes after it. Kelsey slipped out the door. I followed.

It was Clare at the piano, his back to us where we stood on the second-story landing that overlooked the living room. I had a feeling that he hadn't slept.

"God, he's good," Kelsey said.

Downstairs, we joined the people who had gathered to listen. Clare was passing the lead from his left hand to his right and back again, like someone tossing a baseball between his bare hand and his glove. He shifted between jazz and blues, occasionally dropping the bridge from a pop song you didn't recognize until just after he'd moved on to something else. I was surprised that he would call this much attention to himself, but it seemed like he had resisted the temptation to play for as long as he could. There was applause when he stopped, and I followed Kelsey into the kitchen as the crowd broke up. I poured coffee for us while she went to the fridge for half and half.

"I'm not a morning person," she said, holding the cup to her face.

"Me neither."

Her phone was ringing.

"Excuse me," she said, putting a hand on my arm before she walked away.

I found Clare on the deck, one hand cupped around a match that wouldn't light. The sky was the color of newsprint and I felt myself slow as I stepped out of the cool house into the heavy air outside.

"Nice set," I said, handing him my lighter. "I lost you last night."

"I went swimming."

Clare ran his finger behind his ear and wiped sand on his jeans. He had been in the ocean, not the pool. I pointed to his thigh and he laughed when he saw the orange "irregular" sticker that had somehow survived the night. I wanted to talk to him—to anybody, really—about Kelsey, but what was there to say?

"Should we get going?" Clare asked.

"Yeah, lemme find a bathroom."

I spotted her just before she walked through the front door, bag in hand.

"I was looking for you," Kelsey said, which seemed like a lie.

"You're leaving?"

"I am. It was nice to meet you. I'll see you at school."

She kissed my right cheek, then my left. Something had shifted in the intervening seven minutes, and whatever had prompted her to brush my teeth and sleep with me was inaccessible now. I stood there, waiting for something else, but she just waved and walked away. I found Clare standing by the car, drumming his fingers on the hood. I wanted to ask him what the rush was as I reached for my keys, but it was starting to make sense. St. Andrews was another exit for him. I was good for those, it seemed.

There was a problem with the oysters, because there was always a problem with the oysters.

"If Jack thinks I don't know the difference between Malpeques and this backwater Virginia shit . . ." my mother said, waving off the second half-shell I had shucked for her. She glared down at the waxy battered cardboard boxes that lined our walk-in refrigerator. I had come home from school to work a party after my Friday morning classes, something my mother rarely asked of me because Lawrenceville held a half day of classes on Saturday, mostly to keep the boarders out of trouble. I knocked back the oyster in my hand, and winced as the weak brine blotted out the aftertaste of stale hazelnut coffee.

"That bad?" my mother asked. "Jesus Christ. I'm calling Jack."

"I'll call him. Did you send Ronnie for more parsley, or do you need me to go?"

"Shit. Can you stop on your way to Roger's?"

The oysters were for a Princeton real estate mogul named Roger Hokenson, who was throwing an eightieth birthday party for his mother and his aunt—twin sisters who had come to America from Norway in the 1950s with their husbands. The men were dead, but the Ladies, as people called them, were alive and well. They sat in on lectures at the university, did the flowers for some fancy restaurants, and shopped the Sunday farmer's market with their silver hair wrapped up in scarves. Both women were still over six feet tall, but Roger's mom was slightly hunched after a riding accident, which was the only reason I could tell the two of them apart. I called our seafood guy as I backed down the driveway, eager to get the oyster situation straightened out and calm my mother down.

"Jack, what the fuck are those oysters? Are you serious?"

"Who's this?"

"Tom Alison."

"Are *you* serious?" Jack snorted when I didn't answer. "I didn't get my shipment today, homeboy. I had to send someone to my guy in Bridgewater for you, and that's all he could spare. I took care of you before I took care of me, you dig? If you'd been awake when I came by, I could have told you that to save you the trouble of calling me, like an asshole."

"I was awake," I said.

"Yeah, well, you weren't around. I told the cook who signed for them that I wasn't gonna charge you because I know what you ordered. How's that?"

"Thank you," I said. "Listen, I'm sorry about the mix-up—"

Jack hung up.

Someone leaned on a horn in the line of cars behind me. The traffic light on Nassau Street had turned green at some point.

"Yeah, fuck you," I said, feeling twitchy and shell-shocked as I hit the gas.

I got to Roger's early to walk through the space, a restored antique barn where a team of housekeepers was already at work, unfolding rented chairs and tables. Roger spent the early '80s managing bands in New York and buying up reams of farmland all around the county with his family's money. His second wife had just left town after what seemed like an amicable divorce. My mother's friend, who slept with Roger while he was still married, used to say that Roger's mom was the most important woman in his life, followed closely by his aunt, and that his ex-wife didn't understand that third place was as close as you could come.

"Looks like we got the weather," Roger said, as he came through the barn doors. "How's your mom? Is she around?"

We shook hands. He smelled like turpentine and aftershave, and there were matching paint stains on his khaki shorts and worn polo shirt. I said my mom was on her way and doing fine.

"Are those Camels in your pocket, kiddo? Can you spare one?"

"You smoke?"

"Perk of divorce. I'll take two, if that's all right."

I held out the pack, and Roger tucked a cigarette behind his ear while I lit the other for him. I was still working through the carton Clare had bought me in Fort Lee.

"I gotta freshen up," he said. "You need anything, you let me know."

Roger crossed the lawn toward the low-slung brick farmhouse he had redone from the ground up. He took his time, dragging on my cigarette, stopping to pick up and pocket something that he spotted in the grass. You would never mistake him for anyone but the man who owned this place. He lived alone now that his wife was gone; the Ladies occupied a large octagonal guesthouse near the stables where they kept their horses. Across the lawn, Roger leaned on one of the pillars that propped up his deep wraparound porch. He lifted one foot and, having smoked maybe half of it, ground out my cigarette against the bottom of his loafer before he disappeared inside. A man emerged from a side door with two women behind him and three highball glasses in his hands. I didn't recognize the women, who looked closer to my age than to Roger's. Another perk of his divorce.

"Hey," my mother said, coming up behind me. "What are you doing? At least act like you're unloading. And wash your hands before you stick a tray in someone's face. You smell like cigarettes."

"I know," I said. "Relax."

My mother flicked my ear.

"Don't tell me to relax," she said. "You know how much I hate that."

The guests showed up at sundown. Because the barn doors faced west, the new arrivals were backlit and indistinguishable until they came in from the hazy glare outside.

"Hey," Roger called to me, slinging his arms around a young couple, "can we get these folks some food?"

I was on my way back to the kitchen when I saw Jocelyn, a classmate at Lawrenceville who was headed to NYU to study acting after four years of playing the female lead in every production the school put on. She was five foot five in four-inch heels, pretty in a sharp, aggressive way, with theatrically enormous breasts. She liked to get high, and once upon a time she had been good for an eighth every other week. Jocelyn was Roger's niece, I remembered now. Of course she would be here. The band was tuning up in a corner of the barn, and I cut behind them so as not to pass in front of her.

"What's it like out there?" my mother asked, hours later, as I walked back into the tented kitchen behind the barn. "Are people having fun?"

"They're getting hammered," I said, scraping scorched and shattered lobster tails into the trash. "We're out of Amstel Light."

"Good," she said. "How are the Ladies?"

"The Ladies would die happy if they keeled over in their cake."

"Jesus, take that back. I'll have Roger blaming those oysters if we kill his mom. He noticed, by the way. Remind me to tell Jack not to pull that shit again."

"I talked to him," I said. "He's not gonna charge you."

"What? What happened?"

I was deciding how to answer that when something in the kitchen shifted. I turned around to find Jocelyn standing in the doorway.

"Tom!" she said. "I thought that was you."

My mother hated when clients tried to poke around backstage, but her expression softened when Jocelyn wrapped her arms around me.

"Hey," she said. "Is this your mom? Mrs. Alison, the food was so delicious. Wow, you two look so much alike."

"Thanks, sweetie. I'm glad you're enjoying everything."

"Hey, Tom, could you help me with something? My grandmother wants some of those little raspberry tarts. Is that them over there?"

I tried to head her off as she walked to the rack.

"Actually, I have kind of an awkward question for you," Jocelyn said, as soon as we were out of earshot. "Are you holding? My brother wants to get a little stoned."

"Sorry," I said. "Not anymore."

"Anyone else I can ask? The bartender with gauges in his ears looks promising."

"Nothing doing there."

"I'm a little disappointed," she said, brushing something off my sleeve that may not have been there in the first place. "Are you off the clock?"

"I'm on probation."

She took a step back and covered her mouth with her hand to show me how mortified she was. I had seen her do the same thing as Roxie Hart in *Chicago.*

"Oh my God, I'm such an idiot," she said. "I totally forgot. I swear I'll stop being so stupid someday. Listen, I'm not going to bother your bartender. Promise. I'll give my brother the bad news. Say good-bye before you leave, OK?"

Anyone still at the party had stayed too long. Jocelyn's little brother was tormenting the band by sitting in while the singer took a break, asking them to play one song after another while he struggled to come in on time, too drunk to stay upright without the mic stand. Roger chased him off when the singer finished smoking, and the band played "Free Bird" to celebrate their liberation from the wasted nephew of the host. Roger was red-faced and smiling, spinning his date around the dance floor with a glass of bourbon in one hand. The Ladies had been put to bed, which gave him an hour to cut loose and bask in the afterglow. Roger didn't have school in the morning.

We were packing up and hauling trash when he filled the barn's back doorway, blotting out the light from inside with five bottles of champagne in the circle of his arms, condensation soaking his shirtfront.

"Hey, can you kids finish this stuff for me? It's past my bedtime. Thank you, all of you. One of the great catering staffs right here. Tom, where's your mom?"

He spotted her before I had a chance to point her out. He seemed less drunk when he spoke to her, and I watched him press a bank envelope into her hand. They embraced for a long time. I had heard Jocelyn inviting people back to the house and figured she had found what she was looking for.

Someone passed me a coffee mug full of champagne, which I gulped down when I saw my mother coming toward me. I checked my watch—nine hours until my first class.

"Can you make sure that charcoal makes it back into the van?" my mother said to Todd, her captain.

"I got it," Todd said. "Do you need a lift to the Ivy? We're all going for drinks."

"That's exactly what I don't need," she said. "Tom's driving me home. That champagne went straight to my head."

"I'm having a smoke," my mother announced, as I turned onto the empty country road. "As long as you don't mind."

I shrugged. We did this dance where I gave her shit for smoking, even though we both knew I smoked too. The first time she saw me with a cigarette, she'd looked at me as if I carried one of those Canadian antitobacco labels with pictures of black hearts and half-amputated jaws. I tried not to smoke around her after that.

"Do you want one?" she asked me.

I shook my head.

"What's wrong with you tonight?"

"Can you watch out for deer?"

My mother lit her cigarette and took a long drag.

"Don't talk to me like some friend of yours because you're driving me around. Is it that girl from school?"

"What girl?"

"What did she really want?"

"Dessert," I said, wondering if she could see my face flush in the dark.

"Did she ask you for pot?"

"No."

My mother said nothing, so I turned to face her.

"She didn't."

"Watch the road. Hold this."

She passed me her cigarette and wrestled out of her chef whites, which she tossed into my backseat. She was wearing a gray Bruce Springsteen T-shirt underneath, a souvenir from some concert at Jones Beach before I was born, worn to transparency under the arms and torn around the collar. She took one last drag before she tossed her cigarette and rolled the window up. When I was little, she would come home from jobs like the one we'd just left, pay the babysitter, and then sit on my bed to tell me about the dessert she had saved for me, smelling like sweat and smoke and her conditioner, which was how she smelled now, sealed up with me inside the Ford Explorer I had paid for with the money I made selling drugs.

"Should I meet them at the Ivy for a beer?" she asked. "Should I pretend I don't know about your fake ID and take you with me? You know what? Let's go. I owe those guys. And then we're going home. And don't let me catch you with a drink in your hand."

"You won't," I said.

The Ivy Inn sounds like one of those Princeton establishments trying to siphon off some of the university's cache, but the squat ivy-green building had been a beer-and-a-shot joint since it opened in the '60s, a bar where servers from around town got drunk after their shifts. It was the last place I wanted to go right then.

"Where are you going?" my mother asked as I drove past the bar.

"I'm not parking out front. The cops watch that lot all night waiting for people to stumble out and get into cars."

"Can you pretend that you don't know that stuff? I hate hearing you talk like that."

"You asked."

"Even if I ask, then."

The bouncer looked up and down the street before he waved me in, but he held up his hand as my mother followed.

"Sorry, ma'am," he said, smiling. "Need some ID."

"Cute," she said, brushing past him.

Things were slow inside, and the room was strangely bright without the usual pack of bodies to absorb the light from beer signs and the jukebox and illuminated coolers full of packaged goods. There were a few career alcoholics stationed at the bar, a Mexican crew running the pool table, and my mother's team at a table in the corner. Eric, the head bartender, had worked for us once upon a time, but he made more sense here, flipping bottles end over end, pouring blind, breaking up fights. He wore the Ivy's signature polo shirt, which read CHARMED, I'M SURE across the back. The armbands on his sleeves were notched to accommodate his biceps. Eric spent his days lifting at Gold's Gym on Route 1.

"Whoa, it's family night in America," he said when he saw us. "What can I get you? Shots?"

"No shots," my mother said.

"I can't hear you," Eric said. "I think you said, 'Two shots.'"

"Am I seventeen?" my mother asked. "I'll have a Bud Light. And he'll have nothing. Hey, Eric, how often does my teenage son come in here?"

"Him? Never. I don't think I know this guy. He's your son?"

"Jesus, are you all comedians? Don't let me catch you serving him."

Todd was calling to her from the table.

"I got it," Eric called after her, as she grabbed her beer and walked away without so much as reaching for her wallet.

"I'll have a ginger ale," I said.

Eric dropped an ice-filled glass below the bar and poured a shot of whiskey into it before unholstering the soda gun.

"Accident," he said. "My bad."

I put my name down on the dry-erase board by the pool table and leaned against the wall to watch and wait. Roberto, who owned the bodega on John Street, was on a four-ball run. He shot pool here every weekend, dressed in sweatpants and shower sandals like he was hanging out in his garage. The older guys all dressed like Roberto, like they had given up, but the younger ones slicked their hair and pressed their polo shirts to come down here and play. I wondered what was happening back at Roger's as Roberto sunk the eight ball on a bank shot. Someone handed me a cue.

I never won at the Ivy, and I was down three balls when I noticed Eric talking to my mother. She was sitting by the taps, as far from me as possible, and he was circling back to her between orders, leaning on the bar with his heavy, ropy forearms stacked on top of each other. He had been hitting on her for as long as I had known him, but her complete lack of interest made it less difficult to watch. She looked ten years younger in jeans and a T-shirt, even with the grandma clogs she wore on jobs. People sometimes mistook her for my much older sister, and I lived in fear of some waiter mistaking one of our dinners out for a date, but we probably looked too much alike for that. I missed a short, straight shot, and looked up to find my mother standing on the foot rail of the bar. She was arm wrestling with Eric, pushing down on his left hand with both of hers, laughing as he forced a yawn and closed his eyes.

"You gonna shoot?" Roberto asked. "It's you."

I tried to focus on the game. Eric had a thing with steroids and probably with speed, and the idea of him alone with her in his shitty condo by the airport made me want shells for the shotgun that my mother kept unloaded in the closet. Part of me wished I was already overseas so she could live her life, part of me wanted to stay here forever. Roberto sank the eight ball; we shook hands. Mark, our bartender, reached for my cue.

"You suck at pool."

"What are you doing here?" I asked. "I thought I saw you fall in love with that desperate housewife."

"Jesus, did you see that? She scared off that hot blond chick."

"Did that girl ask you for weed?"

"Yeah, maybe. How'd you know that? Did your mom say something?"

"No," I said. "Wild guess."

"She asked you too?"

"She asked me first."

"Fuck 'em," Mark said. "So you're at Lawrenceville and your mom's still working you like this?"

"Not that often."

"Well, good for you. It's a pain in the ass to do two things at once."

Eric had talked my mother into taking a shot with him, and I watched her wince into the back of her hand as she held the empty glass out to him. I shouldered through the crowd as Eric moved down the bar.

"Hey, can we go?"

"Hey!" she said. "Did you clean up at pool?"

"Not really. I'm ready to get out of here."

"Already?" Eric asked, pulling a beer from the tap.

"I have school tomorrow."

"At least come up with a better story. Tomorrow's Saturday. You can tell me you're too fancy for my bar now. It won't hurt my feelings."

"He does have school," my mother said, grabbing a handful of my hair and tugging my head back and forth. "That's how people get ahead in life, Eric. They go to school on weekends."

She seemed genuinely glad to see me, as if we had just run into each other here.

"Well, it's not a school night for Mrs. Alison," Eric said, winking at her. "He's a big boy. You don't need to tuck him in, right?"

For a second I was afraid that she would stick around, and I would have to go home by myself and lie awake waiting to hear her car in the driveway like I was five years old again. Instead, my mother stiffened, and blinked as if she had just remembered something.

"You know what?" she said to me. "Let's get out of here. I'm wrecked."

"Hey, I'll call you this week," Eric said.

She gave him a tight smile, and dropped one of Roger's crisp hundred-dollar bills on the bar.

"That's for them," she said, pointing to Todd's table as she shouldered her purse.

My ears were still ringing from the band at Roger's when we got back to our empty house. My mother disappeared into her room and turned off her light without saying goodnight to me, which was strange because she always said goodnight, even if it meant waking me where I had fallen asleep reading by a night-light to save on electricity, which I was about to do. I was nodding off midsentence when my door swung open.

"Can I ask you something?"

I sat up, squinting in the light.

"Where would you go?" she said. "Let's say you could go anywhere."

"Fiji."

"Really?"

I nodded and waited for her to ask me why.

"I wouldn't go anywhere," she said. "I was thinking about that tonight when I was watching you. I was wondering where you were in your head. I used to think about all the places I'd go, but I just don't anymore."

"Maybe it's an age thing."

"Are you saying I'm old?"

"No," I said. "You're not old."

"Right," she said, "of course I'm not."

She shut my door.

Smacking the steering wheel to stay awake at red lights on my way to school. My short Saturday schedule meant English and then econ before I could go home and back to sleep. I cut through the glassy modernist dining hall to get a cup of coffee before giving my Modernist Literature reading one more shot. The cover on my copy of *The Waste Land* was badly creased where I had rolled on it after losing consciousness halfway through a section titled "What the Thunder Said." I had no idea what the thunder said, and I needed caffeine and Advil and a place to read in the twenty-five minutes before an hour of small-group discussion. Lawrenceville used the Harkness teaching method, in which twelve students and one teacher sit around an oval oak table to talk about the Ottoman Empire or the impact of privatization on capital market growth. It aims to foster engaged and egalitarian discussion, which makes it hard to sleep in class. I took my coffee for the road.

The sprawling campus was deserted except for a few distant figures speed walking awkwardly under the weight of their books. I shouldered through the door of Memorial Hall and moved down the cool hallway of the old building as quickly as my coffee would allow. The stairs were solid blocks of stone, each bearing an indentation deep enough to hold water thanks to two centuries of climbing and descending students. I was headed for the second-story teachers' lounge, which was usually empty on weekends. The door was closed, and when I opened it, the head of the English Department looked up from an interview with a woman in a navy business suit. Mr. McCarthy had been on the disciplinary board convened to hear my case, and while he had voted against expulsion, it was clear that I had used up whatever currency or empathy I had with him. Most of the faculty I had been close to kept their distance now, there being no time for redemption between my arrest and the end of the year.

"Mr. Alison," Mr. McCarthy said. "Can I help you? We're in a meeting here."

"I'm sorry," I said, backing away, closing the door. "My fault."

I crossed the grassy circle that's the focal point of campus, designed by the same architect who did Central Park, and ringed by the boys' Circle Houses, where the boarders lived for their sophomore and junior years. Day students were also assigned to a house and I had been in Hamill, where the administration put everyone they weren't sure what to do with: the son of a cotton magnate who hung a Confederate flag in his window, Canadians, a clique of kids from Taiwan.

In the library, I took the wide stairs down to the basement and a windowless science reading room with plush couches that no one really used. The motion-sensing lights had already been tripped when I opened the door, and it was Clare who turned his head to see who was invading his solitude. We hadn't really spoken since we'd put two hundred miles on my car and decided to spend the next four years at the same school in another country. There was a pause after I sat down, a conversational game of chicken.

"Hey," Clare said, "did you get a housing assignment yet?"

"I'm in Andrew Melville."

"That's the hotel, right? I was gonna request that one. Is that OK?"

"Yeah, why not?"

The only thing we had to talk about was our future shared living arrangements, which was almost funny to me. I settled into the couch and waited for Clare to say something else. And then I realized that he had no book in his hands, that his bag was closed, that he had just been sitting there, staring out across the room. I took out my book and tried to find my place.

The WXPN weatherman reported a record high on the heat index as I drove my mother to my high school graduation. She did her makeup in the vanity mirror; I spun my tie into a four-in-hand at a long red light. We jogged across the parking lot together, and she split off toward the seated crowd while I joined my class behind the chapel, where they'd been marshaled in an alphabetical and single-file line. The girls wore short white dresses for the ceremony while the boys sweated in blue blazers and long pants. I could see the families gathered around the sunken bowl of grass in the middle of campus where our chairs sat empty in the sun—parents and grandparents and godparents squinting at the long formation in the distance, wondering which upright streak of navy blue or white was theirs. I spotted Clare, separated from me by the letters *A* through *S*, hands in his pockets, sunglasses hiding his eyes. I wondered where his parents were this afternoon.

The crowd dispersed as soon as the ceremony ended, seeking shade. I saw my mother making her way through clots of family members toward the empty chair I was leaning on. She stopped in front of me and spread her arms.

"I'm so proud of you," she whispered in my ear, before pulling back and looking me in the face. "Look at you. You're done. You're leaving."

Her eyes were wet, full of pride and something that looked, to me, like fear. Was she afraid for me or afraid to be alone? I couldn't tell, and couldn't ask. It was just the two of us, and I had spent all morning waiting to feel embarrassed and to hate myself for feeling that way, but that wasn't happening now. And then Clare was standing at my mother's shoulder, his hands in his pockets again.

"Mom, this is Clare."

"Hi, Mrs. Alison," Clare said. "Pleasure to meet you."

"Diane," my mother said. "I've heard so much about you."

When I saw Clare stiffen, I tugged on my right earlobe—a gesture my mother and I used at parties to communicate that it was time to shut up or change the subject.

"What happens now?" she asked. "What's next?"

"We go to some parties," I said.

"Can we give you a ride, sweetheart?" my mother asked Clare. "We've got plenty of room."

"Some of those people are unreal," my mother said, as I drove us to a party near the university. "The woman next to me kept going on about how she just went back to work after twenty years, and now she's got her real estate license, and just *adores* showing properties. It barely feels like work, apparently. She asked me if I'd gone back to work and I said, 'Honey, I've been working this whole time.' "

"They're not all like that," Clare said. "Most of them would never think of working."

My mother laughed. I plucked the cigarette from her lips, took a drag, and tossed it out the window.

"Stop smoking," I said.

I wondered what had happened to Clare's Saab as we crisscrossed Mercer County, driving from party to party, encountering faculty members with more and more white wine on their breath as the day wore on. My mother took the wheel after she caught me swigging from a flask of bourbon with a classmate and his uncle, who had asked me if my dad would like to join us for some twenty-three-year-old Pappy Van Winkle, to which I shook my head. Our last stop was out in Ringoes, Central Jersey horse country, where the split-level ranch homes of the people who tend to the animals alternate with the estates of their owners. My mother took the long driveway very slowly, ducking her head as the house came into view over the hedge that surrounded it. Everyone was gathered on a bluestone patio by the pool, and I lost Clare in the crowd while my mother let herself into the house to find a bathroom. Feeling lightheaded from the whiskey and the heat, I decided to watch the party from a hammock in the shade. My mother seemed to be enjoying herself, chatting up the varsity soccer coach, a square-jawed ex-National team goalie from Croatia. In a simple navy dress and modest string of pearls, she was indistinguishable from the women around her. She had seen dozens of graduation parties in her day. She knew what people wore to them.

I wondered if she liked being a guest here instead of running things behind the scenes, work she actually enjoyed. And then she refused two consecutive hors d'oeuvres plates proffered by college kids in dinner jackets. We had skipped breakfast and the only time my mother doesn't eat is when she's working or nervous. Then the soccer coach was gone, dragged off for a photo op with someone's family, and she was left alone in the crowd. I watched her shield her eyes and scan the faces gathered by the pool before she reached into the outside pocket of her purse for a cigarette. Don't, I thought. She stopped midreach, as if I had shouted to her, and looked around to see if anybody else was smoking, which they weren't. I swore at myself for leaving her alone, and stood up too quickly for my low blood pressure to handle. My vision collapsed to a pinpoint, and everything outside of that went white as the blood drained from my head. I staggered toward the pool, wondering how my mother would feel if my adult life looked like the jagged party scene in front of me, full of gold-buttoned navy blazers, horses, and big lawns. I searched for her as the crowd came into focus, but she was not where she had been.

I went looking for a girl named Ashleigh who had been close with Courtney since our freshman year. I found her in the buffet line and asked what she knew about Courtney's cousin, Kelsey, which, as it turned out, was not much. Kelsey's father had been a contractor in Spring Lake, and had built enough big houses to build one of his own. The family had risen on the wave of new money down the shore. Ashleigh was saying that Kelsey might be seeing someone when we were interrupted.

"Hi, excuse me," my mother said, placing her hand on Ashleigh's arm. "Can I borrow my son for a second?"

I followed her through the crowd to the corner of a fence where two chestnut horses stood grazing.

"I've had all the fun I can stand," she said.

"What happened?"

She had been talking to the man who owned the house when he spotted Clare at the buffet, and wondered aloud who had brought him. My mother said that she had, and our host told her emphatically that Clare's family hadn't been invited.

"Not that they would have been able to make it," she said, scoffing, imitating him, exaggerating his disgust and pomposity. He had asked my mother if she knew what Clare's father had done with the money people had entrusted to him. My mother runs a business that requires her to come prepared, especially to parties. She told the man that she had no idea what Clare's father had done, or how anyone could blame a child for it.

"The fucking nerve on this guy," she said, lighting a cigarette.

"Did he tell you what happened?"

"No, Tom, that's not the point. And don't repeat that story."

In the car, she adjusted the rearview mirror to find Clare's face.

"Is there anywhere you'd like to go, sweetheart? Anywhere else we can take you?"

"That's OK," Clare said. "My things are at school."

My mother turned to face him.

"Where are you going when they close down campus?"

I hadn't thought about that. Clare didn't answer.

"Why don't you stay with us?" my mother said.

The cash register woke me, and the ring of the drawer became the ring of my mother's laugh as she made change for one of her morning customers. Clare and I had stayed out until just after 3:00 a.m. at a party thrown by a boy named Sky. When the last keg was kicked, I drove us back to Lawrenceville, and we had just passed through the gates when Clare asked if my mom meant what she had said, if he could really crash with us for a while. I told him my mother always meant the things she said, and that it was fine with me as well. I waited with the engine running while Clare packed a bag, trying to imagine how this would play out, and what Clare would think about the way we lived. I had a clear memory of driving home and a less clear memory of bringing Clare upstairs and showing him the couch and finding him a blanket. Some combination of alcohol and nervousness had clouded my mind, and I woke up hungover and unsure what had happened in the end. I pulled on dirty clothes and walked down into the shop, pausing at the stairs to see if Clare was still asleep. The couch was empty, the blankets folded neatly on one arm.

"Need help?" I asked, pushing my hair out of my eyes.

My mother shook her head without looking up at me, so I walked back into the kitchen for a slug of orange juice. When I closed the refrigerator, wiping my mouth with the back of my hand, she was standing just behind the door.

"Jesus Christ," I said. "You scared me."

"Really? I scared you? How do you think I felt when I woke up at 2:00 a.m. and you weren't home, hadn't called, hadn't said where you were going?"

"I'm sorry," I said. "We went to a party."

"How many times do I have to tell you about driving home when you've been out like that? You're on probation, Tom. And let me tell you something else, because obviously nothing that I've said so far has sunk in: if you get pulled over, or wind up with the cops for any reason, I won't be there to get you out. Do you understand me?"

I nodded.

"Watch the register while I grab something from the back and then you can go find Clare. He helped me set up this morning while you were sleeping it off."

She was on her way out when a man in a suit walked in and set his briefcase down.

"Do you have the *Times*?" he asked, filling a paper coffee cup from a carafe.

"No, sorry, didn't get it today," my mother said. "Looks like they forgot us."

"There's a stack of papers by the back door," I said.

My mother tugged on her right earlobe.

"Could have been yesterday's," I said, grabbing a rag and wiping down a clean counter.

"Sorry," my mother said. "Check back tomorrow."

The man waved it off.

"Go put those papers in the recycling," she said to me when he was gone.

"Why? It's definitely today's."

"There's an article about Clare's dad in there," she said. "I don't want him to see that in my house."

I walked back through the kitchen, and grabbed a paring knife to cut the bailing wire.

The story was just below the fold: MORE QUESTIONS THAN ANSWERS IN CASE OF FUGITIVE FINANCIER. I dropped the papers into our blue bucket, and headed up to my room with the top copy tucked under my arm.

The article read like a follow-up to whatever piece had announced that Michael Savage was on the run. It began by describing how Clare's dad had gone out on his own after a long spell on the commodities desk at Lehman Brothers, where he had made a small fortune for himself and a much larger one for the firm. The third paragraph described the opening of Savage Asset Management: "The street address on the fund's letterhead—1793 Carriage Way, New Hope, PA—offered no hint that the offices shared a suburban strip mall with a Wawa convenience store, a dry cleaner, and a nail salon." Clare's dad had employed half a dozen young, hungry traders and some light back-office staff. The reporter had talked to the clerk at the neighboring Wawa, who described the day they took possession of the space. A team of young men in suits had come crashing through the doors in the bitter cold hours before sunrise, demanding two gallons of coffee and every can of Red Bull they had. I pictured them acting like drunk teenagers, tossing things over the aisles to each other, tearing into packages before they had paid. They bought cigarettes, batteries, Tylenol, Sno Balls, Pepto-Bismol. Like men heading out to sea, the clerk said. She'd had to ask one of them to activate the unscratched corporate card he offered her as payment. And she remembered a man—old enough, she thought, to be their father—who stood outside on the sidewalk, talking on his cell phone.

The story went on to quote an old *Forbes* profile of Michael Savage and a former colleague's theory that his trading savvy stemmed from the severe color blindness he had suffered all his life—that it was like a missing sense that sharpened all the others. The knowledge of things he couldn't see compelled him to seek out every piece of available information, whether he was picking stocks or cars or sofas for his office. But his desire to have every fact extended to the kind of nonpublic information that can land a man in jail. And his traders, it turned out, had been chosen for their connections as much as anything else: a college roommate at a big consulting firm, a cousin at Pfizer.

He was driven to know everything. How could you stop that kind of momentum before you crossed a line? To come across some vital knowledge and then say: Wait, I can't know that. There would be no way, I thought, to pull up short. I remembered the freshman at Lawrenceville who, back in January, ran straight at me as I walked out of the library, and then ran into me, unable to slow down in time. I laughed at his frantic sputtering. I told him to relax. "Dean Doyle is looking for you," he said. "Two cops with him. Looking everywhere." And then I was running for my car.

Michael Savage had been reported anonymously for insider trading, blindsided. I wondered who that would have been. A principled whistle-blower? A former colleague, stuck at Lehman, who resented his success? Or maybe it was someone who stood to gain from being an informant. I knew more about that situation than I cared to admit, and put that thought aside. A raid on the offices turned up piles of falsified trading records. There were large chunks of capital that were either missing altogether or not where Michael Savage claimed. But there had also been two big redemptions that he'd had no trouble meeting, a sign that he was making money and had cash on hand, although no one could be quite sure how. There had been no massive losses and, as far as anyone could tell, no extravagant lifestyle financed by unwitting investors. No polo team, in other words. No private islands. The Savages lived relatively modestly in an old Pennsylvania farmhouse on the Delaware. The *Times* had asked a forensic accounting specialist to comment on how long it would take to untangle the paper trail and figure out where all the cash had gone. Years, he said, especially without cooperation. Decades, even. I tore the article carefully along the fold, tucked it into my wallet, and dropped the rest of the *New York Times* into the trash.

Clare and I had plans to drive to Maryland that afternoon. Lawrenceville was the southernmost of the old prep schools, and every year the newly minted graduates followed the southern boys to parties at their houses on the Chesapeake and plantations in Virginia, sometimes road tripping as far as West Palm Beach before they went their separate ways.

I walked into town alongside a stream of women driving alone in expensive cars, which made me wonder how Clare's mother had spent her days while her husband was doing god knows what with other people's money. Clare was walking toward me, looking fresh and rested and completely unaware that his family was all over the news.

"How'd you sleep?" I asked him.

"That couch is actually really comfortable. And your mom is great. That was the best omelet I've ever had."

"Cool," I said. "Listen, everyone's meeting behind the field house to drive down to Bethesda. Do you need anything from your room before we go?"

"Nothing from my room, but could I borrow your car for an hour?"

"For what?"

"I need to pick up something at my parents' place."

He wouldn't say what, and clearly wanted to do this alone, but that, as my mother liked to say, was a personal problem. The *Times* had run a small aerial picture of the house, and there was no way I was passing up a closer look.

"I'll drive you," I said. "No big deal."

"This is it," Clare said, pointing to a gravel drive that filled a freshly cleared gash in the woods between the Delaware River and the narrow winding road. It was a service road for the construction of an outbuilding behind the house, a capillary connected to the wide main drive. The unfinished guesthouse was covered in DuPont weatherproof sheeting, and bookended by two Dumpsters splattered in that smooth, light-colored mud that's peculiar to construction, the lifeblood of a building site. No way to know when they broke ground that all the planning and the sketching and the permits and the lumber would lead this far and no further.

The main house was long and low and made of stone. Clare unlocked the door and led me through the dark entryway into a living room that overlooked a pear-shaped pond. The room was sparsely furnished, and I saw from the marks and discoloration on the wide pine boards of the floor that things were missing—rare antiques, I imagined, family heirlooms that couldn't be replaced after an asset sale. There was nothing flashy about the house, nothing that looked less than a century old. Michael Savage wasn't interested in displays of wealth, which distinguished him from almost every wealthy person I had ever known. Clare was standing with his toes on the fringe of a threadbare Persian carpet, staring down at the deep imprints of piano wheels, like fossilized hoof prints in the dark knotted wool. He walked briskly out of the room, and I heard him pacing and pausing, hunting for the instrument. I wanted to tell him I was sorry, but as he walked back into the room we heard the sound of heavy wheels on gravel. Clare's head jerked toward the window. I followed him outside.

A moving truck was idling beside my car. Two men in boots and back braces jumped down from the cab, paying us no mind as we came down the front steps, the shorter one telling a story about a weekend in the Poconos that ended with a shotgun full of rock salt. Clare and I stood behind them as the hinged metal door flew up to reveal a brown leather sectional. The men climbed inside and began shifting the pieces to unload.

"Your folks here?" the one with the shotgun story called.

"They don't live here anymore," Clare said. "They moved."

The men stopped. The quiet one spit on the floor of the container.

"What do you mean, 'They moved?' " the shorter one said. "This is when they told us to show. Last time the color was wrong and now you're saying they don't live here?"

"They're gone," Clare said.

"Listen, kid," the man said, jumping down, coming toward us. "This thing is paid for. It's a custom piece. I can't take it back again. If it don't go here, then tell me where it does go so I can get it off my hands."

Clare punched the cigarette lighter into my dash for the second time in ten minutes, rolling a Camel Light between his fingers, waiting for the coil to heat. The couch had shaken him. We sat staring through the windshield at the cinder block wall of Lawrenceville's hockey rink waiting for everyone to assemble.

"You play?" Clare asked, holding up a guitar pick he had spotted in my cup holder.

I learned guitar from a cook who worked for my mother, a big Texan man who gave me his Yamaha acoustic when he left us for a restaurant in New Orleans. One day I was playing in my room, figuring out a chord change in "Over the Hills and Far Away," when I looked up to find my mother in the doorway, clutching the frame as if she was expecting a hurricane.

"Who taught you that?" she asked.

"No one," I said. "What's wrong?"

"Your dad loved that song."

It was the first time she had mentioned him in three years. Someone upset the string of bells that hung from our front door, and she was gone.

Clare jumped as Bart Higgins rapped his knuckles on my window.

"We're riding out," he said. "It's 95 South most of the way. Stay close."

Bart ducked his head to see who was riding shotgun, and from the expression on his face, it was clear that he had seen the *Times*.

"Hey, Clare," he said, giving me a sideways smile.

Clare nodded to him and I dropped the car into reverse.

"Hey, can you just drop me off back at the dorm?" Clare said.

"What?"

"Just let me out here."

"You don't want to go?"

Clare shook his head.

"What are you gonna do?"

"You're going to miss them," Clare said. "Just let me out."

"We can stick around, if you want. You know what? I hate Maryland. Let's stay here, crash the Princeton eating clubs or something."

"Are you sure? It's your last chance to see everyone."

I was sure. And I was unsure now why I had planned to go in the first place, why I had even considered driving two hundred miles in a caravan of people who regarded me with a mix of sympathy and apathy now that I wasn't dealing anymore. The party promised six uncomfortable waking hours followed by an uncomfortable night of sleep on a sofa or in the front seats of my car. Clare was the excuse I had been looking for.

"Put your seat belt on," I said.

I cut my wheels toward home.

Back at the house, Clare disappeared into the bathroom while I unpacked my bag. My mother heard us come in and ran up from the shop, motioning wildly for me to follow her back down. I laughed when I saw the couch, which took up most of the room.

"What am I supposed to do with this?" she whispered.

I shrugged. "I tried to call you."

"Where the hell am I supposed to put it? Do you have any idea what this thing costs?"

"Leave it there. Give people a place to sit."

"There's no place to *stand,*" she hissed, watching the stairs as Clare's boat shoes appeared on the landing, and began their descent. "What are you doing back? I thought you were driving to Virginia."

"Maryland," I said. "We decided to stay here."

"Is everything all right?"

"Everything's fine."

"Clare, sweetie," my mother said. "I don't know what to say."

"You don't like it?"

"No, it's beautiful. You're sure your parents can't use it? I'm sure they'll want it back."

"I don't think so," Clare said. "They're getting rid of stuff. We can take it out to the curb if you don't want it."

"No, no, no," she said. "Don't do that. I'll figure something out. And I want you to know that you're welcome to stay here for as long as you need to, Clare. And that's not about the couch."

When I was younger, my mother and I lived on Long Beach Island, a barrier island seventeen miles long and three blocks wide that runs along New Jersey's southern coast. LBI gets thinner every year; the Atlantic will swallow all of it eventually. Today it's covered in water parks and yacht clubs and expensive second homes. In a thousand years, it won't exist.

I was in sixth grade when we moved to Princeton, and there were days when I would wake up and imagine that I could still hear the surf through my open window. And then I'd smell the air and realize there was no salt in it, that we were inland now, that the sound outside was from a passing truck. When people asked why we were moving, my mother cited the rising cost of living and the plunging standards at the schools. She said there was more money to be made in Princeton, but mostly she wanted me to grow up somewhere else. Living on the island means weathering the winters, when no one comes, when the traffic lights on the boulevard flash yellow, as if even the traffic authority has moved on. The dead stretches harden you and breed contempt for the crowds who show up only when it's hot and sunny. And thanks to my Saturday classes, I only made it down to LBI in summer, when school was out. I was a tourist now;

I had to call my best friend, Casey, and make sure he was around so Clare and I would have a place to crash. It was not a call I liked to make. My father was a Long Beach Island tourist once.

"What's your plan?" my mother asked. Clare had gone upstairs to pack a bag, and I was sprawled out on his parent's unclaimed couch with my second cup of coffee.

"Meet up with Casey, maybe take Clare surfing if it's good."

"You watch out for him down there," my mother said.

I scoffed and flipped my coffee cup into the trash.

Clare fell asleep before we hit the highway. He slept through Allentown, and the entrance to 539 West, a two-lane road that cuts through the Pine Barrens to the shore. When I cracked a window to smoke, Clare opened his eyes and offered to drive. I shook my head, killed the radio, and focused on the road.

Casey worked mornings at a sandwich shop called Subs Up, and I timed our arrival for the end of his shift. When we were younger, our mothers had waitressed together, vacationed together, split the cost of babysitters for occasional nights out in Atlantic City. Casey was two years older, and after "toughening me up" as a kid—a personal project of his that never really took—he had looked out for me in elementary and middle school, where everyone knew that picking on me meant dealing with him. He was the one person I didn't lose touch with after we moved away. Clare woke up as I pulled into the gravel lot behind the clapboard building where Casey worked.

"We're here," I said, and Clare stumbled out into the sunshine, squinting at his new surroundings.

Casey was alone inside the shop, drying his hands on a filthy dishrag. He faked a one-two punch, and then leaned across the counter to embrace me, palming the back of my head like he always did.

"This is Clare," I said.

"Nice to see you," Clare said, offering a conventional handshake. Casey's hand was higher up, his forearm at a 45-degree angle. He held it there until Clare brought his hand up to meet it.

"You eat?" Casey asked.

"Can I get a sausage, egg, and cheese on sesame?"

Casey nodded and thrust his chin at Clare.

"That sounds good," Clare said.

Casey turned his back on us to crack the eggs, and Clare stood at the window, watching traffic. He reached for his wallet when Casey finished our sandwiches, but Casey shook his head and slid the bag across the counter. The door opened behind us. It was José Manuel, the Mexican kid who worked the afternoon shift.

"Qué tal, amigo?" Casey said. "Todo bien?"

"Sí, bien, bien," the kid said, giving Casey a quick fist bump before he jumped the counter and snatched an apron off the wall.

"I'm clocking out," Casey said. "Meet me at Eleventh and Atlantic."

We were three blocks from Subs Up when I heard the whine of Casey's black Volkswagen GTI behind us. He swung out in front, making time before the speed traps, which I used to know by heart. I pulled up next to him at the entrance to the surfing beach, and the three of us walked over the dunes. A set of waist-high waves rolled in just as the sea came into view, each one closing out to form a wall of whitewater as a messy southeast wind blew everything to shit.

"Is it worth waiting for low tide?" I asked.

"It's your vacation, big guy," Casey said. "It's been blown out all week. We should probably just scurf on the bay."

"With whose boat?"

"Rob's. You remember Rob."

I remembered Rob. Rob dated my mother before I was born.

"He never uses that jet boat anymore. Gave me the keys. Ever scurf before?" Casey asked Clare.

Clare shook his head.

"You've surfed, right?" Casey asked him.

"Sure," Clare said. "I've tried it a few times."

"It's surfing with a tow rope, behind a boat," I explained, as Clare and I followed Casey to the marina on the bay. "No straps, though. You pop up on the board when the boat gets up to speed, like you're dropping in. It's what you do down here when it's flat."

Clare was watching Casey weave through traffic in front of us.

"You're losing him," he said.

"I know where we're going, Clare."

Casey was talking to the dockmaster when we pulled up to the marina. He waved and then pulled his shirt over his head and turned his back on us for the second time that morning, revealing the tattoo that spanned his upper back from shoulder to shoulder. It was an image of the Lower Trenton Bridge over the Delaware River, which has a neon message spelled out across the suspension cables: "Trenton Makes, the World Takes." Casey wore only the "Trenton Makes" half, with the neon lettering in some mix of red and white that looked lit up, even in direct sunlight. His skin was stretched tight across his muscular frame, and the ink looked like something viewed through heat waves as he walked down the dock, rolling his shoulders with his stride. When we were younger, our PE teacher had compared him to her car-chasing Pomeranian because they were both compact and fearless.

"You got sunglasses?" Casey asked Clare, lowering himself into the pink and teal pleather interior of a shiny white jet boat. "Gets bright out there."

"In the car," Clare said.

I tossed him the keys.

"How's things?" I asked Casey, as I jumped into the boat behind him.

"They're good," he said. "Been busy as hell. Big night at the Sailfish last night. Two fights over the same chick. Bouncer took some guy down with a Maglite."

Casey filled in occasionally as a shift manager at the Sailfish Bar in Beach Haven. He had been supporting himself since he was sixteen, when his mother married a man he couldn't stand. They split up two years later, but Casey was comfortable on his own by then. He'd had the Subs Up gig for as long as he'd had working papers, but by then it was mostly for tax purposes—a few hours a week to show the government some income. Casey sold cocaine to people who cut it and resold it to street dealers who delivered it to bachelor parties, taxi drivers, outcall strippers, and anyone looking to take their vacation up a notch. The coke came to Casey through a Mexican connection, the cousin of some line cook at the Sailfish who no one but Casey and the cook had ever met.

"What's this guy's deal?" Casey asked, nodding in the direction Clare had gone.

"I told you about him. He's living with us. His folks skipped town."

"This is him?"

"Yeah. Clare."

"I thought Clare was a chick. His dad's fucked, right? It was on the news last night."

"Sure," I said, as Clare walked up.

"Sorry," Clare said. "I'm ready."

"No worries," Casey said. "We're waiting on one more. She's almost here. If she brings her cousin, just call the cops and report a homicide. He put a hole the size of a softball in my long board yesterday."

I heard a car skid into the lot behind us. I knew who this would be.

"The clown car's here," Casey said as our friend Mike jumped down into the boat followed by his cousin Melissa, Casey's girlfriend. "Hey, Mike, just use my board for target practice next time."

"Whoa, someone woke up on the wrong side of the bed this morning," Mike said. "Did your four-hour work day make you cranky? I can't help it if your stupid board likes rocks."

"I invite you on my boat, and this is what I have to deal with."

"This ain't your boat. You gonna introduce me to your friends, or what?"

"This is Clare," I said. "Clare, this is Mike."

"I'm sorry," Mike said, offering me his hand. "Have we met?"

For two humiliating seconds, I actually believed he had forgotten who I was, but this was a dance he did with anyone who had grown up here and moved away.

"Go fuck yourself," I said.

Mike ripped off his sunglasses.

"Tom? Tom Alison? Jesus Christ, Melissa! It's our old friend Tom!"

"Can you please stop talking for ten seconds," Melissa said. "I can't take it anymore. Hi, Clare. Nice to meet you."

"Hey," Mike said, shaking Clare's hand.

Inked down the length of his right arm was a Japanese girl on a bicycle being chased through mountains by a dragon. The monster shuddered with the force of his grip. Mike had gone away for just under two years after the police showed up at a construction site where he was working and found a trailer containing not invoice-stuffed file cabinets and orange cones, but a hydroponic growing system and forty-five marijuana plants in full bloom. Mike's partner in the grow was supporting his ex-wife and a set of twins, so Mike took the hit and spent eighteen months at Southern State

Correctional, which he referred to as his time in the country. He made a living playing poker, online and in Atlantic City, now that he was out. He said it was like chess that paid.

Melissa kissed me on the cheek. She had been with Casey since their freshman year, and managed a chain of surf shops on the island while she pursued an urban planning degree at Rutgers. She was the only person whose judgment Casey didn't question, and she was digging through her bag when Casey tossed her some lip balm that, from the look on her face, was the thing she had been seeking.

"Let's go, already," Mike said, clapping his hands in Casey's ear.

Casey shook his head in mock disgust, and turned the key in the ignition. The engines coughed and spit out water and exhaust. Casey eased the boat out of the harbor, accelerating as we cut between the channel markers, and letting it run out on the bay. Melissa had been sitting on the back bench with her knees against her chest, but she stood up as the boat leveled off, and put her arms around Casey's waist from behind, pressing herself against his back, propping her chin on his shoulder. She had at least three inches on him in her bare feet. He turned his head and kissed her cheek. She let go and fell into a captain's chair as Casey swung the boat to starboard and threw it into neutral.

"Who's first?" he asked, untangling a towrope from the floor compartment.

"I'll go," I said.

I jumped off the back deck, straight through the balmy shallow water of the bay, and into a layer of silt studded with broken shells. I let the air out of my lungs and fell slowly backward until I heard my board break the surface as Mike slid it off the boat.

Scurfing works like this: You lie flat on a surfboard with one hand on the handle of a towrope and the other hand flat on the deck of the board. As the boat picks up speed, you push down, pop up to your feet, and ride. I watched the boat get smaller as Casey pulled away from me and Mike paid out the slack in the rope. Melissa was talking to Clare, and I was grateful for that, because Mike and Casey were suspicious of anyone they hadn't known all their lives. I wanted to fall back in with them, but there was Clare—the poster child for the life that I had left them for. The nose of my board popped out of the bay as Casey eased onto the throttle.

I loved scurfing when I was a kid, flying across the flat water between the island and the mainland on a board that's meant for something else. If your boat was big enough, you could ride the wake without a rope. Casey used to say we'd know we'd made it when we had a boat like that. That was the hook—you could always get a bigger boat. They called it foot-a-year disease down the shore.

I got to my feet as easily as people get back onto bikes. There was some chop on the water, but even with the wind and the spray and the glare, I could make out who was who on the boat in front of me. They each occupied a captain's chair—Mike facing backward to keep an eye on me, Casey at the wheel, Clare and Melissa gazing out to port and starboard. My calves were twitching with the strain of staying upright, but I held on to drown out the sadness that was starting to come up in me. Finally, I let the rope go, and let the board sink underneath me. I paddled back toward the island as Casey swung around to pick me up.

Mike dove over me as I hauled myself aboard.

"Watch him while I drive," Casey said.

Mike was up as soon as we were moving. He fell hard jumping the wake of a Coast Guard boat, and called for us to swing around and give him back the rope, which Casey did. I saw Clare stiffen when Mike finally let go.

"You ready?" I asked.

"Yeah," he said, folding his sunglasses and looking for a place to put them until Melissa held out a hand.

"You're gonna love it," Mike said, water streaming down his body as he caught his breath with his hands propped on his knees.

"Just push down with your free hand and jump up," I said. "Don't think too much."

Clare jumped in feet first, keeping his head above water, and swam out to the board.

"Watch him," Casey said. "Tell me when he's off."

"Who is this guy?" Mike asked.

"He's crashing with us for a while," I said.

"That's cool," Mike said. "Was it awkward the first time you guys had sex?"

I pegged an empty water bottle at him, unsure how else to react. How many people had looked at the two of us and had that thought?

"You know his dad," Casey said to Mike. "You know of him, anyway. Michael Savage?"

"The guy with all the clubs in Philly?"

"Never mind," Casey said. "Don't you watch the news? I know you can't read."

"Hey, Casey. Fuck yourself. Who is he?"

"The guy who made those peoples' money disappear."

"No shit," Mike said. "That's him? I thought that guy was in his fifties."

Casey shook his head.

"He's sweet," Melissa said. "Be nice to him."

"Could you not say anything about it when he's here?" I asked.

"Don't worry, buddy," Mike said, wrapping his arms around my neck and grating his knuckles against my scalp. "I'm not gonna embarrass your friend. What the fuck could I say, anyway? 'Ha ha, your dad's a criminal?' The only one of us without a record is Melissa."

Clare waved to us to say that he was ready.

"Watch him," Casey said. "Here we go."

I felt a rush of pride when Clare got up on one knee, but he stayed there, listing back and forth as the board sliced left and right beneath him. He hit a wake, knifed sideways, and disappeared.

"He's off," I called.

Casey swung the boat around and planted the towrope in front of Clare with a tight turn.

"Just push down and stand up," I said as we passed.

Clare nodded without looking at me.

He was up on his knees and down again in less time.

"Drive for a minute," Casey said to me, lighting a cigarette. "Come up nice and slow. He's ready."

I pointed the boat toward Shelter Harbor, and we were almost up to speed when Casey told me Clare was down again. I realized I had never seen Clare fail at anything. I was nervous to have him back onboard, unsure how he would react.

"Watch him," Casey said to Mike. "He doesn't trust it."

Mike nodded. "He thinks it won't set unless he holds it there."

"OK, coach," Melissa said.

They occupied the back bench while I drove, Melissa with her back against her cousin's shoulder and her feet in Casey's lap. I felt the weight of the entire life that I had left behind here when I saw them like that—still, silent, propping one another up.

"He's ready," Casey said to me without turning around.

"He's down," Casey said, not half a minute later.

Clare raised a hand for me to stop as I swung the boat around again.

"You're good?" I asked.

He nodded.

"Is this your first time here?" Melissa asked him when he sat down next to her.

"Yeah," Clare said. "First time."

We ate at the Sailfish that night. It's a big, loud restaurant anchored by an oval bar in the middle of the action, a place where people come to overspend on seafood in the last throes of vacation. No one brought us menus, and the first round of appetizers hit the table before I had a napkin in my lap—coconut shrimp, artichoke dip, crawfish cakes covered in Jersey corn. For the main course, two waiters carried out a six-pound lobster that had been on prominent display at the raw bar. Mike split the shell with his hands, exposing the glistening white meat and the sea-green mess of the organs. He snapped off a claw and offered it to Clare. Mike and Casey had warmed to him after seeing him humbled on the water.

"That guy's watching us," Clare said, and I looked up from my scallops when I heard the worry in his voice.

"It's his place," Mike told Clare. "He's watching all this food coming to our table and counting all the money he's not making."

I turned to see Rob Mancuso, the owner of the Sailfish and the boat we had been scurfing with. He was standing at the bar, shorter than some of his seated customers, his bald head gleaming under the lights. Clare was wrong—he was watching me, not us. I nodded to him when our eyes met, and he nodded back.

"He has a bunch of restaurants," Mike went on, "and spends his whole life driving from one to another in his SL55, breaking balls, and making sure no one has a good time while they work. He has more money than Jesus Christ. He fuckin' hates me. He loves Casey like a son."

"You ever cater for him?" Casey asked Mike. "He's out there hauling trash with the Mexicans on every job. Works harder than anyone alive. Maybe you should have charged people for drinks once in a while and not served sixteen-year-old girls. Your shifts were like a fucking ad for statutory rape awareness."

Clare laughed so hard that his Arnold Palmer gushed out his nose.

"You mean the jaywalking of sex crimes," Mike said. "Anyway, he hated me before that. He's only got love for you, big guy."

"I'm sick of people talking about him like he walks on water," Melissa said. "He's lucky he's not locked up."

Clare wasn't laughing now.

"Rob's been on LBI since you were a gleam in your daddy's eye," Mike explained to Clare. "He ran this crew back in the eighties, moving tons of weight, making fuck off money, and this,"—he waved a lobster claw at the space around us—"is what he did with all that cash. This and a bunch of other places like it. Not bad, right?"

"Mike, shut up," Melissa said.

"What, Rob reads lips now?"

"He's coming over," Casey said. "He's going to tell you to get the fuck out of his restaurant because you're a loudmouth idiot."

There were hands on my shoulders.

"How's the food?" Rob asked.

"Hey, Mr. Mancuso," I said, turning around in my chair. "It's great, everything's great."

"Yeah, they do a nice job. Tommy, can I talk to you a second?"

Casey's expression gave me no sign that he had seen this coming. I dropped my napkin on the table and followed Rob to the bar with blood pounding in my ears over the din of the packed dining room and the Bon Jovi on the stereo.

"What's your poison?" Rob asked.

"Vodka tonic."

"Try again."

"Ginger ale."

"Ginger ale," he called down the bar. "And a club soda. Lots of ice, lots of lime. How you been?"

"Good," I said.

"Good to be back? Hey, Maurice, send a split of champagne to twenty-three, OK? What the fuck is taking so long over there?"

"Yeah," I said. "Always good to be back."

"How's your mom? I hear she's doing good up there."

"She's good. She's busy."

"School's good? You're done, right?"

I nodded, wondering how long it would take for him to get it out.

"Good for you. That's a pretty good school, huh?"

"Yeah," I said. "I learned a lot."

"I got this nephew who's thinking he might want to go there. Real smart kid. Not much of an athlete, but basically a genius. You liked it, right?"

"Yeah, sure," I said.

"I was thinking you could meet my nephew sometime, talk to him about the place. Give him some pointers, maybe look over his application."

Right, I thought. Of course.

"Sure," I said. "Whatever I can do."

"Would it help to have you talk to people there, or is that not a good idea after what happened?"

"You heard about that?"

"Yeah," Rob said. "I heard. I figured you were smarter than that, but what do I know. I hope you learned your lesson."

"I think I did."

"You think? Don't think."

"I did."

Rob nodded and smacked my shoulder.

"You boys paddle out today?"

"No, it was all blown out."

"I was out this morning," Rob said. "Couple nice sets came through. Don't be so picky. You're here for what, two days? Take what you can get. Most important thing you'll ever learn."

I laughed.

"They don't teach you that at Lawrenceville?"

"No," I said. "I guess not."

"Can't be that good of a school, then," Rob said.

Cops were gathering in the street outside the restaurant, anticipating the crush of a summer night, the inevitable fights.

"Sure you brought enough guys?" Mike called to them, as we headed for the car.

"Come over here and say that to my face," one of them said, flipping his baton into the air and catching it above his head. He and Mike went way back.

"Take your cousin to Disco's," Casey said to Melissa. "And Clare too. Me and Tom are going to Rommel's for something to drink."

Clare had been sticking close to me, but Casey was a good manager because he made directions sound like prophecy.

"Pick up smokes for me," Mike said.

"No," Casey said. "This is the third time this week."

"That's how I know you love me."

"You drive," Casey said, tossing me his keys as we walked to the car. The sun was down, the traffic on the boulevard transformed into one long stripe of red and white light. I eased out of the space and threw the GTI into gear.

"You should come visit me at school," I said. "Take some time off once I get settled."

"I should," Casey said, arching his back and digging in his pocket for his phone.

"Yeah," he said. "I called you five hours ago. Tuesday's fine. As long as Tuesday means Tuesday. No, we'll take my car. Four a.m. Yes, I'm serious. Hey, you got any more of those books-on-tape? OK. We'll come by later."

"Who was that?" I asked as he hung up. It seemed like he was extra careful not to discuss business with me or around me after my arrest, although that might have been my own paranoia.

"Disco. The guy with the bar in his garage."

"You guys going someplace?"

"Hey," Casey said, pointing at the road.

The car in front of us had stopped to make a left. I slammed on the brakes and something slid out from under the seat and smashed into my heel as we skidded to a stop.

"You should find a better place for that," I said, nudging the gun back where it had been.

"You should learn how to drive," Casey said.

At Rommel's Liquor Store, Casey grabbed a bottle of Patrón and a Diet Dr. Pepper for Melissa. He pointed to a corkboard on the wall behind the counter as we waited in line. A hand-lettered sign above the board read BUSTED PUNKS and every inch of cork was covered in confiscated fake IDs.

"We're still up there," he said. "Hall of Fame."

And there we were, side by side, our faces rounder and smoother, the cheap ink on the fake Maryland state seals faded by the sun. Our invented dates of birth would put us in our late twenties by now. Years ago, we had swaggered in with freshly minted licenses, and put cheap vodka on the counter. I looked up at the board after we'd handed the cards over and saw a row of identical IDs, printed by the same tattoo parlor in Wildwood. The clerk pulled an electronic scanner out from underneath the counter, and told us we could put the vodka back or spend the night in jail. As we left the store I watched him pierce the plastic cards with thumbtacks and stick them to the board like butterfly specimens, the holograms glinting under the fluorescent lights like iridescent dust on fragile wings. Casey didn't need ID here anymore.

"Babies," Casey said. "Remember that?"

"What's that?" the clerk asked.

"Nothing. Let me get a pack of Newports too."

We killed two hours in a garage speakeasy called Disco's, run by a kid called Disco who had long white-blond hair and a tattoo of a horseshoe on the inside of his bicep that stood right side up for luck when his left arm was at his side. Casey took him into a corner to talk as soon as we walked in. The garage looked like a yard sale: sun-scorched surfboards, stolen beer signs, driftwood, movie posters, and threadbare furniture that people down in Harvey Cedars left by the curb at the end of every season. A lifeguard turned nineteen that night, and we all stepped up for birthday punches until the boy's shoulder was red and badly swollen under his dark tan. Clare, I was surprised to learn, could hit. The lifeguard barely braced himself, not expecting much, but Mike whistled through his teeth as

Clare's punch sent the boy sprawling into a tangle of rusted beach cruisers. Clare apologized and tried to help him up, but the boy waved him off, laughing.

"I feel like a man!" he yelled.

Our next stop was a poker game held on a yacht tied up at the Shelter Harbor Yacht Club. It's where the bartenders on the island take their tips and play until someone takes the pot. The owner of the boat is a fantastically fat orthodontic surgeon from Philadelphia who doesn't play cards, but loves the game for the party it creates and the girls it brings around. He was sitting in a recliner with a massive rocks glass in one hand and a female lifeguard perched on each arm of the chair. There was a constant sway from people coming aboard and going ashore, and most of the crowd was gathered around the spot-lit table in the galley, where the game was underway. Mike had long since been banned, and a bartender from the Sailfish was up $3,000 when I slipped through the sliding door onto the deck without anybody noticing. Clare had disappeared into the bathroom with two cokehead girls who worked at the boardwalk candy store, and I figured he'd be busy for a while. I jumped the gap between the boat and the dock, headed for the parking lot. Casey's keys were still in my pocket from the drive. I unlocked the car, shut myself inside, and reached under the seat.

It was a beautiful piece. I turned it over in the glow of the streetlights, a bright, heavy .357 Magnum in stainless steel. The grips on the revolver's handle were polished cocobolo wood—veined, translucent, smooth to the touch. I thought back to Casey's love of woodshop, of wooden Alaia surfboards, of the wooden-wall Jeeps we'd grown up with. The gun was not something he had picked up on the fly. I broke the cylinder open and spun it with a slap of my hand. The six rounds blurred into a brass ring, and became distinct again as they slowed. I closed the cylinder and held the gun below the dash in both my hands. I thumbed the safety off.

Six months before, when I was arrested for selling drugs at Lawrenceville, I gave Casey up in a Lawrence Township Precinct interrogation room that smelled faintly of bleach. I allowed myself to remember it now, locked in a car with a gun in my hands. The police asked me for the name of my supplier and I gave it without hesitation, praying it would buy me time or leverage, as scared as I had been when an older kid had held my head underwater at the public pool. A female cop with a ponytail asked me for the spelling and jotted it down on a notepad. Later, she told me I had done a good thing, that there was still time for both of us to straighten out our lives. Casey never asked if I had given him up because it was inconceivable to him that I would do that. I tried not to think about it, but there were days when it was the first thing in my mind when I opened my eyes. Was it possible that I'd inherited, instead of my mother's fierce, unyielding sense of right and wrong, the kind of moral compass that compels a man to never see his kid or sell out his friends for nothing? I wiped the gun down with my shirt and slid it back under the seat.

The bartender had taken the pot by the time I got back to the boat. The tension of the game had dissipated, and Clare was walking toward me, running his tongue across his teeth.

"Where'd you go? Everyone was asking."

"Just out for some air."

"We're staying here, right? That's the other thing everyone was asking."

"You don't seem ready for bed, but yeah, we're staying at Casey's place."

Clare blew a long breath through pursed lips. I didn't touch coke, mostly because Casey didn't. Casey used to say that people cut the shit out of the stuff he sold, and I figured that whatever Clare was doing was as good as it got.

"This place is great," Clare said. "I don't want to leave. Your friends are amazing. Are you upset? Is something wrong?"

"No," I said. "I'm fine."

"Are you sure? You seem kind of down. Hey, can I ask you something? I feel like you spend all this time looking out for me and I never do anything for you. I'm not a shitty friend, am I?"

"No. Not at all. You'd do the same thing."

I wondered if that was true.

"Yo," Mike said, slapping both of us on the back. "Should I leave you two alone? We're getting outta here."

The boat cleared out, and the whole party took a walk down to the bank. We all packed into the blinding, air-conditioned ATM vestibule, and people started chanting at the bartender as he entered his PIN and stuffed the bills into an envelope. What would you like to do? the machine asked. Make a deposit. Amount? $4,700. The slot popped open, and the whirring gears inside almost ground to a stop as they tried to swallow the brick of cash. A yell went up when it went through. The bartender held up the receipt. He was sweating, smiling at the floor, talking about the game, like this was an Olympic victory interview just after his event. Outside, a cop banged the butt end of his Maglite on the glass, pointing at the bartender.

"At least I know who's buying at Nardi's tomorrow," he said. "Now go home, you motherfuckers. You're disturbing my peace."

The seafood market in downtown Princeton was packed with people picking out tuna steaks and yelling into cell phones about dinner plans and lobster tails. Clare and I had just come from a job at a country club in East Brunswick, which Clare had insisted on working, even after my mother told him that we had plenty of hands. She had asked us to pick up scallops on our way home. I watched the guy behind the counter pop a scrap of Nova Scotia salmon into his mouth before he called for the next customer to please step up.

"Hello?" Clare said, cupping his hand over his mouth as he spoke into his phone. "Yeah, hang on. He's right here."

Clare passed me his phone, mouthing to me that I should just give her my number already.

"Hi, Kelsey," I said.

"How are you?"

"Great," I said, shouldering through the door so we could understand each other.

"So I'm in Princeton with my cousin and she's not feeling so hot. I was thinking we could have dinner. Are you free?"

Kelsey had said 8:00, and just after 8:15 the hostess at the restaurant assured me again that no one had come asking for me, that she had three parties on dessert, that she couldn't seat me by myself. I crossed the street and sat on the stoop of a framing shop to wait. I wondered if Kelsey was going to show, or if I would end up back at the house with Clare and my mother and the bottle of sauvignon blanc that was sweating through the paper bag at my feet. A big Japanese tour group stopped at the restaurant's door to read the menu, and sent a runner in to ask about a table for fifteen, which the restaurant didn't have. I saw Kelsey as they moved on, checking her reflection in the glass, looking up and down the street, waiting for me. She saw me as I stood on the double yellow line, gauging the gaps between a string of eastbound cars.

"Hi," she said. "Thanks for meeting me. Sorry I'm late."

"Thanks for calling," I said. "Do you want my number so you don't have to keep calling Clare?"

"Not really," she said. "What's the point? You'll have a UK phone the next time I need to talk to you."

The hostess sat us right away, but there was a moment where we stood awkwardly across from each other while a busboy wiped our table down, both of us passing our eyes over the people around us and the plates in front of them, searching for something to say. I wondered if this had been a bad idea, but Kelsey smiled as soon as we sat down, and asked if I had been getting down the shore. She had cut off most of her hair, and wore what was left at an even length of a few inches, the spiky points echoing her petite nose and the points of her ears. The kitchen sent out a dozen oysters, courtesy of a cook who used to work for us. Kelsey didn't seem to notice, too caught up in a story about a snapper she had caught the week before on someone's sailboat off Mustique, a Caribbean island that I had to look up later. The rich bronze of her skin seemed to suck up the buzzy yellow light of the dining room. She slurped an oyster from its shell, and I wondered who she had been with on the boat. We were drinking fast, and the bottle was empty and upended in the ice bucket by the time our entrees dropped. Luckily the table next to us had gotten carried away with the BYO policy; they offered us an open, untouched Chardonnay as they swayed and struggled with their blazers and their purse straps. Kelsey thanked them, and a woman asked her where she'd found the coffee-colored linen jacket she was wearing. Kelsey told her it was something she had made herself.

"How's your friend Clare doing?" she asked me.

"He's good," I said. "You heard about his dad?"

"That's why I asked."

"I mean, he's a little weird, but I think he's doing fine. He's staying at my place, actually. Shit, I meant to tell you: he's coming to St. Andrews. He just got in last week."

"I love how it's everyone's plan B," she said, brushing capers off a piece of lake trout with her fork. "What made you decide to go there?"

"My guidance counselor said I should hang out there for a year, lie low, maybe transfer."

"That's what she told you? Lie low?"

"Yeah. I think that's exactly what she said."

"I don't think she knew what she was getting you into."

"What do you mean? It sounds like you hate it."

"No. I love it. It's not for everyone. It works for me. Why do you think Clare is going? Is it because of you?"

"No," I said, shifting in my seat, remembering Mike's reaction when I told him Clare was staying with us. "He didn't really have another option. Maybe he wants to get out of the states for a while."

"He picked the wrong place to escape what happened to his dad, if that's what you're saying. Anyway, I'm sure you'll both do fine. Is there anything you want to know?"

There was nothing about her that I didn't want to know, but I realized she was talking about the school, which I had barely thought about since I mailed my deposit.

"How long is the flight?" I asked.

"The flight's not bad. You take a sleeping pill and wake up there."

"How about academics?"

"They're amazing."

"I was kidding."

"I know."

"How's your fish?"

"It's great," she said. "I'm not kidding about that. I guess you have good taste."

After dinner, I walked her to her car, a blue Lexus SUV that Mike would have called a mom mobile, parked just off the Princeton campus. She was digging for her keys and I was trying to think of some way to keep her there when someone called my name. The voice seemed to come from the illuminated rectangle of an open door in a long windowless brick wall. I looked harder and saw three men in white waiter jackets taking a cigarette break just outside the light.

"Who's that?" Kelsey asked.

They worked for my mother on and off, and they were waving me over. I heard music as we drew closer, the strains of a live band taking "Brick House" too fast and too hard somewhere inside.

"Good to see you, bro," said a cook nicknamed Pollo for his skinny legs.

"Nice to meet you," Kelsey said to them.

"What's the job?" I asked.

"Party," Pollo said. "Some lady turning sixty. You two should check it out. Night's young, you know?"

"Yeah?" Kelsey said. "You think we could pull it off?"

"No," I said. "Not a good idea."

"Cute white kids like you?" Pollo said. "Come on, man. Who's gonna tell you no?"

Kelsey took my hand as we crossed the kitchen and stopped at the twin windows on the swinging doors that opened into the ballroom. Pollo looked over my shoulder and gave us the lay of the land.

"Yeah, that's the birthday girl," he said, pointing to a woman with a helmet of graying hair and geometrically precise bangs. "There she is. Been in that spot all night. Long as you steer clear of her, you're fine. Her name's Marla. She works here; she's a dean or something. She likes her champagne not *too* cold, you know?"

Kelsey and I pushed through the doors onto the dance floor, and as I spun her away and pulled her close to "Wild Horses," we hammered out a quick history, talking in each other's ears. She tugged a ring off the middle finger of her left hand and slipped it onto her ring finger.

When the song was over, we sat down at an empty table, and were immediately joined by two couples at least twice our age. A server came over to take our order, and winked at me when I asked for two glasses of champagne. He had been outside with us, I realized. He knew who we were.

"So, how did you two end up here?" a woman asked, spinning a lock of hair around her finger, while her husband's eyes moved slowly over Kelsey's face as if he were cataloguing her features.

"I'm a friend of Marla's cousin John," I explained.

"I'm his fiancée," Kelsey said.

They asked how long we had been together (almost four years), and Kelsey told the story of how we'd gotten engaged two months earlier on a sailboat in Mustique. The wedding would be in Spring Lake, she added. Another couple joined us. I was a second-year analyst in fixed income at Lehman Brothers, I told them. Kelsey was going back to school for design.

"Where has Marla been hiding you two?" someone asked.

Kelsey laughed, took my face in both her hands, and kissed me on the mouth.

"We'll have to ask her to invite us to these things," she said.

We made a lot of friends during the hour or hours that I experienced as noise and liquor aftertaste and color-saturated snapshots. Kelsey snapped a flower off a centerpiece, and was tucking it behind my ear when someone threw open a side door that led straight out into the night. I took a small step back, unsettled by the block of darkness fifty feet away, the inverse of the bright hole that had brought us here. Of course it's dark outside, I thought, because there's nothing out there now. I wanted to believe that our fabricated life had supplanted our reality, that we would go on like this when the bar closed and the lights came up. I wanted to slow down and sober up a little. My thoughts felt like water rushing down the hallway of a ship.

A man from our table had asked us to show him how one took tequila shots with the salt, the lime, the whole nine yards. I was wincing into the back of my hand when a woman standing at my shoulder asked me how we wound up here.

"I'm a friend of Marla's cousin John," I said, turning around. "And this—"

"I'm Marla," the woman said.

And there she was. How dare you, I thought, too drunk to be embarrassed at how comfortable I had been inside a lie. Marla wasn't finished.

"I'd call security, but everyone thinks that you're cherished family friends. People asked why they weren't seated at your table. So why don't you just say your goodnights, and leave on your own."

"Happy birthday," I said. "Thanks for everything."

Kelsey and I stumbled back to her car.

"OK," she said. "This is where I leave you. Jesus, wish me luck driving to Courtney's."

"You're leaving?"

"I can't sleep in the car."

"You can crash with me. You can't drive home right now."

"You have company already," she said, meaning Clare.

I felt the sharp foil corner of a condom wrapper prick my thigh through the thin pocket of my chinos. I moved in to kiss her, but Kelsey turned her head away. She kissed me on one cheek, and then the other.

"You better get used to that," she said, after her second kiss missed my face as I pulled back to ask her a question with my eyes. "It's always two where we're going."

PART II

In the parking lot at Newark Liberty International, Clare eased his mother's BMW into the sea of cars we had seen from the overpass. We hauled our things out of the trunk, and Clare lit out for the terminal, his oversized suitcase listing behind him from wheel to wheel.

"What about the car?" I called.

Clare stopped short.

The car came into our lives after Clare answered a call from a Connecticut area code. There was a woman on the other end whose name, when Clare parroted it back to her as a question, sounded Dutch. We were with Mike and Casey at the Tropicana in Atlantic City. When the blackjack dealer asked Clare to take his conversation somewhere else, I followed him into a food court, where the woman on the phone explained that she had an SUV belonging to his family at her home on Fishers Island, and asked Clare if he'd be so kind as to come and pick it up. Had Clare's parents been vacationing at someone's beach house when they heard the law was closing in? I imagined them boarding a ferry before dawn, ditching their vehicle, offering a cab driver a stack of hundreds for a lift to

Teterboro and a waiting plane. I never learned what their car was doing there. If Clare knew, he didn't let on.

Two days later, a demure Eastern European woman—not one of the family's regular chauffeurs, judging by the jerky, overcautious way she handled the Mercedes wagon—met us at the Fishers Island ferry dock. The house, hidden by tall privets, ran along a slice of land between an unmarked street and a rocky beach. Our visit lasted under five minutes and followed a tight script: give the boys the car keys from a silver dish on the wet bar in the study, offer them a glass of water or a diet soda, suggest a nearby B&B where they can spend the night. We could hear a dinner party in some distant wing, but no invitation was forthcoming. I imagined someone scratching Clare's name off a to-do list as we sped down the narrow island roads in his mother's silver BMW X5, now stranded in Newark.

Clare turned to face me without setting down his bag. He would have left the car to rust if I had kept my mouth shut.

"It's long-term parking, right?" he said.

"I don't think a year is what they had in mind."

"What should I do?"

"Just leave the keys on the back left tire. I'll have my mom come pick it up."

The big airy terminal was full of sunlight and echoing boarding announcements. I was halfway through the check-in line when I sensed someone closing in on me; Clare was three steps away when I spun around. He stopped just short of the retractable nylon barrier and swallowed hard.

"They're charging me this fee," he said. "My stuff weighs too much."

Behind him, the attendant at the American Airlines counter was craning her neck to see where he had gone, waving his passport in the air.

"How much?" I asked.

"Three hundred. There's this fucking hold on all my cards." Clare opened the backpack slung over his shoulder and took out a blue felt shoe bag. He bounced the shoes in his hand, as if trying to guess their weight for a prize at a fair. "Do you see a trash can?"

"Wait," I said. "Slow down. You're gonna throw stuff away? Why don't I just spot you the money and you can pay me back when we get over there?"

"Can you do that?"

Maybe, I thought, balancing my checking account in my head. I handed Clare my card.

"Can you come over and sign?" he said. "They know I'm not you."

A mother of three, eavesdropping behind us, agreed to hold my place in line.

"Hi," the counter attendant said. "Is everything OK?"

Clare stood with his back to her while I paid his fee, pretending to keep an eye on my bags. I signed the receipt and she told Clare, over my shoulder, to enjoy his flight. It took me a second to understand that she was talking about the plane ride, and not making a joke at Clare's expense.

He was almost through security by the time I joined the line, and I watched the TSA agents stop and search him from my place at the back. They had him spread his legs and raise his arms like Da Vinci's *Vitruvian Man* while a woman in uniform traced the outline of his body with a plastic wand. Another agent flipped through his passport and riffled through his bag. I wondered if they knew him as his father's son, if the family name was now a big red flag.

I didn't get a second look on the way to my flight. When the captain announced that we'd be taking off shortly, I dug my phone out of my pocket and called my mother one last time.

"Hey," I said. "It's me. You want a car?"

"What's your purpose here?" the customs officer asked.

She was my first British accent on foreign soil, but my excitement at this fact was not contagious. The sun had just risen over London, Heathrow. I had a connecting flight to Edinburgh. She did this all day.

"School," I said. "St. Andrews University."

"You're a first year?"

"Yes, ma'am."

"I need your matriculation letter."

I handed her all the paperwork I had.

"None of this is any good," she said.

I asked if she would mind checking again. She flipped quickly through the pile, but gave no sign that she had found what she was looking for.

"This is your visa," she said, pounding a stamp into my passport. "You can come and go til June."

Clare and I sat in a glass bus stop outside Edinburgh airport, watching double-decker coaches cough black exhaust into a darkening sky. The sun had set by the time the university's chartered bus pulled up and opened its doors. Everyone on board looked American and jet-lagged. A short stint on the highway was followed by a long ride on a country road that barely fit the bus, wet leaves brushing past my face behind the window. After about an hour a woman near the front stood up, tapped a microphone, and welcomed us to

St. Andrews in a thick brogue. I saw the town through the windshield, its streetlights flaring and fading like fireflies, blotted out by high-pitched rooftops and towers and spires as the landscape spun in front of us with the winding of the road. On our left, the woman said, was the Old Course, where golf was first played. It was all low grassy hills in the darkness, a patchy expanse of black land. To our right was Andrew Melville Hall, where Clare and I were meant to live.

"One of the finest examples of new brutalist architecture in all of Scotland," our guide said. "If you look closely, you'll see that it resembles two giant steamer ships crossing paths in the night."

I saw what she meant about the building as we pulled up to the spot-lit entrance, situated where the bows of the glass and concrete "ships" met at an angle. Clare and I dragged our bags into a lobby full of plastic plants. In a far corner was the kind of store you find in hotel lobbies, selling magazines and medicine in single doses. Andrew Melville Hall functioned as a hotel in the summer, when the school rented rooms to golfers, and still felt like a hotel now—muffled, thick walled, sterile. The woman behind the reception desk summoned a porter to take our bags up to our rooms. Dinner, she informed us, would be ready in an hour in the top-floor catering hall. She handed us our keys.

Clare and I rode the elevator in silence, a thickset Scottish porter between us. We stopped on three to drop Clare off, and I pushed through fire door after fire door as we walked the long hall on the port side of the ship. Between each set of doors, an axe and an extinguisher were buried in the wall behind a pane of glass, signaling a fear of fire that seemed strange in a town where you spend most days expecting rain. Outside in the darkness, balls of rainfall were visible around the orange streetlights that ran along the empty road.

"Can you wake me up for dinner?" Clare asked, his key in the lock. "You have an alarm, right? Mine just died."

The urgency in his voice was about more than missing a meal. He looked exhausted, and seemed afraid to close his eyes in a new place with no one there to wake him. I told him I would come by later. The porter showed me to my floor.

"This is your room," he said, opening the door.

The porter waited in the hall while I dragged my bags inside. The rooms were small and square, the walls covered in corkboard to prevent the tacks in tie-dyed tapestries and Joy Division posters from ruining the sheetrock. I had my own bathroom for the first time in my life, which was something. But the disappointment I felt took me back to the first time my mother brought me to our house in Princeton, led me up the back stairs, and opened the first door on the second-story hallway. The room she showed me, my new room, was empty except for a wash of grime and loose change along the far wall, like something left by an outgoing tide. The paint was peeling and the windows looked over a small parking lot dotted with trashcans. This was not what I had imagined when she told me she had found the perfect place in Princeton. I wished that we had never left the shore.

"Everything in order, sir?" the porter called from the hall.

"Yeah, totally," I said, tipping him ten pounds because I hadn't broken any bills.

When he was gone, I lay down on the blue duvet and stared at the reflection of my body in the dead screen of the TV aimed down at the bed—270 nights here, give or take.

Dinner was a barely edible British take on lasagna: boiled vegetables pressed like botany specimens between layers of overcooked noodle, topped with half an inch of mystery cheese. The plastic cups, smoky with scratches and fraying at the rims, reminded me of summer camp. Getting-to-know-you banter was swelling all around us. I had imagined—what? A more exotic and egalitarian version of my high school? I couldn't remember.

"Are you gonna finish that?" Clare asked me, pointing his fork at my plate.

He had been tucking into his food across the table. Either the twenty-minute power nap had done wonders for him, or this drab scenery and bad food were exactly what he'd hoped to find. I pushed my tray toward him. Finally, a girl in a red sweatshirt stood on a chair to say that she would take us out for the evening, that all we had to do was follow her.

After dinner, she walked backward toward the town, leading a parade of international students. She took questions from the people near the front, and recited facts as a light rain began to fall again. The population of the town doubles between orientation and exams, she said. There are three main streets in St. Andrews proper:

North Street, South Street, and Market Street—four if you count the Scores Road, which runs along the water and ends at the Old Course Club House. There are more pubs per capita in St. Andrews than anywhere else in the world.

Our first stop was the Victoria, a second-story bar and lounge on Market Street. The parade became a mob as people crowded into the stairwell to get out of the weather. On the step above us, a boy and girl were doing their best to talk about us without seeming rude. The boy turned around after some audible prodding by his companion, and stuck out his hand.

"Clayton Jacks," he said. "Pleased to meet you."

He wore the family name engraved on what looked like a medical ID bracelet, the links of which were as thick as his skinny fingers. He was well dressed and overeager. I tried to guess which boarding school he hailed from.

"I'm Tom. This is—"

Clare had fallen back and turned away.

"I think you were on my flight," Clayton said, over my shoulder. "The seat behind me?"

Clare turned, and the two of them shook hands. I couldn't tell whether Clare recognized these people personally or recognized them as a type that he was eager to avoid.

"Clayton Jacks," Clayton Jacks said again. "Pleased to meet you. And you know Tom?"

"We went to school together," I said.

"So did Chantal and I. Chantal saw the two of you at dinner and said we had to meet you."

Chantal had very white skin and small hands that shook slightly. A child's face, expensive clothes.

"Where were you at school?" she asked.

"Lawrenceville."

"Lawrenceville, of course," she said. "We were at Exeter together. And where are you from?"

Clare said he was from New Canaan, which was either a lie or not the answer to the question she had asked.

"It's nice to meet people from boarding school," Chantal said.

They hadn't asked where I was from, and in the silence that followed, I realized that Clare hadn't really introduced himself.

"I didn't catch your name," Chantal said to him.

"It's Clare."

Chantal waited for the other name to drop.

"Hey, let's go somewhere else," I said. "I know somebody here. Does anyone have change for a phone call?"

"Here," Chantal said, producing a sleek silver cell phone from her bag, "use this. It works all over the world."

Just before we parted ways in Princeton, Kelsey had torn a corner off a map of Ocean County, written down the number of her Scottish cell phone, and slipped it into my back pocket. I had been playing with the paper all night, and now it was as soft as cotton, the number illegible, which didn't matter because I had memorized it weeks before. I was eager to find Kelsey and lose these people both for Clare's sake and because I had a feeling they were also here because something had gone wrong in their lives. Pick up, I thought, after three single-note ring tones. The noise that broke through on the other end was deafening.

"Hello?"

"Kelsey. It's Tom."

"Hi, Tom."

"I'm here."

"Be more specific."

"This place called the Victoria."

"Walk out the door and go straight until you hit the Scores. It's the one by the water. Turn left when you see the beach. Ask someone for Ma Bells."

"We'll be right there."

"I'll be right here."

I led the way, and Clayton fell in step beside me. He was determined to find some common ground, and we managed to come up with the Gold and Silver Ball the year before, and a New Year's party at the Warwick in Manhattan that I had heard about but not actually attended. He wondered aloud how we had never met, while I split my attention and gave the other half to the conversation Clare was trying not to have behind me. He stuck to the New Canaan story, and implied that he had always been a boarder. Chantal mentioned people we had gone to school with, and Clare pretended not to know them, politely excusing himself from the life I was pretending to lead three steps ahead of him.

The scenery came to Clare's rescue as we hit the Scores. St. Andrews Bay was black in the darkness, and a white stripe of reflected moonlight ran perpendicular to a hundred yards of rolling breakers. The white of the surf became the white-sand beach that ringed in the Old Course and the bedrock foundation of the town. The smell of salt water took at least two time zones off my jet lag.

A group of girls tottered by, and one of them pointed backward over her shoulder when I asked her where Ma Bells was. The bar sat below the street, behind a sunken concrete courtyard filled with people clutching pints and smoking and talking at one another. The bouncer on the door wore an earpiece connected to a coiled wire that snaked down his thick neck, and beside him was a man in a long gray overcoat who was not here to pick up college girls, judging by his officious demeanor and the way he looked us over as we started down the stairs. Kelsey appeared in the doorway, wearing a low-cut white T-shirt with what looked like a little boy's tuxedo jacket. She whispered something to the bouncer, who waved us in as she disappeared.

Soft rock played on the jukebox inside, but the mood was frenzied and the room was packed. There was something prefatory about the noise people were making, like the atonal mess of an orchestra tuning up. Kelsey was waiting for us inside the door, a cigarette in one hand, a highball in the other. She came to me first, draped her arms over my shoulders, and crossed her full hands just behind my head. Holding her for those four seconds was like picking up a guitar to find it in a strange tuning, where nothing you play sounds the same. I tried and failed to catch her eye as she kissed Clare hello and introduced herself to Clayton and Chantal.

"Come sit down, you guys," she said, taking Clare by the arm and heading for a table in the back. "Did you just get in?"

Before I could answer, I realized that Prince William was sitting at the table Kelsey was leading us to, talking to an older man dressed like he had just walked off the golf course. This explained the extra man on the door, and a second man, identically dressed, watching our table from the opposite wall. And this was more like it. Clare seemed as shocked as I was, but Chantal and Clayton gave me these weird congratulatory smiles, a show of appreciation for helping them fall in with the right crowd on their first night. William wore the uniform of my Catholic grammar school: blue button-down, pleated khakis, boat shoes. Sitting next to him was a boy dressed in a black belted racing jacket and a white dress shirt, the kind of thing you'd expect royalty to wear for a night out. He wore half his shoulder-length hair tied back in a kind of samurai pony tail, and had a navy ascot knotted at his throat, which told me that he took this British upper class thing very seriously, or not seriously at all. Kelsey made her way around the table and slid into the empty seat next to him. He turned as she sat down and I watched him cock his head and kiss her on the mouth. Her face followed his as he sat back and resumed his conversation with a dark-haired girl I couldn't see. Kelsey slapped his thigh.

"This is Julian, who can't be bothered to introduce himself."

"Jules," he said, shaking Clare's hand and then mine. "You're first years, then?"

"I met these two at my cousin's birthday," Kelsey said.

Jules squinted at Clare.

"Looks a bit like Will, doesn't he?"

This was a good excuse to look at William, whom we had been pretending to ignore. Clare's nose was broader on the bridge, and his jaw was less angular, but the resemblance was astonishing when you saw them side by side. Jules hit the prince of England on the shoulder with the back of his hand.

"Mate, have a look. Your long lost twin's just turned up from America."

William, laughing, shook Clare's hand.

"Great face," he said.

"I'd lose the American accent if I were you," Jules said to Clare. "Have your hair cut. Pass yourself off."

The girl sitting across from Jules was named Mary. Her deep tan and her hair, which had the color and sheen of obsidian, made her look like Disney's Pocahontas. She barely turned her head when she was introduced to us, which made it seem like someone had told her to hold still in this shifting sea of bodies, although she didn't look like she took orders.

"Thanks so much for bringing us," Clayton said, wiping gin off his mouth with his sleeve. Martinis had materialized around the table. Kelsey stuck her fingers in her boyfriend's drink, fishing for an olive, her hot pink nails magnified by the liquor and the convex glass.

"Cleveland," Clayton said, in answer to a question that I didn't hear. "Shaker Heights."

"No, which hall are you living in?" Jules asked.

"Oh, Andrew Melville."

"Who lived there our first year?" Kelsey asked.

"Damien," Jules told her. "Lasted a month. We should take this lot over to the Old Course and pay him a visit. He'd enjoy some company."

"I don't know," Kelsey said. "They just got here. Maybe save that for another night. Are you guys hungry? You're not eating hall food, are you?"

"I couldn't even tell what they served us tonight," Chantal said. "I didn't touch it."

"You must be starving," Kelsey said. "Let's get you some Indian food, and then we can have a drink at my place."

We all nodded, half drunk now, one appetite igniting another like a chain of flares. Kelsey checked her boyfriend's watch. She seemed dependent on him for small things—an olive, the time of day. Clare asked where the bathroom was, and I followed him when he stood up and shouldered through the crowd. I couldn't sit at that table anymore.

I found Clare at the bathroom sinks, leaning on the counter in a standing track start, staring down at the place where the mirror met the marble. I washed my hands at the sink next to him, and caught his eye in the glass. There was no relief for him in the crowd we had just fallen in with, and we had both looked at each other when it became clear that Jules and Kelsey were a couple. Clare's reflection laughed.

"So here we are," he said.

In the street outside Ma Bells, Kelsey announced that we were going to Balaka, an Indian restaurant that served takeout until midnight. Clayton was imitating the man who had been talking to William—a Frenchman who had apparently been trying to get the prince to join him for breakfast. Kelsey, laughing, snaked her arm around Clayton's waist and said he must have known that guy for ages. I wished that I had found a way to leave Clayton and Chantal where we'd found them. In my fantasies about St. Andrews, I had imagined only me and Kelsey, with Clare somewhere in the periphery. Kelsey dug her phone out of her bag and called her flatmates to see if they had cigarettes and say that we were on our way.

"I'm with these precious first years," she said. "I'm bringing them home."

The chicken vindaloo that Clayton ordered, along with three bottles of champagne to go, was the hottest thing I had ever tasted. We took one bite at a time, huddled over takeout containers at Kelsey's kitchen table, and then raced each other to the fridge for vodka, lager, soy milk—anything to ease the burning before going back for more. Clare and Chantal tried to see who could stand the spice for longer, laughing through tears and stamping their feet as if the pain was music they were dancing to. Kelsey's flat was filling up as the bars emptied out. Her flatmates lit cigarettes and leaned against the kitchen walls and counters, watching us. The light from the naked fluorescents overhead cut through the smoke and hit their glossy lips and diamond studs and the whites of their eyes. Someone wondered aloud what we'd be like in six months, and I tried to imagine what kind of change they were anticipating. Clare put a hand on my shoulder, dabbing at his glistening forehead with the cuff of his shirt. "Enough," he said. "Get that shit away from me."

The stairwell coughed up visitors in twos and threes. Jules

appeared behind a pair of twin boys I had seen at Ma Bells. I nodded to him, but he gave no sign that he recognized me. He was wearing scuffed-up velvet tuxedo slippers that I had seen men wear at the benefits we catered, and his jacket looked much older than he did. His clothes were threadbare in a way that looked not shabby, but aristocratic. No one in New Jersey dressed like that. Jules stepped aside to make way for two girls on their way out in a show of good and effortless manners.

Back in the kitchen, Chantal was getting hit on by the twins.

"You kids need some parents," Kelsey said, as Clare and I walked in together. "Has anyone explained this to you?"

"No," I said, warily.

"It's called academic parenting. It was about academics back in the 1400s, but it's more of a mentorship thing now. Third- and fourth-year boys adopt some first-year girls—that usually happens first—and girls adopt some first-year boys, and when someone has a suitable flock, they combine with someone they know or someone they sleep with to make an academic family."

I pictured the title grid from *The Brady Bunch* filled with drunk first years leering at each other while mom and dad looked on with pride. Jules filled the doorway and told Kelsey he was heading over to see Damien. When he was gone, Kelsey picked up her phone and motioned for me to follow her as she walked down the hall, ordering taxis for her guests. She opened the door to her room, and waved me in.

"Sit while I fix myself up," she said, pointing to her bed.

There was a landslide of silk and denim and cotton piled against the foot of the mattress, outfits considered and discarded. Necklaces and bracelets poured out of a jewelry case on her dresser and a pile of books stacked beside an antique radiator had collapsed like the bricks of a demolished wall. Hanging above her bed was a small portrait done in oil paints. It was Kelsey in the painting, but it could have been an older sister, or her mother in her younger years; she looked like someone had tapped and drained some of her youth. She seemed to be doing something with her hands, but her hands were just below the edge of the canvas, the gesture lost. She was topless in the painting, and either her tattoo had been left out or her ink was more recent than this artwork, although I doubted that.

"Who did that?" I asked her.

"Jules."

"He paints?"

"We broke up last spring," she said, ignoring my question. "I saw him this summer and we got back together. Old habits die hard, right?"

"Or they don't."

Kelsey's mouth was frozen open as she put on her mascara.

"Yes, he paints," she said, finally. "It's almost all he does."

"Where are we going?"

"The Old Course Hotel. This guy named Damien is living there until he finds a house, which is ridiculous."

"He's a student?"

Kelsey nodded, snapped her compact shut, and turned to face me.

"Are you having fun?" she asked.

"It's two fifteen," I said, after the girl in the front seat of the taxi turned to ask me for the time.

"It still feels so bloody early."

"That's where we're going," Kelsey said, squeezing my thigh and pointing.

The Old Course Hotel, the largest and brightest building outside the town, came into view as the driver spun around the traffic circle that launched us out of St. Andrews proper. We piled out under an enormous awning and revolved through the lobby door. I was expecting the kind of opulence you find in big American hotels, but the ground floor was all beige walls and cream-colored carpeting. This was where visiting parents stayed, Kelsey told us, and where people came to hole up for the weekend when there were good drugs in town. She led us to a room at the end of the third-floor hallway, and knocked.

The first thing I saw over Kelsey's shoulder was a motorcycle helmet on a dresser, and the second thing was a boy sitting on the bed with his back against the headboard, one loafer on the king-sized duvet, and the other planted on the floor of the suite that he was using as a dorm room. On the nightstand beside him was a disassembled set of throwing darts that he was piecing back together, a dart shaft tucked behind his ear. He didn't acknowledge us until he had inspected the point on a steel tip in the lamplight. Jules sat on the other side of the bed, ashing a joint onto an empty bottle of Bordeaux. Two new girls occupied the sofa, their legs tucked under their bodies like birds.

"This is Damien," Kelsey said. "He's from New York."

He was handsome in a way that made him seem unknowable, the product of generation after generation of good breeding, of men fucking a long line of successively more attractive women.

"Welcome to St. Andrews," he said, as if we'd just officially arrived.

"Wait until you meet the rest of these kids," Kelsey said, crossing the room to kiss the two girls on the couch. "The memories come rushing back."

The other taxi had stopped for cigarettes and its passengers were coming down the hall now, with Clayton in the lead.

"Isn't this place just *dripping* with charm?" he shrilled, trying on an English accent.

"This one's a scream," Kelsey said.

Clayton had a bottle of champagne in each hand when he burst through the door.

"There we go," Damien said. "You all should be ashamed for coming empty-handed."

Mary went straight for the TV and flipped through the local weather, *BBC News,* and a scene from a spaghetti western. She settled on a rap video set at a house party with tanks full of mermaids.

"You two can sit down," Jules said to Clare and me, nodding at the bed. "Remind me what you're called?"

"I'm Clare," Clare said. "And this is Tom."

"Clare?"

"Lutèce," Clare said.

It was his mother's maiden name, according to the *New York Times*. And this, I thought, is how far he's willing to go.

"What are you studying?" Damien asked.

"History of art, music."

"You came all this way for that?"

Clare explained that he loved the UK, and golf, and that he had wanted to go here for the longest time. He was trying to align his life with theirs, but even I could have told him that he was getting it wrong. These people hadn't come here just because they wanted to.

"What about you?" Damien asked me. "What are you studying?"

"Econ."

"No points for originality. You and I get to hit the books while Clare and Jules over here are surrounded by girls dressed to the nines, waiting for Will to trip in the aisle so they can help him up and get a shot at the throne. History of art is basically required for your M.R.S."

"Your what?"

I looked to Kelsey for an explanation, and saw that everyone was deliberately looking at anything but her. And then I figured out the acronym.

"The M.R.S. degree," Damien said. "Half the girls in this town came up here to be the queen of England, and when they realize it ain't gonna happen, they start fighting over the scraps, like the poor man's Prince William here."

"Oh, naturally," Mary said. "I've always wanted to marry some wanker like you and spend the rest of my life in some shit hotel like this." She turned to Clare. "Don't listen to a word he says."

"Anyway," Damien said, "first-year econ is a cakewalk."

"Have you taken 3001 yet?" I asked.

"I'm in it now. That's the third-year course. You've got a while before you have to do any work."

I had been placed in 3001, but decided this was not the time to bring that up.

"Hey," Damien said, "do you boys have academic parents yet?"

We shook our heads.

"Jules, you want in on this?"

"Jules doesn't want kids," Kelsey said. "Do you, Julien?"

"I don't blame him," Mary said. "Why don't you Americans adopt your own kind and Jules and I can spoil them from time to time?"

"Done," Damien said, popping some of Clayton's warm champagne. He took a long draw, and passed the bottle to me.

"Drink up, kids," he said. "Welcome to the family."

Damien opened the nightstand drawer, and produced a glossy visitors' guide to St. Andrews, taking great pains to hold it level. It seemed like the beginning of some ritual presentation, until I saw that the cover, a photo of the crumbling castle by the sea, was covered in cocaine. There was a pile like a white island in the water and a row of lines cut across the sky that looked like jet trails left by planes. Eventually, it came to me. As I leaned in with Damien's £100 note in my right nostril, hoping there was no special trick to this, I couldn't be sure if cocaine smelled like money, or if it was the other way around.

Afterward, I sat on the bed, listening to other people talk. The coke, as it hit, reminded me of paddling a surfboard straight into an oncoming set, scratching to get over the top of the first wave before it begins to break. There's a moment when you know you've made it, a breathless feeling as your body floats over the peak. My first taste of cocaine was that split second, on loop. I thought of Rob, of his empire on LBI, built on an appetite that I didn't understand until then. I imagined everything he owned, every stud and inch of wiring, every chair and table. It made sense to me now. I had been staring at Kelsey without registering her. She caught me and winked.

"He's nice enough," Jules was saying about some friend of theirs who was taking a semester off.

"Right," Damien said. "That's one of his problems."

There was no one at the reception desk by the time we stumbled through the lobby, and no taxis outside. Clare said he knew the way on foot, that it would be faster to walk home than to wait for a cab. I had no idea where I was, but Clare had some heightened sense of direction, like a bank robber who maps out an escape route as he rides into town. We crossed the highway, and a dew-soaked field. As our hall came into view, I had a clear picture of the two ships that made up the building, the hills behind them like frozen waves. The guide had said the ships were passing each other in the night, but that seemed like an optimistic view of the design, because the ships were actually smashing into each other, their bows joined at the point of impact. We were living in an accident. I hung back as Clare and Clayton and Chantal went inside. The clock in the church tower struck four. I unscrewed the crown on my watch, popped it loose, and changed the time.

Registration took place in an old concert hall on North Street. A bundle of bright-colored electrical cords ran from the foyer down the long center aisle and up to the stage, where a team of administrators sat behind long tables covered in file boxes and welcome packets. Clare and I signed in at the door, and I was drifting off in an overstuffed theater seat when someone called my name on the PA. I followed the wiring and found myself on stage, facing a Scottish woman with wind-burned skin and thick hands.

"You're American, then," she said, opening my file.

A passport photo, taken at a CVS in West Trenton, was paper clipped to the corner, and I remembered my mother telling me to cut my hair as I left the house. The administrator flipped through a photocopy of my application, my standardized test scores, and a personal statement that detailed my desire to "broaden my perspective." She stopped at a letter on Lawrenceville stationery and tilted her head back to skim it through her glasses.

The letter, addressed To Whom It May Concern, explained that on the morning of January 23, two officers served a warrant for Thomas Alison, eighteen, of Princeton, who was suspected of drug possession with intent to distribute. I could recite the whole thing from memory, and it was playing in my head like an audiobook as her eyes ran down the page. Mr. Alison fled on foot when the officers approached him on the corner of Craven Lane and U.S. 206, and was later apprehended.

By a cop who stood down on my ankle in silence, bending the bones while he waited for backup. My hands were cuffed behind my back, my face pressed against a grassy knoll behind the hockey rink, a hundred yards from my car, which I had been making for as fast as I could run. All I could see was a thin line of trees that rose out of the ground to wildly different heights, like a graph of some unimaginable volatility. A police radio crackled and spit out reports from around the county. I wondered if anyone else's life was crashing down right then, if I could call out to them through the radio.

A half ounce of marijuana was discovered in my vehicle. The distribution charge was later dropped, leaving me with a misdemeanor violation that was just enough to torpedo my college plans and preclude me from interning with an investment banking firm, which I had hoped to do that summer. I was suspended for a month, my sentence was suspended by a judge, and I successfully completed one hundred hours of service to the Lawrenceville community. And if this fucking nosy Scottish administrator had any further questions, she could address them to the dean of students, whose number was printed just below his signature.

The woman licked her finger and turned the page. Behind the letter was the thing she had been looking for: a blue sheet of paper with a gold seal in the corner that told her my tuition had been paid in full. There was a box of student ID cards in front of her, and her stubby fingers ran through a dozen that were not mine before she handed me a piece of plastic with my name and face on it.

"Here you are," she said.

I snatched it from her outstretched hand, and looked out into the audience for Clare.

"Can you check again?" Clare said.

He was also on stage, two tables away. A woman was sifting through the papers in his file.

"It doesn't seem to be here," she said. "There's not much I can do without it, I'm afraid."

His tuition hadn't been paid yet.

"I'll get it taken care of," Clare said. "I need to buy a phone. Where can I do that?"

"Hey," I said, putting a hand on his shoulder, keeping it there when he flinched. "We passed a place on the way here. Let's go. I need one too."

In the Vodafone store, a salesman explained that without proof of permanent residence, the best he could do for us was a plan where you bought minutes as you used them. I watched Clare pacing in the street outside as the clerk sold me the same model that Clare was now using to make a call. His head snapped up when someone answered, and he said something in French and walked out of sight.

I found him on a bench by a dry fountain at the end of Market Street.

"Everything cool?"

"Let's get lunch," Clare said. "The menu at Ma Bells looked good."

"It looked a little spendy."

"I'm buying," he said. "Don't worry about that."

There was a round of applause as we ducked in off the street. Kelsey beckoned to us from a back table where she sat with Mary and the two girls from the couch in Damien's suite. All of them had sunglasses pushed up on their foreheads. The sun had not been out all day.

"They'll have two Newcastle salads, the venison, and the fish and chips," Mary said to the waiter, before we had a chance to read the menu. "That's a proper lunch. And two very dry martinis. These were perfect."

I thought: Thank Christ this is on Clare.

"You two were at college together?" a blond girl named Lucy asked.

"College?"

"High school," Kelsey whispered.

"College," Mary said. "This is university. College comes before. You'll have to learn to speak proper English now that you're not in the colonies anymore."

"What if we're not here that long?" I said.

"Ah, I see. You're the clever ones who got into trouble at some fancy college in America. We get dozens of your type." She turned to Clare. "What crime did you manage to commit?"

The waiter arrived with our drinks, and Clare put his lips to the quivering dome of gin in his glass. I was on the hook now, bait to draw attention from him.

"You got me," I said.

"I did, did I?" Mary shifted in her chair to face me. "Tell us about your trouble, then."

"I was selling pot at school. At the 'college' we went to."

"And you were found out how?"

"I sold to one of our teachers, and she made a joke about it at a dinner party. Someone didn't think that it was funny."

"Are you serious?" Clare asked.

"I don't think the admissions office here minds things like that,"

Mary said, ignoring Clare's surprise. "Helps your application, I'd say. Sign of a budding entrepreneur."

Our salads hit the table, and we listened to the girls talk shit—who slept with whom over the summer, who was suspiciously thin. All the food was well cooked and well seasoned, a far cry from the oily pub fare I had been expecting. Mary snapped up the check when the waiter dropped it between Clare and me. It was cold outside when we pushed through the door and into the courtyard, the sun hidden behind a smear of clouds, the town cast in a sharp half light.

"Come by my place tonight," Kelsey said, as she kissed my cheek. "Bring your friends."

I let Clare get ahead of me as we headed for the hall, and called my mother on my brand new phone. She told me she'd been worried, and lit a cigarette as I read off my number, the flick and spark of her lighter carried across the ocean to my ear. She was smoking inside, which usually meant something was wrong.

"Where are you now?" she asked.

"Heading back from lunch."

"How's the food there? What'd you have?"

"Bunch of stuff. Why don't we do more venison loin?"

"It makes people think of road kill," she said. "And I don't love it. Too gamey most of the time. How'd they serve it?"

"Pan roasted and sliced real thin, with this black-truffle-celery root puree."

"Black truffle? That's part of your meal plan?"

"Someone took me out."

"That must be nice," she said, exhaling. "Give me more good news. I have to fire Carla in a few hours, and I don't want to think about it anymore."

"I'm looking at the ocean," I said, which had been true a hundred yards before and which always made her happy. "Was Carla skimming tips or something?"

"I don't want to get into it."

"OK."

"I'm sorry, honey. I'll call you tomorrow. Say hi to Clare for me, OK?"

Clare and I were almost home. A dozen Americans were playing Frisbee on the lawn in front of Andrew Melville Hall, ignoring the threatening shade of gray the sky was taking on, pretending that September in Scotland is as mild and predictable as it is in the American Northeast. This is one way to exist in a strange place: Ignore the weather and play with things you brought from home. Another is to get drunk at lunch and sleep it off before going out again. Clare and I cut cautiously through the game and went our separate ways to bed.

"Morning," Clare said, standing in my doorway, his polo shirt tucked into his khakis.

"Where are you going all dressed up?"

"Golfing. Damien just called me and told me to meet him on the links. You up for a round?"

"I don't know," I said. "I've never played before."

"So you didn't buy a links pass."

"That's a safe assumption."

"Well, whatever, you can walk the first hole and then play through. We're meeting at the clubhouse in half an hour. Clayton's coming. You never used the course at Lawrenceville?"

"I used it. I got high there on the weekend sometimes. What do I wear to this?"

"Something with a collar. Don't wear jeans, if you can help it. You can use my clubs."

"When did you get clubs?"

"They showed up a few days ago."

"They showed up?"

"My dad had them sent from his club in Pennsylvania."

There was actual fallout from the explosion of his father's

life—all these things, bought in better times, that kept crashing down out of the sky.

"I'm gonna swing by my room and grab them," Clare said. "Meet me in the lobby."

Damien and Jules were waiting for us in front of the towering stone clubhouse that overlooked the eighteenth green. Damien had a big driver laid across his shoulders, his hands hanging over the head and the handle like a country club crucifix as the wind blew his hair into his face. Jules was texting furiously, and Clayton was coming from the direction of our hall, dragging his clubs, stopping now and then to catch his breath. An old man in a plaid driving cap informed us that we could tee off in ten minutes, that the schedule was light.

"Are you going to make it?" Damien asked as Clayton dropped his bag in front of us and braced himself with his hands on his knees. I couldn't see his eyes behind his sunglasses, but there were dark sweat stains in the places where the breeze had blown his silky polo shirt against his body. He was trembling, swallowing visibly every few seconds. It didn't look like he had been to bed.

"Did anyone bring water?" he asked.

"Clare, is this your caddy?" Jules said, ignoring Clayton, and nodding toward me without looking up from his phone.

I blinked, shocked. I had put on a pair of pleated suit pants, a white polo I used to wear on jobs, and Adidas Stan Smith sneakers, which, from a distance, could have passed for spikes. Jules gave me a dry smile to let me know that it was both a joke and not a joke. I tried to imagine what Kelsey would have told him about me. Some kid from Jersey, single mother, fancy high school, friends with Courtney. Nothing to worry about, in other words.

"You lads are up," the old man called, waving us over.

"He's just along to watch," Damien explained, jabbing his thumb at me as the rest of them flashed their links passes to the man's approving nods.

We followed the towpath to the tee box where Clare lost a coin toss to Jules and had to tee off first. His practice swings looked tight and powerful, but he shook his head and clenched his jaw after each one. He sliced his first shot, cursing as he let the head of his club hit the ground. Jules hit a ball halfway down the fairway, but he was back on his phone before it had bounced twice. Clayton hooked his first shot off the course.

"Want another?" Damien asked.

Clayton shook his head.

"Watch," Damien said to me, settling down into his stance. "Keep your left arm straight and bring the club up just past vertical. You wind your body up, create the tension, and then you let it go. Down and through." He swung and I watched the ball shoot straight off his club. "Short," he said under his breath as the ball skipped down the fairway.

They all fucked up their putts once everyone was finally on the green. Mini golf is essentially a varsity sport on Long Beach Island, and I wondered if any of that training was applicable here. I watched Clare drive a second time, beating back my instinct to grab a club and give it a shot. As Damien was teeing up, Clayton dropped his clubs and ran for a sand trap cut into a rise in the green.

"Get it all up," Damien called, squinting down the fairway. His second shot was as good as his first, and he turned to me before the ball stopped rolling, holding out his driver. Clare was attending to Clayton, who was doubled over, hawking up long beaded strands of saliva as his stomach searched for something to expel. Jules took a call.

"Jesus, just tell her to meet us at the ninth hole," Damien said.

Jules turned his back to us, and I heard him running through the kind of low-toned reassurance you use when the person on the other end is crying.

"It's not baseball," Damien was saying. "You're swinging down and through. Stand back from the ball a second."

He stood behind me, and arranged my grip on the handle, interlocking my right pinky and left forefinger, wrapping my hands with a loose grip that was half cool leather glove and half warm palm.

"Good," he said, and tapped the back of my right thigh, forcing me to bend my knees while he pressed himself against my back, directing my stance with his body and a low tone that I felt as a hum and hot breath behind my ear.

"Keep your upper body loose, point your outside foot like this, and tell me what it's like to fuck Kelsey sometime. I can't decide if she'd be any fun or not, and Jules doesn't kiss and tell. Spread your legs a little more. Keep your eyes down when you bring the club back, and once you're all wound up, just let go and follow through. Always follow through. Take a few practice swings."

A gust of wind dispelled the heat of his body as he stepped back and left me standing on my own, my hands twitching as I lifted the club. I swung down and through.

"Good," Damien said. "Keep doing that."

I tried it again and again, waiting for my heartbeat to settle before I stepped up to the ball.

"Keep your head down," Damien said.

I heard Jules tell Kelsey that everything would be fine, and something else that I was sure I could make out if only I could turn around and read his lips. My first swing missed the ball completely.

"You were high," Damien said. "Kill the grass, if you have to. Follow through."

I caught air again and looked to Damien for guidance, but he folded his arms and raised his eyebrows. It was on me now. Down and through. I felt the club connect with something and a patch of sod burst in the air in front of me. Damien pointed at a low bank of clouds just as my ball seemed to fall out of it. It bounced along the fairway a hundred yards or so in front of us. From the way that Damien was looking at me, I gathered this was not the norm.

"Can you do that again?" Jules asked, his hand covering the speaker of his phone. "Or was that beginner's luck?"

Damien took another ball from his pocket and teed it up in front of me. I fixed my grip and swung, remembering to lift my head as the ball soared and then slowed as though the atmosphere was thicker just above us. My second shot went farther than my first and then bounced off the course into the high grass. Clare started toward me, but Clayton grabbed on to his ankle.

"Wait," he said. "Stay here."

Damien cocked an eyebrow at the two of them, which prompted Clare to kick his leg free, leaving Clayton on all fours in the sand. Damien placed another ball in front of me.

"You've done this before," Clare said.

I shook my head and fixed my grip.

"Kid's a natural," Damien said.

Hey," Clare said, as I opened the door to my room. "I know this is last minute, but my parents are here. They want to meet you. Can you come to lunch?"

He was showered and dressed and visibly disappointed to find that I was neither, that his knocking had woken me. It was almost noon.

"Fuck," I said. "Yes, of course. Give me five minutes. Less."

My head filled with blood as I snatched my dead phone off the floor. I swayed and realized that I wasn't sober yet. We had closed Ma Bells, and then the bar at the Old Course, which had a long-standing tradition of staying open until the last guest retired, which had been sometime after 5:00 a.m. I had a splitting headache that ran around my skull and down my throbbing neck. I blew my nose into some toilet paper, and stared down at the composition of thick yellow snot mixed with clotted blood and caked white powder. I remembered looking at my watch as Clare and I were walking home and thinking, in a moment of coke-sponsored overconfidence, that four or five hours of sleep would be plenty. What were his parents doing here? I felt steam slipping around the edges of the shower curtain, and tried to decide what to wear to lunch with a wanted man.

"You boys in the service?" the cabdriver asked, smiling at us in the rearview mirror after Clare told him we were headed to RAF Leuchars. For the first time in my life, I felt worse after a hot shower.

"Why are they flying into Leuchars?" I asked as we drove past the Old Course, ugly in daylight, the grounds surprisingly bare and unkempt. Leuchars was an air force base.

"They don't do chartered flights at EDI."

"Your parents have a plane?"

"They're borrowing it. They're flying back tonight."

As we pulled into the parking lot, I saw a single off-white jet in front of a yawning hangar, the pointed body of the plane shaped like a rifle cartridge. Two figures were standing on the tarmac by the tail. Mr. and Mrs. Savage saw us pull up and step out, but whatever they were discussing took precedence over our arrival. Clare asked the taxi to wait, and we closed the distance between them and us on foot.

Michael Savage hugged his son and closed his eyes for a few seconds just before he let Clare go. He looked thinner than he had in his portrait in the *Times,* his cheeks padded out with a well-groomed salt-and-pepper beard. His eyes were narrow enough that I couldn't make out their color, and every angle of his face—the slope of his bald forehead, the slant of his jaw—seemed to culminate in the sharp point of his nose. He was holding a Dopp kit cut from heavy leather, and I wondered why he had brought toiletries if they were just here for the afternoon.

"Nice to finally meet you, Tom," he said, and shook my hand.

Camille, Clare's mother, was asking Clare if the shirts she sent had fit him properly, and I picked up a whiff of a French accent in her fluent English. Wire-rimmed glasses sat neatly on her tan face, and a cool breeze kicked up the ends of her dark blond hair. She had clinically perfect posture; the line of her back was as straight and firm as the heels on her shoes. She kissed me on both cheeks.

"You two look like a hundred bucks," Mr. Savage said, as we headed for the cab.

"Yeah," I said, with a nervous laugh. "Long night."

The restaurant Clare had chosen, a café at the east end of North Street, was a casual lunch spot with a menu chalked up on a blackboard. Clare was quiet, studying the people around us in a way that made me wonder whether his father would be recognized. Mr. Savage had his Dopp kit on the table underneath his right hand. Mrs. Savage asked what trouble we had found so far.

"We were at the Old Course Hotel last night," I said, triggering a memory of shooting tequila past my numb front teeth in the bathroom of Damien's suite.

"The Old Course," Mr. Savage said. "The bar there is famous."

"They look as if they've discovered that already," Camille said.

Camille asked if Prince William was still here, and I told her how Jules had called them out as twins.

"What have I told you all these years," she said to her son as our food hit the table.

"How's the living situation?" Michael asked. "Is the dorm nice?"

"It's nice," I said. "It's a hotel in the summer."

"It looks like a prison," Clare said, spreading his napkin across his lap.

My eyes flashed back and forth between Michael Savage and his wife, as if the two of them were playing tennis. He smiled when he caught me staring.

"I heard you two ran into a friend of mine in Ridgewood."

Clare looked as surprised as I was. His father turned to me.

"So Tom, Clare tells me you're a future business leader of America. Tell me about the public perception of this thing. It's hard to understand from the inside."

"I don't know that much about what's going on," I said.

"You must have the broad strokes by now. It's a terrible story, am I right?"

I looked to Camille for help, but she was smiling at her husband with her hands folded in her lap. Clare was applying ketchup to his side of roast potatoes, somewhere else in his mind.

"It's not the worst story I've heard," I said.

"No, I don't imagine it is. What's the worst story you know?"

"You want to hear it?"

Mr. Savage took his hand off the Dopp kit.

"I do," he said.

My mother's friend Amanda was beaten almost to death one night at Somerset Medical Center, where she worked as a nurse. No motive, lead pipe. The police knew who had done it, but they fucked up the evidence gathering and the arrest, and had to let him go. With her settlement check from the hospital she bought a place near the ocean in New Hampshire and a 12-gauge shotgun. My mother went to visit her and came back with the gun, but Amanda killed herself anyway, with enough pills to let everybody know she meant it. She was thirty-four, unmarried, haunted by the figure who had appeared in a doorway behind her, who watched her run the copy machine in silence until she turned and saw the length of the scrap pipe in his hand. She didn't really survive the attack.

I stopped then, realizing that I'd just betrayed the memory of my mother's friend and demonstrated for a master class in How to Change the Subject. There was no returning to the topic of the

Savage family's legal troubles now. I hated myself for being baited, and hated Michael Savage twice as much for baiting me.

"What made her do it?" Michael asked. "In your opinion. I mean, she was probably safe where she was."

"She ran out of options," I said.

"What makes you say that?" Camille asked.

"She felt like she didn't know people after that. You get cut off from the crowd, you look for the exit."

"There must have been some other legal channels she could have pursued," Michael said. "I mean, come on."

There was an urgency in his voice that made it sound as if he had something at stake here, as if he had a lot riding on the legal recourse of my mother's dead friend.

"Who told you that?" Camille asked me, ignoring her husband now. "About why she did what she did?"

"No one."

"Good for you," she said. "Would anybody like dessert?"

"Clare and I have to stop by a bank," Michael said to his wife in the street outside the restaurant. "Maybe Tom can give you the grand tour, and we'll give you a call when we're finished."

"Let's walk by the water," Camille said to me. "I'd like to see the beach."

The Scores Road was deserted, and a stiff breeze was blowing off the bay. We walked in silence, seagulls shrieking overhead.

"You handled yourself well at lunch," Camille said, finally.

"Thanks. I don't know why I told that story."

"I do. And I don't apologize for Michael, but I'm sorry to hear about your mother's friend."

"I didn't really know her."

"That's not important, is it?"

My phone was buzzing against my leg.

"It's Clare," I said. "Hello?"

"Hey, stupid question: Who are you banking with here?"

"I'm not banking with anybody."

"Where do you get cash?"

"At an ATM. The Royal Bank of Scotland on Market Street. The fee's cheap."

"Do they have safe deposit boxes?"

"No idea," I said. "Why?"

"Never mind," Clare said. "I think we're good."

The Dopp kit didn't contain toothpaste or aftershave or hair product. It was Clare's tuition, in cash, and then some. Camille smiled at me as I hung up.

At the end of the Scores Road, we found the path that wrapped around the eighteenth green of the golf course and led down to the beach. The sand was white and surprisingly fine, and the water was shallow for what looked like half a mile out. An endless succession of low breakers had worked the sand under the surf into a pattern like a fingerprint. We cuffed our pants, carried our shoes, and threaded our way between the kite fliers, the yellow labs, the children building sand castles. Camille slung her coat over her arm and revealed a frame that I could see had not always been this thin; the tension in her shoulders betrayed the ghost of a fuller figure they no longer had to bear. She was silent until we were beyond the crowds.

"When Clare told me the story of how you found each other, I thought to myself, 'Ah, this is something.' You don't know yet what it means to a parent, especially a mother, to have someone look out for your son when something terrible has happened and you have to leave your home." She stopped, and look back toward the town. "I think it's good for the two of you to be out of America, to see something else. I wasn't born there, but I came just in time for its moment, I think. You're too young to understand this. You've never known anything else. It's changing now. It's good to be away. It's an exciting time, for both of you. You can become whatever you like this far from home." She threaded her arm through mine and we started back. "Who knows what can happen," she said.

We met Clare and Michael in front of Ma Bells and walked back to Andrew Melville Hall. The Dopp kit was gone. Clare was having problems with his computer, and Michael seemed happy to put on a fatherly air and fix something before he climbed back in his borrowed plane and flew away. Camille sat next to me on the bed facing the window, and we watched a cluster of rabbits feeding at the top of a sharp slope behind the hall while father and son hunched in a corner to play with the laptop. The cat seemed to come up from the grass. It was crouched so that its legs looked like the wheels of a locomotive as it took three quick steps and sunk its teeth into a rabbit, just behind the ears. The cat shook its head once, hard enough to break the rabbit's neck, and dragged it out of sight. Camille let out a quiet laugh and turned to me. The other rabbits didn't move.

"This could be the problem," Michael said to his son.

In the cab back to Leuchars, I listened to Michael apologize for the brevity of their visit, and explain that the plane was only free for the afternoon.

"Look at this place," he said, as we drove past the Old Course. "I don't know why you two would ever leave. Travel Europe, play golf on days that end in *Y*."

"We were just speaking about that," Camille said, turning to me.

We watched them board the plane, and watched a pair of hands reach out to close and seal the door. I would have stayed for takeoff, but Clare told the driver to go. His father had paid the fare both ways.

"Hello?" Clare said, into his phone. "Yeah. Is it OK if Tom comes? He's with me now. Seven. Sure. We'll see you there."

"Who was that?"

"Clayton wants to have dinner at that Indian place."

With you, I thought. Not with me.

"Let's just go straight there," he said. "I need a drink."

At Balaka, Clare told the waiter that we were waiting for a third before we ordered. He checked his watch for the third time in ten minutes, drumming his fingers on the table in time with the sitar music. He was tense, but present. Back in the world. I wondered how much of that had to do with being flush again, and just then Clare fished out his wallet and handed me six fifty-pound notes, crisp as the napkin in my lap.

"Thanks for the spot at the airport."

"This is too much."

"Buy me a drink sometime. I wonder what's keeping Clayton."

"Where's Chantal?"

"Having dinner with one of those twins. Sounds like she's in love."

How do you know that? I wondered. What conversation did you have that I wasn't there for?

"Was Kelsey with Jules when you met her?"

"Unclear," I said. "She says they broke up and got back together."

"Classy," Clare said, laughing. "I guess that's Jersey for you."

There was an edge in his tone that shocked me like a paper cut. I thought: There must be some equation to correlate lack of empathy or visible disdain with net worth or cash on hand. Clare was looking over my shoulder to where Clayton was threading his way between the tables, apologizing as he came.

We ordered martinis, wine with dinner, Scotch in place of dessert. I dropped out of the conversation sometime after our appetizers were cleared, and sat there, listening to them talk London shirtmakers and tell St. Barts hotels. Clare placed his hand on the black leather folder when the check dropped and said that he would take care of this one. Clayton insisted that it was his idea, his treat, and covered Clare's hand with his. I watched Clare's tall water glass topple as he jerked his hand free. Work one shift in a kitchen and you realize that we can rest our skin on a scalding surface for a few seconds before we register the pain. There was no delay in Clare's reaction, as if it were born of some older instinct, the recognition of a threat that predates fire. Clare dropped his napkin over the spill and motioned for the waiter. I thought: What's this?

Orientation lasted two full weeks, and I had almost forgotten that we were here to take classes when they finally began. Clare and I had signed up for an art history course on the European modern movement, and on the first day, Prince William walked to the front of the lecture hall with half a dozen people in tow. He took what looked like careful notes while his entourage whispered and turned around to ensure that, yes, everyone was watching. The lecturer lost his patience halfway through the class and stopped to glare at them, the colors of Cezanne's apples cast over his face as he paused between the projector and the screen. He had just finished explaining that the phrase *still life,* in any romance language, translates to "dead nature."

The School of Art History was the best in the UK, the reason the prince was here. He was one of the few second years who actually showed up for lectures after the first week. Grades, or "marks," as Mary insisted we call them, didn't count toward your degree until your third year. Third years were scarce on the social scene as a result, toiling in the library stacks while their carefree academic children were playing in the streets, day drinking, staying out all night.

Clare and I had history of art and English lit together, but I took

Econ 3001 alone while Clare stayed on the quad for private piano instruction. My professor was head of the School of Economics. He had been the chairman of finance in New Zealand before he was asked to resign because of his drinking. He lectured at Dartmouth after that, then McGill, moving from post to post and fleeing the fallout of his alcoholism with the same cross-continental leaps. He landed at St. Andrews, finally, and had somehow managed to sober up in a town full of bars. I had e-mailed him early in the summer, attaching a paper and my AP scores, and asking if I could place out of the entry-level courses. He replied an hour later, telling me to see him after the first lecture. I arrived early, took a seat near the front, and listened to the room fill up behind me. I looked around for Damien before the lights went down. He never showed.

When the professor had described the arc of the course and listed the exam dates, he told us that we might as well enjoy our only early dismissal of the semester. I made my way down to the lectern while he packed his briefcase.

"Professor Watkins? I'm Tom Alison. I wrote you about taking this course and you said to see you after class?"

"All right," he said, scanning his enrollment list.

"I sent you a paper in August?"

"I was sent several papers in August, Mr. Alison. I'm afraid you'll have to be a little more specific."

"It was on currency. The case for a gold target."

"That was your work?"

"Yeah," I said. "Is it all right if I take your class?"

"Yes, I'd say you're in the right place. How old are you, if you don't mind my asking?"

"Eighteen. Would you mind signing this for the registrar?"

"You know," he said, uncapping his pen, "it's unusual for someone your age to be thinking about currency like that. There are traders twice as old as you who wouldn't understand what you wrote. You're wrong, of course, but it was a nicely articulated delusion if I remember correctly. I'm assuming this will be your concentration?"

I nodded.

"Tell me something," he said, holding my form to his chest, taking it hostage. "If you don't mind my asking. What is it you'd like to do?"

"Hedge funds, eventually. Probably investment banking first. I'm not really sure."

"That's the most awful waste I can imagine."

"Well, thanks for letting me take your class."

"Of course," he said. "It's my pleasure. I wish you all the luck in the world."

Darling," Jules called, as he opened the door to Kelsey's flat. "Your children are here."

Raisin Sunday, an ancient St. Andrews tradition, took place during the first weekend in November. It was designed as a bonding experience for the fledgling academic family—breakfast at mother's house, followed by a long night out with dad. No one I asked knew where the name came from. The unofficial holiday had morphed, over the years, into a kind of loosely sanctioned shit show—six thousand students unleashed on the town after an alcohol-soaked breakfast, Monday classes canceled in advance. Residents stayed off the streets or left St. Andrews altogether. Clare and I had put on ties and jackets, per Damien's instruction, before we presented ourselves for breakfast.

The smell of bacon and burnt toast had almost masked the ashtray perfume of Kelsey's flat. Her long dining room table was draped in a patchwork of tablecloths and covered with dishes, glasses, carafes of orange juice, piles of pastry, and sweating bottles of sparkling Italian wine. I walked into the kitchen, where Kelsey, in high heels and a printed floral dress, was checking something in the oven.

"Can I help?"

"No," she said, straightening up, smoothing her apron. "This is the one meal I can pull off on my own. Go sit down. Make yourself a drink."

She planted a kiss just behind my ear, and slapped me lightly on the ass.

In the living room, Damien was mixing Clare a Bloody Mary that was mostly vodka.

"I blacked out around noon my first Raisin Sunday," Damien was saying. "Lost half of an amazing pair of shoes and woke up in a bunker on the sixteenth hole. Not a good look. I'm not saying you shouldn't push it, but let's not be those people today."

"To pushing it," Jules said, looking straight at me. "Cheers. I'll drink to that."

Clayton and Chantal showed up. A cork shot out of a bottle neck, glanced off the ceiling, ricocheted around the room. After two drinks, the alcohol under the sludge of tomato and spice had a constricting effect, as if it was dehydrating me and everything in Kelsey's flat. The surfaces, the sunlight shooting through the windows—it all seemed harder, brighter. I wasn't used to day drinking. My spine felt like a coiled spring.

"What do you have planned for the next generation?" Mary asked Damien.

"Football matches, afternoon tea with Jules, party at Will's place, the Westport. We can go back to my suite after that, if anyone's still standing."

"How long do you plan on living in that awful hotel?"

"Until I find something to buy. Paying rent here is like burning money."

"As opposed to what the Old Course charges."

"Burns a little brighter that way."

"Ah, to be a noveau riche American."

"Watch it," Damien said, with an edge in his voice that I had never heard before.

"Everyone sit down," Kelsey said, balancing a baking dish in each hand as she swept into the room.

I was about to ask Kelsey what the dish was, but stopped on an inhale when I saw the way Jules was looking at me. I held his flat stare until he pushed back from the table, took the vodka off the sideboard, and asked if we were actually going to start drinking, or what. Shots were poured and passed around. Clare caught my eye, and I saw that he was choking back a smile to mask his excitement at this weird pageantry. There were catcalls from the street below, the voices of people who had started ahead of us. Kelsey stood up and raised her glass.

"To my wonderful children," she said. "Happy Raisin Sunday. Put something in your stomachs, for the love of Christ. You'll need it."

Because Clare and I had split a cab from Melville Hall, I didn't notice the shift in the town until we spilled into the street. The police were out in force, with light riot gear over the traditional white shirt, black tie, and navy sweater. They had orders from the university to step in only if students posed a danger to themselves or others, and they seemed relaxed and jocular, chatting and calling to one another over the tops of their Plexiglas shields. It was easy to see why the residents didn't stick around for this: ten til noon by my watch, and already the sidewalks were choked by roving packs of students, drinking openly, and dressed in costume, in pajamas, in unseasonable scraps of clothing. My outfit was starting to feel like a costume in a different way: I was pretending to be someone who got dressed up to get drunk at breakfast.

Down the block, one of our fellow first years was standing in the garden outside his mother's flat, preparing to drink from a long plastic tube connected to a funnel that was being held by his mother out of a first-floor window. I had seen this done at Princeton parties, but usually the drinker took a knee while someone poured beer through a funnel held above his head. The boy closed his mouth around the clear tubing that ran down from the spout. He tipped his head back, opening his throat as far as it would go just before his academic father poured off a full bottle of red wine, which filled the tube like blood inside a vein. The boy folded after four or five agonizing seconds, splattering red across the stone walkway as he hacked and choked.

"That's fucked up," Clare said.

"Remember what he's wearing," Damien told him. "He'll be fun to watch later on. We ready? Is everyone with us?"

Everyone was not with us. Jules and Kelsey were halfway down the block, locked in conversation. He had a shoulder against a high garden wall, while she was upright with her back to us, doing all the talking. They stood toe to toe after she stopped, which reminded me that I had no claim on her attention or affection that could lead to a tense silence like the one they were still sharing. I wanted something between me and Kelsey that could start a fight.

"Uh-oh," Damien said from behind me. "Did you get someone in trouble?"

"What are you talking about?"

"What am I talking about?"

"Is that about me?"

"Is what about you? Are we still playing stupid? Here, carry these," he said, and handed me three bottles of Prosecco. "Let's go. They know where to find us when they're done."

Done with what? I wondered. Had Jules caught the kiss she hit me with upstairs? I was losing the bottle trapped between my bicep and ribs, and dropped another bottle as I tried to catch it. The glass shattered, bubbles flaring up and then vanishing into the pebbled sidewalk as the wine bled out. Someone cheered. A policeman stabbed two fingers at his eyes and pointed to me from across the street.

We followed Damien to the athletic fields cut into a rise behind Andrew Melville, where three shockingly organized soccer games were under way. Across the first pitch, I saw a thickset middle-aged man moving through the crowd along the sidelines, dressed in vestments of the Catholic Church. A woman trailed behind him, wearing a long dress that laced up in the front and pressed her breasts together. I heard Mary explaining that the man was not actually a bishop, as he liked to be called, but an old queen who liked to dress up as a member of the clergy. The woman was a failed London actress who worked in a nearby castle now.

"One of those horrible places where they dress up in Renaissance costume and teach you to make bread," Mary said, lighting a cigarette.

Jules was sitting on the sideline, prying off his wingtips. He replaced them with a pair of borrowed soccer cleats, laced those up, shed his blazer, and took the field. Someone had talked him into playing. He jogged backward to the halfway line, his eyes on the ball, regarding it with the same even intensity he had used with Kelsey, who was nowhere to be seen. I turned back to the game as a forward from the opposing team headed a long pass out of the air and beat a midfielder on the run. He was charging downfield now, dribbling, unaware that Jules was coming for him. In his trim gray slacks and crisp white shirt, Jules looked like a spectator who had wandered out onto the pitch. I thought: he'll never make it. I had underestimated his commitment. Jules laid down into a long-shot slide tackle, his left leg leading, his right leg underneath him like the bent arm of a paper clip. I winced, mostly for his clothes. He planted a hand in the grass as his foot connected, catching the ball and then the ankle of the opposing forward, who pitched into a somersault. Jules used the last of his momentum to pop back to his feet. He caught the ball before it traveled out of bounds, and then shot downfield along the sideline. His teammate was streaking into the penalty box, and Jules landed a pass neatly in front of him. The boy took a shot that glanced off the crossbar, shook his head, spat, and then raised his hand to Jules in salute. Jules didn't notice. A streak of dirt and grass ran down the left side of his body, broken by a stripe of clean white fabric where his shirt had come untucked. I had no idea that he could play. There were hands on my shoulders.

"May I offer a blessing to the first years?" the bishop said, when I spun around.

He was holding out his hand, and I was just Catholic enough to know that you were meant to kiss the ring. There was something wet and white in the corners of his mouth, and something inscribed on the ring's surface that I was too drunk to read. His complexion was paint-by-numbers splotchy, and a pair of thick, Coke-bottle glasses magnified his bright blue eyes. Clare, Mary, Clayton, and I joined hands with him and his companion. We bowed our heads.

"Da, quaesumus Dominus, ut in hora mortis nostrae Sacramentis refecti et culpis omnibus expiati, in sinum misericordiae tuae laeti suscipi mereamur. Per Christum Dominum nostrum. Amen."

Clare raised his head and opened his eyes. He stared at the bishop. The bishop continued.

"Heavenly Father, we offer you these young men. May you enrich their hearts and their minds and may they walk in your way as they enter their life in this place. In nomine Patris et Filii et Spiritus Sancti. Amen."

"Amen," his companion said.

Everyone was trying not to laugh except Clare, who was in no danger of laughing. Mary broke the tension by passing me a spliff, but I needed weed in my system like I needed a broken arm. I offered it to Clare, who took a quick hit and coughed it up.

"That wasn't a translation," Clare said, through the smoke. "What he said after the Latin. What the bishop said."

"What?"

"The Latin was the Prayer for a Good Death."

"Are you sure?

"I took Latin for four years. Yes, I'm sure. Why would he recite that?"

"Who knows," I said. "It's the least weird thing I've seen all day."

The cohesion of our group was astonishing when you considered the hour at which we'd started drinking. People would peel off, vanish, and then casually reappear. I wondered if this was how families functioned, if all the members were subject to a force like gravity. When everyone but Kelsey was assembled, Damien announced that tea would be served shortly in the art studio Jules rented from the university. It was time to go.

The wind was blowing hard onshore, and the police seemed less relaxed now. We passed two students getting sick in the street on our way through town, a boy in an oversized flight suit, and a girl in her civilian clothes. Jules led us to the art department's administrative building on the Scores and unlocked the front door. We burst into the empty building and barreled down the stairs, breathing in the smell of dust and decomposing paper, the acrid fumes from oil paint and clay. There was music coming from an open door at the end of the underground hallway. The room Jules rented was divided into studio space splattered with paint and something like a living room. A Persian carpet—blood red, blue, and brown—covered one corner of the rough cement, bordered on adjacent sides by a leather sofa and a credenza that held a record player, speakers, and a cluster of liquor bottles like a model skyline. The particulars reminded me of Casey, and what he would have done with a space like this: nothing accidental, everything just so. Kelsey had changed into a slouchy loose-knit sweater, black leggings, and boots, and was moving around the room, prepping. She brushed past me to fill an electric kettle from the water fountain in the hall. People I had never seen before were filtering in, third and fourth years, friends of Jules's. In the corner, a janitor's orange mop bucket was filled with ice, beer, and wine. Someone put on "Sticky Fingers" by the Rolling Stones. It felt like we had retreated into a bunker while the world came to an end outside.

When the water had boiled, Jules lined up a set of chipped china teacups and dropped a tea bag into each. Damien produced a Baggie of gray powder from the inside pocket of his jacket, held it to the light between two fingers, flicked it twice.

"Anyone who doesn't want a dose, speak now or forever hold your piece."

"What is that?" I asked.

"It's fairy dust. It's what'll get you through the night."

"It's Molly," Mary said. "MDMA. It's very good, if it's the batch from the Dutch boys."

"Fuckin A, it is," Damien said. "OK, show of hands: Everybody in?"

The doses were measured out with a tarnished silver coffee spoon. I stared into the steam from my cup, letting the tea steep, hoping the heat would burn off some of the drug. I had never done this. The bitterness of English breakfast gave way to the taste of a chemical whose first effect was to twist and contort every muscle in my face. Damien laughed.

"Holy shit, that's terrible," I said.

Mary pinched my cheek and hummed the first few bars of "Spoon Full of Sugar" from *Mary Poppins.* We had never touched before, I realized, as she walked away.

Jules was sprawled on the couch, directly across from the folding chair I had dragged to the edge of the rug. I felt hands on my shoulders for the second time that day. It was Kelsey, and it seemed like she was locking eyes with Jules, their stares meeting somewhere in the space above my head. It took everything I had to keep from turning to see her face. I could smell her perfume and then I couldn't, like someone floating through warm and cool patches of a lake. Jules blinked and then raised his eyebrows, almost imperceptibly. I felt her fingernail graze the top notch of my spine as she tucked a tag back inside the collar of my shirt and walked away.

The Molly hit me all at once. I was alone in the hall, drinking water from the fountain, and when I straightened up, it felt like warmer, thicker blood had rushed into my head. I steadied myself with both hands on the wet stainless steel. Everything seemed to have a pulse that I could see only in my peripheral vision, so I kept casting my gaze around, trying to catch the corkboard or some distant floor tiles before they froze again. Clare appeared in front of me when I opened the studio door, bouncing a little on the balls of his feet, the party in full swing behind him. He took a deep breath and let it out through pursed lips.

"Right?" I said. "Jesus."

"Be a darling and do a charcoal portrait for me," Mary was saying to Jules. "I want something to hang over my mirror so I can't see how fat I'm getting."

"I don't draw on command," Jules said. "It's not a party trick. I'm not in the mood."

You're lying about that last part, I thought, as he rubbed his palms together and wiped them down the length of his thighs. Mary lost interest and turned her attention to the bar. Jules stood up.

"Fine," he said.

"Change of heart?"

Jules ignored her, placed a massive pad of paper on an empty easel, and flipped to a blank page.

"Clothes or not?" Mary asked.

Damien laughed.

"Stand just over there," Jules said.

Mary walked to a blue piece of tape in the middle of the filthy white sheet on the floor.

"Here?" she asked.

Her shirt seemed to fly over her head and into a corner. Her bra followed it, and then she popped the button on her jeans, hooked her thumbs into the waistband, and peeled them off, decelerating as she worked them down around her ankles. When she stood up, she was wearing nothing but the silver bracelets on her wrist. Jules pursed his lips and squinted at her.

"Unlock your left knee," he said. "Put your left hand behind your head if you can."

Mary ran her left hand through her hair and down the back of her neck so that her fingers rested just between her shoulder blades. There was a tight swell to her stomach, a symmetrical roundness she hid under baggy or elaborate shirts, amplified as she thrust her hips forward with the pose. Her breasts were much whiter than the rest of her, one stretched taught and flat across her ribs with the tension in her arm, the other hanging soft and weighty like a piece of fruit. She stood with one foot on top of the other, a jet-black wisp of hair barely visible between her legs. Jules beckoned to Kelsey, who walked straight past her naked friend and leaned on the wall behind the easel. Most of the people in the room seemed or pretended not to notice, but I spent the next ten minutes wondering when this would be over, unsure what to do with my eyes. The drugs were ramping up, and I was breathing hard, bracing myself, unsure how far this would take me, and how much more I could take. Finally, Jules tore the portrait off the pad, folded it in quarters, and tucked it into a portfolio.

"Let me see it," Mary said.

Jules shook his head.

"Why not?"

"It doesn't belong to you."

"You're such a wanker."

Jules shrugged. Kelsey, smiling, pushed off the wall and trailed a hand across his lower back as she walked away. I couldn't imagine what he had done or what she had seen in it. To watch the two of them explode and then resolve, a wave followed by a glassy lull, flat water with no memory. Someone's phone was ringing. My phone. Lit up with a call that registered as a string of zeroes.

"Hello?"

"Tom?"

My mother. I wanted to hang up, but I knew how that would look.

"Tom? Can you hear me?"

"Yeah," I said. "Hey. Hi."

"Did I wake you up?"

"No, not really."

"Is everything OK?"

"Yeah, sorry, everything's fine," I said, moving into a corner to get away from the music.

"Really?"

"Yes, really. I'm fine."

My voice sounded flat inside my head, but any emotion I tried to layer over it made me feel like an actor on a radio drama. This was not going well. I could sense my mother's reaction an ocean away, her heightened awareness, some alarm sounding in her head.

"Is that your mom?" Clare said, getting up from the couch. "Can I talk to her?"

"Mom, hang on a second. Clare wants to say hi."

"No, Tom, I need to talk—"

But Clare had already pried the phone off my ear.

"Hi, Mrs. Alison," Clare said. "Hey, I just wanted to say thank you again for taking me in and everything. I really miss Princeton. And your cooking. I know, I know. You didn't have to do any of that, and it was so amazing of you."

He went on like that for a while. I was sure she was embarrassed—and embarrassed for him—but she played along. I could picture her tight, patient smile.

"You too," Clare was saying. "Yeah, he's right here, hang on."

Clare blocked the speaker with his thumb, mouthed "Do I sound high?" and handed me the phone.

"Hi," I said. "Sorry."

"Is Clare still with you?"

"Yeah," I said, confused. "He's right here. Do you want to talk to him again?"

"Tom, I need you to go somewhere else for a second. Somewhere he can't hear you."

I smiled at Clare and crossed the room.

"OK," I said, closing the door to the hall behind me. "What is it?"

"Do you remember Chuck LaPolla? Marcy's cousin who works at Goldman Sachs?"

"Yeah," I said. "Sure."

"He came by the shop this morning because he heard from Marcy that you and Clare were over there together. He told me that Clare's dad was into some bad shit with some really scary people, that those people might be looking for him now, that they might even be looking for Clare. He was trying not to scare me, which scared the shit out of me. I mean, he drove here from Red Bank to tell me that. He's never even come into the shop before. Has Clare said anything to you?"

"No," I said. "Definitely not."

"Please tell me you're being extra careful."

"Of what? What am I supposed to do? Start packing heat?"

"Please don't be smart with me, OK? I'm having a fucking heart attack right now. Clare's parents haven't been there, have they?"

"No," I said.

"Are you telling me the truth?"

"Why would they come here?" I asked, realizing it was a fair question.

"I don't know."

"Did Chuck say what he was doing?"

"Remember how the *Times* said there was all that money that the Feds couldn't find? Apparently it got funneled into all of this black market stuff. Chuck said people knew that he was up to something weird, but no one knew how bad it was. He wouldn't tell me any more than that. He said he wouldn't have told me anything, but he was worried about you hanging around Clare all the time."

She had read up on Michael Savage, after pretending for three months that she didn't care what Clare's dad had been doing. The drugs were muting the fear I should have felt about all the things she was telling me. It was like watching someone scream while you wore headphones.

"There's nothing to worry about," I said.

“Why do you both sound stoned? It’s the middle of the afternoon, isn’t it? What did you guys take?”

“Nothing,” I said.

“Don’t bullshit me. Is this how you spend your Sundays? Fucked up on drugs? Do I need to come over there and haul your ass home?”

“No,” I said. “Relax. It’s this holiday here. Raisin Sunday. Something you do with your academic family.”

“Your what? You better have an amazing explanation when I call you tomorrow, mister. Just tell me it’s not opiates. And don’t tell me to relax.”

“It’s not opiates. Stop worrying. I’m fine.”

“I still have this fucking car sitting in my driveway. I’ve been trying to get Bruce Cassidy on the phone all week to make sure I’m not going to have the FBI kicking down my door for accepting stolen property or something.”

“Just enjoy it.”

“Oh no, honey. You are not in a position to be giving anyone advice right now.”

She was quiet for so long that I wondered if the call had dropped.

“Hello?”

“Tom? I’m here. Be careful, OK? I hope you two are looking out for each other.”

“Don’t worry,” I said. “We are.”

We were leaving for hours. There would be a general movement toward the door, but there was always another side to the record, another skinny spliff, another short pour of champagne all around. Kelsey was tidying up when Damien killed the music, cut the lights, and held the door until the last of us were out.

We filled the street as we flowed over to the party on Queens

Gardens, where William's guards were holding back a crowd that spilled down the front steps. William threw parties at the flats of well-heeled friends because entertaining at his place was a national security risk. We stood across the street with Damien, who made a phone call and gave a sign that we should wait. I was lighting one cigarette with another when William emerged, pointed down at us, and whispered something to a guard. And then we were in: in plush club chairs under the high pressed-tin ceilings, in the kitchen where the prince of England jumped up on the marble island and poured tequila into upturned mouths, and finally up on the rooftop, looking out over the town. There was a strong sense that we were all in this together, having come this far. Every cigarette was passed from mouth to mouth, every beer and cocktail was communal. We were taking key bumps of the Molly, which Damien had cut with coke to keep us going. Back at the studio, someone had accidentally switched the record player from 45 rpm to a faster setting, which had the same unexpected and distorting effect on the music that the coke was having on me now. Damien put his arm around me and walked me to an uncrowded corner for a private conference.

"Hey," he said, offering his cigarette. "That thing between Jules and Kelsey? It's a little more complicated than I made it out to be when I was breaking your balls this morning. Jules used to date Mary, years ago. I don't know if anybody told you that or not. They grew up together. She thinks this thing with Kelsey is something he'll get over. Don't get in the middle of it. In fact, stay far as fuck away."

I was squinting at him, trying to get all this new information through the blockade of everything in my blood. I needed air, but we were already outside. I needed water.

A bathroom on the second floor. I was drinking from the faucet when Mary opened the door, which I could have sworn I had locked.

"I was thirsty," I said, as if I owed her an explanation.

"Don't mind me," she said.

She brushed past me, worked her jeans over her hips and sat down to pee.

"Good show so far," she said, tearing off a few sheets of toilet paper, and running them between her legs. "I'm impressed you're all still standing. You must come from good stock."

I stepped aside to let her use the sink, but Mary matched my movement and then stepped into me with an expression that was equal parts blank and impatient, her breasts brushing against my shirt, her eyes flicking back and forth between mine, too close to focus. Finally, she cocked her head and kissed me on the mouth. Past her lips—so soft they felt deflated—she tasted like cocaine and rotten fruit. She bit down on my bottom lip and pulled me to the bathroom floor on top of her, looking over my shoulder at the ceiling as she fumbled with the closure on my khakis. She set her jaw, finally, and tore them open, which sent a single button skipping across the tile floor. I was shocked to find my pounding heart had sent blood to my cock before I had had a chance to process what was happening. She pulled me to her and I took a sharp breath as we collided, but the friction was too much. I put a hand to my mouth for saliva, only to find that my mouth was also dry, at which point Mary lost her patience, dug her nails into my hips and pulled them to her face. I had my hands on the edge of the bathtub and I remember being shocked that the world could contain two sensations as different as the cold, hard porcelain against my palms and the impossible heat and softness of her tongue as she took me all the way into her mouth and coughed me up again before pulling me back down. I felt her shudder as her legs closed around my back, and then she had her nails in me again, and I started fucking her, working her body across the floor until her left shoulder and the left side of her jaw were pressed against the tub, her eyes locked with mine. She stuck a hand between her legs to get herself off, her nails scratching me as I fucked her harder and harder. And then I felt her shudder, and her expression changed. Her eyes rolled back slightly in her head, and her skin seemed to go taut over the bones of her face. She hissed twice in quick succession and shuddered so hard that she almost shook me off. I wasn't done, but that evidently didn't matter. She lay under me with her eyes closed until she got her breath back, then put both hands on my chest and pushed me off. She left as soon as she had everything back on.

The landing was empty when I finally stepped outside, and then Clare stepped out of a bedroom and closed the door behind him. He took the stairs without so much as acknowledging that I was standing in the doorway of the bathroom, staring at him. Damien emerged a minute later. He wasn't zipping up his fly, or tucking in his shirt, but somehow I understood what I was seeing. Damien gave me a pat on the back as he passed.

I found Kelsey in the kitchen. She didn't seem eager to talk to me, but by then I didn't care. I told her what I had just seen. She smiled without looking at me.

"Is Damien gay?"

"He just does what he feels like doing," Kelsey said.

"Is Clare?"

"I have no idea, sweetheart. If anyone would know, it's you."

"Why is Jules upset?"

"It has nothing to do with you. Stop talking about this stuff, OK?"

I was searching for something else to say, when William appeared beside us. He placed a hand on Kelsey's shoulder and a hand on mine.

"Is everyone well?" he asked, beaming.

"What?" I said.

"Are we all doing well?"

"I'm perfect," Kelsey said.

"Brilliant," William said.

"So friendly," Kelsey said, as William walked away.

Damien came by to collect us. We were off again.

For 364 days a year, the Westport was a mellow, modern English pub with ample seating. Tonight the tables had all vanished, and each of the three rooms was a sea of people dancing. The strobe lights made it feel like I was looking through one of those View Master children's toys, loaded with a thousand stills of the crowd, and set to a rapid fire click through. I was dancing with Mary and then the lights went out, and it was Damien up against me, and then Clare. Jules was going wild, swinging his hair around, and waving his body as if all his joints had just been oiled. At one point, he put one hand on my lower back and his other hand on Kelsey's and tried to bring the two of us together. I wondered how his hand felt to her, if there was a difference in pressure as he pushed us into each other. She reacted by turning her body into his, avoiding me as if we were both positive magnets with no choice but to remain apart.

I remember the mouthful of champagne that took me to the edge and forced me to close one eye to see anything at all. Hang on, I kept saying to myself. Just hold on and everything will settle. I found a wall, and let it carry my weight. The music stopped, the lights came up, the crowd poured out the door like water. I remember heading north, thinking I was finally going home. Clare was acting as my guide.

I came to in the sand. My head was clearing as the sun came up, adding depth and detail to the world. The beach was flecked with clusters of people, all us of looking like we had just washed up on shore, shipwrecked, marooned. Jules lay in the sand with his fingers laced behind his head. Kelsey lay perpendicular to him, her head on his stomach. I was feeling less and less with every passing second. All I could think about was the way the ground caves in and falls away in movies about the end of the world, a giant sinkhole, everything cratering. There's no end to this, I thought. This mushrooming void has to be replaced with something, anything. I stood up, and walked toward the water.

"Tom," Kelsey said, sitting up. "Tom, where are you going? What's he doing?"

"He's going in," Damien said. "He'll be fine. Tom, it's pretty cold."

"It's freezing," I heard Kelsey say. "Tom, come back here."

I stopped just long enough to untie and shed my shoes, thinking back to the story Damien told at breakfast, wondering if a loss of footwear was a rite of passage. I dropped my phone into the sand.

The water, when it hit my feet, felt like pinpricks. It soaked through and up my pant legs, swallowing my lower body. I didn't feel the temperature until it hit my crotch, and suddenly I was sucking in air like my lungs had sprung a leak. I dove, my head breaking the surface of what felt like half-frozen cement. Crushing cold. I opened my eyes and kept them open.

Come shopping w/ me?

The text from Kelsey arrived just as I was heading to a lecture. Twenty minutes later she pulled up to Andrew Melville in a black Audi A3, a more expensive, European version of the car that Casey drove. It was the Wednesday after Raisin Sunday, and the sky had been threatening to unload on us all morning. Kelsey stepped out with the engine running and walked around to the passenger side.

"You drive," she said.

The seats were cool and hard, and the interior was pristine—no spare change, no tangle of car chargers, nothing dangling from the rearview mirror. My car looked like that for about fifteen minutes after I drove it off the lot. I tested the clutch and shifted into first gear, which I had never done with my left hand. I wondered what would happen if I crashed gently enough that we both walked away unharmed, how Kelsey would explain it. I knew whose car this was.

Kelsey turned on the stereo, but the CD changer was empty and the radio was mostly static. She turned it off.

"Where are we going?"

"Waitrose," she said. "For groceries. It's just outside town."

The rain started as we stepped out into the parking lot. Kelsey grabbed my hand and broke into a run for the doors.

I still wasn't used to British grocery stores with their champagne displays and shelves of unrefrigerated eggs. Near the entrance was a freezer case full of dead fish on ice.

"Look at that one," Kelsey said, pointing to a tuna that had been halved to show off the muddy, marbled flesh. "It's so dense."

"They can kill you," I said.

"How?"

"This fisherman from South Plainfield hooked one off of LBI and got his feet tangled in the line. The thing swam off and pulled him under."

"I can't tell if you're fucking with me or not."

"I'm completely serious."

"I thought you meant the mercury."

"The what?"

"The meat is full of mercury. You're not supposed to eat it if you're pregnant. Your mother never told you that?"

I shook my head. My mother hadn't been pregnant in a long time, and she served tuna for a living.

"What do you need here?" I asked.

Kelsey shrugged. This was not, I realized, about grocery shopping. It was about getting out of town to a place where no one knew her—to see me and not be seen. A woman with two children in her cart was scanning a high shelf, talking to herself. An elderly couple shuffled by in rain gear and matching Velcro shoes. There was no one from St. Andrews here.

In the produce section, Kelsey found a pair of decorative wine barrels, boosted herself onto one, and patted the surface of the other.

"Thanks for coming with me," she said. "I couldn't face another day alone in the studio."

"How's the collection coming?"

"I think you'll be into it. I can see you in all the men's stuff. Where's your other half?"

"Clare? I don't know. I haven't talked to him today. Hey, thank you for not saying anything about his dad."

"You don't have to thank me. It's not like people are asking and I'm having to lie. I still can't believe no one's put two and two together. I guess it didn't get the same coverage over here."

"He's using his mom's last name."

"I know. I've heard him. Do you think he regrets coming here?"

"It's hard to tell with him. Are you going home for the holidays?"

"No," she said. "I won't be back in Jersey for a while. It's hard for me, actually. To go back."

"Can't keep you down on the farm, huh?"

"No, that's not it. I had a boyfriend in Ocean City who died right before I came over here. The summer that I graduated."

"Jesus," I said. "Fuck, I'm sorry. That must have been terrible."

"Some woman ran a stop sign and hit him on his bike at ten thirty in the morning. On her way to Dunkin' Donuts. When I think of all the times he could have killed himself. He was a dealer, like you were. He had some ugly people in his life, but he had such a good heart, I can't even tell you. He wore out his luck."

She stopped and shook her head. I was trying to decide if I believed that everyone came into the world with a fixed amount of luck that you tapped, periodically, like a commissary account.

"What was his name?" I asked.

"Why do you want to know that?"

I shrugged.

"Brandon Di Massi. Did you know him?"

I shook my head, and wondered if Casey might.

"Remember when you asked about my earrings at that bar in New York? He gave me those and I lost one the week after he died. That's why I was only wearing one. Anyway, where did you live on LBI?"

"Beach Haven. Do you know it?"

"My aunt had a place in Harvey Cedars. That Ferris wheel in Beach Haven is the first place I got kissed. Why did you leave?"

"My mom owns her own business, and things got slow after Labor Day until people started showing up again. She caters parties."

"What about your dad?"

"He was a big fisherman. And he played guitar. They were never married. I mean, I don't know him. We've never met."

"I bet he was handsome. Unless that's all your mom."

"Can I ask you something?"

"Of course."

"What are you doing here?"

"I thought that's what you were going to say. I saw the way you looked at me when Damien said that thing about girls who come here to get married. Is that what you think?"

"I don't think anything."

The stock boys were working around us as if we had some right to be here that superseded the need to do their job.

"Tell me what you want to eat," she said. "I'll make us something. Let's not go out to lunch."

"I'll cook," I said.

"You cook?"

"You don't believe me?"

"Show me," she said, as she jumped down.

Her flat was empty, her flatmates out of town. In the kitchen, I pulled a chef's knife from the wooden knife block and tested the edge against my thumb. I minced a clove of garlic and mashed it to a pulp with the flat of the blade, adding rosemary, sage leaves, and sea salt that made a sound like sand between teeth as the knife steel crushed everything into a paste. I threw a handful of chopped pancetta into the cast-iron pan on the stove, and let it cook while I quartered plum tomatoes. Kelsey handed me a glass of cold white wine, but kept her fingers on the stem when I tried to take it from her. That was when I should have kissed her, hindsight being what it is. I could hear the pancetta crackling on the stove behind me, the snapping of the fat over the flame. I wanted to get this right. Kelsey let the glass go. I scraped the herbs and salt and garlic onto the hot pork, splashed wine from my glass into the pan, watched it turn to steam. I added the tomatoes, stirring as they cooked down. The butter and cream went in next, and when that had combined, I grated pecorino over the sauce and watched it melt into the surface. Kelsey had cooked the pasta, and had done some shopping of her own at Waitrose: a bunch of kale, a bag of grapes, walnuts, paprika, more garlic, pears. I had figured she was stocking up, but now I saw that all of it was going into a salad, which seemed like a bad idea, a dish I'd have to pretend to enjoy. The walnuts were cooking in a pan with oil and spices while she shredded the kale with her hands. She set the table while I served our plates.

"Needs black pepper," I said, tasting a piece of pasta.

"Why are you so tense?" she asked. "This is perfect."

The dish had turned out just shy of how it was supposed to. It felt like the first thing I had done right in a long time. The salad was a delicious mess, the kind of thing I'd never think to make. Kelsey stood up and leaned across the table to wipe a spot of sauce off my chin before she licked it off her thumb. I had that feeling you get on trains, when the doors close and you brace yourself for movement and it doesn't come.

"What am I going to do with you?" she said.

All Damien had said in his voice mail was to be outside Andrew Melville Hall in fifteen minutes, ready to go. I got no answer when I called him back. The night was clear and unseasonably warm. I lit a cigarette and upset the early evening stillness with a stream of smoke.

"Hey," Clare said, coming up behind me. "I just stopped by your room. He called you too? Do you know what this is?"

I shook my head.

Fourteen minutes later a chauffeured black Mercedes pulled up to the curb. I climbed up front with the driver while Jules stepped out so Clare could sit bitch for whatever journey we were undertaking. Jules and Damien, loose jawed and smiley, had clearly been drinking.

"Where are we going?" I asked.

"Edinburgh," Damien said.

We had just killed a pint of Irish whiskey when the car turned down Princes Street, above the grassy valley that divides the city. Down in the valley was a spot-lit castle on a chunk of cliff, which I had figured for a photo-shop job or a theme park attraction when I saw it on the postcards sold in St. Andrews. The car stopped on a quiet residential block where a line of dark row houses faced an empty park. Damien told the driver that we wouldn't be here very long. We walked to the corner, where Damien hit a buzzer for flat number 4C. Static, laughter. Damien leaned in.

"Tell Nick it's Johnny Rockets," he said.

The lock on the wrought-iron gate began to sing. This was a *Boogie Nights* party, Jules explained as we climbed the stairs. Which meant turntables, aviators, Afro wigs, roller skates, and short, short skirts. Nick was in the kitchen, someone said, pointing to a roomful of people at the end of a long hall, where someone on skates was spinning on a table like a figure skater, a blur with occasional limbs.

"Nick," Damien called from the doorway.

The spinning column seemed to condense, and became a blond-haired boy in fresh-cut jean shorts, sunglasses, and a suit vest that hugged his lean, bare torso. He motioned for the people below him to make way and skated off the table, landing neatly on the floor.

"This is Nick," Damien said, as Nick toe-braked to a stop.

"Boys," Nick said. "What an honor. Please, follow me."

Two people stopped Nick as he skated down the hall in front of us, and expressed slurred admiration for his performance in a show that, judging from the photocopied programs scattered on the floor, was *How to Succeed in Business Without Really Trying.*

"We closed tonight," he explained over his shoulder. "Hey, *pardonnez-moi.*"

A girl was leaning on the door that he had stopped in front of.

"Nick, you were fantastic," she said, staring up at him. A stylized desert scene was printed on her pink T-shirt, the word *Iraq* scrawled in script underneath a palm tree.

"I appreciate that," Nick said, pounding on the door over her shoulder as she stepped aside. "Be decent!" he called into the wood, taking a key from his vest pocket and fitting it into the lock. Nick reached inside and hit the lights, which triggered a shriek and a string of profanity. There was a couple in the queen-sized bed, hiding themselves, using the top sheet as a shield. The boy, in boxer briefs and nothing else, squinted up at us while the girl rolled out from underneath him and pressed herself against the wall, her arm over her breasts. Her limbs seemed to multiply as she flailed in a tangle of clothes and bedclothes, and I realized it was not one girl, but two.

"Mate," the boy said, "are you taking the piss?"

"I told you, no guarantees," Nick said, skating across the hardwood. "Get dressed. This'll take a minute. Hey, you found a third! That's great!"

The boy was hopping into his jeans while one of the girls, a blonde with thick ankles and narrow shoulders, snatched her shirt from the nightstand and stormed into the hall. The other girl was trying to get dressed under the billowing tent of the sheet. That was the first time I saw Jules laugh out loud.

"Come in, come in," Nick said, locking the door behind the last of his evicted guests. He produced a pair of jeans from deep in a mesh laundry hamper, pulled a wallet from a back pocket, and fished out a stack of homemade envelopes the size of business cards. He held one out to Damien, who made no move to take it.

"That's the garbage you sell to the drama club, but where's the stuff I'm here for?"

"Why don't you try some before you cop a fucking attitude with me? Jesus, are you gonna be this big a dick your whole life?"

"Tom," Damien said, "play guinea pig."

Nick dipped his big brass key into the powder-filled valley of the folded paper, and held it to my face. Behind the mirrored lenses of his aviators, his pupils were flitting between my nose and the small mountain of coke coming toward me. He looked like someone trying to feed a child. I cleared a nostril and leaned in.

"So how's life on the water?" Nick said, as I winced.

Jules asked after a friend, a sculptor who went to school down here. Nick said he was having people over later, that we could all find ourselves a threesome if we showed up at his flat around 5:00 a.m.

"It's coke," I said, finally. "It's nice."

Damien took out his wallet.

"I'll take whatever you've got there," he said.

Fits and starts of music were coming from the next room—the tuning of an electric guitar, a splash of low notes from a keyboard. The guitar player hit a minor chord, gave himself more volume, and launched into something by Nirvana.

"Who's that?" Clare asked Nick, pointing to the wall that the noise was coming through.

"This band one of my flatmates plays in. They're trying to get me to sing with them. What do you think?"

"They're terrible," I said.

Damien threw back his head and laughed. "Is this shit that good? Maybe we should all do some."

"Wait a goddamn second," Nick said. "You thought you could just pick up your gear and be on your merry way? Do I look like some nigger from Bed-Stuy to you? Stick around. Have a drink." He turned to me. "Let me guess: you play guitar."

"Not really," I said.

"He's lying," Clare said, blinking in the aftermath of an enormous bump. "Tom, I've never heard you play. Let's sit in."

"No thanks," I said. "It's been too long."

"Believe me, it doesn't get much worse than those guys," Nick said. "Maybe Jules can explain why English people have no rhythm. The drummer's good, but he's from Wales."

"The drummer's all right," Clare said.

"Can we do some more of that?" I asked.

"If we're staying," Damien said, "then we're all doing some."

Nick rolled into the living room ahead of us, waving his arms like an umpire.

"Enough!" he shouted. "Lay down your weapons! Out!"

A boy in a sleeveless T-shirt reluctantly gave up his guitar, which was cheap and not in tune. Clare was playing with the controls on the keyboard, testing the amp. The drummer stayed.

"What do you play?" Nick asked me.

"What do you sing?"

"I make shit up. Play some blues."

"In E," I said to Clare, tapping the distortion pedal with the toe of my sneaker. The red light popped on, the amp began to hum, and I stole a lick from B. B. King's *Live at the Regal*. Nick spun on his skates, and started singing about a woman who used to make her own paychecks. He was down onto one knee, his chin on his chest, and I was staring at him in disbelief, not because he knew the words, but because he was channeling a black man twice his weight and three times his age—the barely contained screams, the best lines delivered like quick right jabs. The drummer was better than he had sounded through the wall, loose and never wrong. People were pouring through the door. Nick pressed his back up against mine, and skated in place while he sang some lyrics of his own:

You know I'm so happy, baby,
That my boy to came to see me
I said I'm so happy, baby
That he's down here to see me
It's good to see his face, Lord
But I wish he'd let these nice boys be

"Lemme hear those keys," he said to Clare.

And Clare laid into it, his fingers hitting the notes and then pulling back as if the keys were scalding hot. It was amazing to me that we could just pick up and play like this, both of us high and flying. Two girls were dancing with Nick. I felt a rush of vaguely patriotic pride.

We went on like that for a while, Nick making things up, Clare and I tossing the lead back and forth. My fingers were aching from playing rhythm, and while I could still feel my way through the pentatonic scale, I couldn't improvise for shit as the coke faded, leaving only a bitter trail down the back of my throat. I gave up when Clare switched keys. He was shifting into jazz with the drummer as I wedged through the bottleneck of the doorway.

"You're not terrible," Nick said, skating up behind me. "Your boy can play."

"I liked your lyrics."

"Well, they come from the heart."

"Can I get a little more of that stuff?"

"Of course you can. Come with me."

With his door locked behind us, Nick tapped a small snowdrift onto the sleeve of a Big Star record.

"How're you finding the St. Andrews Academy for Misfits and Miscreants?"

"Is that what they call it?"

"That's what I call it. It's like the bar scene from *Star Wars* up there. Every kind of weirdo under one roof."

"Are you from New York?"

"I'm from West Palm. I met Damien at summer camp a thousand years ago. Imagine what a shit he was as a little kid. It almost deserves a moment of silence. Is he showing you a good time?"

I nodded.

"He's fun to watch, right? He'd save the planet if he was a car.

Runs on his own steam." Nick did a line, and used the breath he had inhaled to say: "He mentioned you, actually, if you're the kid from Jersey. I don't really know you, but I feel like you're playing this place the way you play guitar, you know? It's all borrowed licks with you. Anyway, I get what you're doing there, but what about your buddy on the keys?"

"What about him?"

"What's his malfunction? What'd he do to end up here?"

"Have you heard of Michael Savage? The financier?"

"No, I'm deaf and blind."

"That's Clare's dad."

It took me a second to realize that rather than imagining myself telling Nick that, weighing the consequences and thinking it through, I'd gone and done it. The coke had me operating two steps ahead of myself. Nick laid down his credit card.

"I'm assuming Damien doesn't know that. Well, I'll be. Jesus, he'd have a field day with that."

Nick went back to work on the two industrial-sized lines that he was racking up.

"Do you make good bank selling this?"

"Good bank?" Nick laughed. "Yes, I make good bank. I make as much as bankers. Don't even think about trying that shit over here. I see how you're looking at this stuff. And you, my friend, are not cut out for this."

"What makes you say that?"

"The fact that you're not arguing. You know, you fucked up if you came here to be like the people you're running around with. Kids like you, they go to a high school full of trust fund babies and they think they can have that if they make the right moves. It doesn't work that way. What you're aiming for and what you're looking at are different things."

Nick finished his line and held the record sleeve up to my face.

"Let's get back out there," he said, and then paused. "Maybe you've figured this out already, but you're either the help or you're not."

I thanked him.

Nick pinched my cheek, pulled an envelope from his vest pocket, and slapped it down on my thigh.

"Be cool, stay in school," he said. "That's on the house."

Nick and I bumped into Damien as we stepped into the hall.

"We're heading to the Opal," Damien said, "You're welcome to join us."

"I'll pass, brother. You can have the businessmen and their bunnies all to yourself. I don't feel like fucking with them tonight. Plus, I'll have seventeen distinct semen samples in my sheets if I don't stick around. But thanks for stopping by."

The driver had fallen asleep with his head against the window. I tried to imagine how it would feel to wake up to four boys coked to the gills, demanding music, lighting cigarettes—to be the help, in other words. We were flying across the city, green lights as far as I could see. Brilliant windows studded the dirty, ornate stone façades. We were all talking at the same time without talking over one another. The driver pulled up to a crowded patch of sidewalk and we seemed to step through the crowd as we stepped out of the car. Damien nodded to a bouncer who unhooked a black velvet rope and ushered us inside. The Opal Lounge looked like a mash-up of New York nightlife as imagined by someone who didn't live there. The host told us he would have a table in a few minutes, if we cared to have a drink at the bar. Damien ordered champagne, something pink and vintage.

"Shit," Damien said. "My wallet's in my coat."

His coat was with the coat check. He handed me the bill.

"Tom, can you get this one?"

At the going exchange rate, this one was a little more than $800.

"Here," Clare said, reading my panic. "I owe you for the other night."

He slapped a card down on the bar, but the bartender had his back to us, so Damien picked it up to tuck it into the check folder. He paused when he felt the weight, and glanced down at the piece of metal in his hand. I watched him read the name stamped into the titanium. Clare pushed past me and shot out a hand to snatch it back, but Damien had already made the handoff. Clare stood at his shoulder while the bartender ran the card. I could see both their reflections in the mirror behind the stacks of back-lit bottles. Damien looked like someone had just put something in his mouth and asked him to guess what it was. I couldn't look at Clare, so I closed my eyes, my guilt magnified by the drugs. Damien offered Clare the check, and Clare scribbled in a tip and signed a name, his real one, I presumed. He reached around Damien, left the folder on the bar, and walked away.

"You knew the whole time," Damien said.

"So?"

"Clare's dad's name is Michael, right? Don't bullshit me."

"I always called him Mister."

"Yeah," Damien said. "I bet you did."

"Did your dad have money with him?"

"That's the stupidest thing you've ever asked me. Please don't insult my father like that."

"What's this?" Jules asked.

"Nothing," I said.

Damien had turned his attention to a couple who were making their way toward us through the crowd. We had cut them in the line outside, and I knew they were American without hearing them speak. The man—he was at least thirty—looked like he had just come from work, his thick pink tie pulled away from his thick neck under a pinstriped suit. He was nodding enthusiastically with the DJ's mix. The woman seemed older and wore pearls, a dark skirt, and a soft white sweater. She looked ready to apologize for whatever he had come over to say.

"Hey, I'm Adam," he said, sticking out a hand. "Could you boys settle a little bet for us? That looked like Prince William who y'all were talking to, but my friend Anna says it's definitely not."

"How did you get in here?" Damien asked.

"Whoa, you're American? Our clients brought us, but they pussed out and went home early. We work for Bear Stearns. Are you guys members or whatever?"

"Let me guess," Damien said. "Sales and marketing."

"Did we meet at the conference?"

"Let's go," Anna said.

"Hang on a second. Was it?"

"Was it what?" Damien asked.

"Was that Prince William?"

"Well, it would be some coincidence if it wasn't, don't you think? He goes to school right up the road. Do you want to meet him? I'm sure he'd love to meet you guys."

"I know that's not him," Anna said, as Damien walked away. "Right?"

"He'll be here in a second," I said. "Just ask."

"Hey, how come you're all American?" Adam asked.

"We're not," Jules said.

Jules seemed unimpressed by this, and I was starting to understand that he didn't share Damien's enthusiasm for theater or performance art, or whatever this was. He liked drugs and champagne and conversation; he tolerated this. I felt the same way, and wished that I could make him understand that somehow. Damien and Clare were threading their way back through the crowd. Clare balked at the sight of our new friends, who had their backs to him, but Damien pushed him forward. He was going to make Clare dance.

"Will, this is Adam and, I'm sorry, I didn't catch your name."

"Anna."

"Anna, this is Will."

Anna seemed more interested in Damien than Clare.

"It's a pleasure," Clare said.

I coughed over a laugh; Clare's accent was so good that I wondered if he had been practicing. I was amazed he had agreed to this, but it made sense—impersonating royalty was easier than lying to New York investment bankers about his last name. One was a game, the other was not.

"So do you come here a lot?" Adam asked. "Is this, like, a place where you hang out?"

"A bit," Clare said.

He was cagey and uncomfortable, which was probably what they expected of royalty faced with tourists.

"So you're really Prince William? This might sound stupid, but do you have, like, ID or something?"

"Adam, Jesus," Anna said.

"Do you think the prince of England has a fucking driver's license?" Damien asked. "He has a driver. Did you see that Benz outside?"

"Fine, fine, I believe you," Adam said. "I was just fucking with you. Sorry if I came off like an asshole. Can I buy you all a shot or something?"

"Sure," I said. "That'd be great."

Damien kept inviting Jules to do the talking, Jules being a close approximation of English royalty, and Adam bought us shot after shot, which seemed to make the coke burn hotter.

"Hey, do you guys do any skiing over here?" Adam asked, shifting his weight back and forth, miming a mogul run. "I got some from our cab driver and we gotta kill it before we fly back."

The bathrooms at the Opal, studio-sized rooms with locking doors and ample seating, were designed for this kind of thing. Adam offered us key bumps from a green plastic bag. Damien rubbed his finger along the inside edge and touched it to his tongue. He shook his head and slipped a hand inside his jacket pocket.

"I wouldn't do my laundry with that stuff," he said. "Flush it. It's disgusting."

Once Nick's envelopes were in rotation, Damien occupied a leather ottoman and Anna, after a few minutes, moved onto his lap. This would be her souvenir from Scotland: a one-night stand with a rich, handsome college kid. I imagined her rehashing it over brunch in Soho with a group of girlfriends, joking that she went all that way to fuck someone from New York. She laughed at something no one had said, and I looked from her face down to her lap, where one of Damien's hands was resting, the broad pads of his fingertips disappearing in the folds in the fabric between her legs. Adam was less stupid than he had seemed, and was determined to do as much of Damien's cocaine as possible. He was arguing with Jules about barrel length in shotguns used for sporting clays. Clare kept trying to catch Damien's eye. Whether he was desperate to explain himself or desperate for something else, I couldn't tell. I was too high to talk.

Finally, Anna said that she was ready to head back. She stood up and pulled Damien to his feet. Jules said he was going to pop by and see what his sculptor friend was up to. Adam followed him; Damien had left the coke with Jules. Clare caught me by the arm as I tried to leave.

"Hey," he said.

His eyes were pointing in slightly different directions as he tried to focus on my face.

"I'm sorry about that thing with the card," I said.

"Whatever, I don't give a fuck about that. I'm going home. I need cash for a cab."

"Just take the car."

"Damien's taking the car. I need cash. I'm out."

"I'm out too."

"How can you be out of cash? You haven't paid for anything all night. All week. You're lying."

He was inching toward me, and I felt time slow to a jagged crawl. Clare grabbed at my front pocket where my wallet was visible against my thigh. His fingers snaked over the hem and found the leather of my billfold. I grabbed his wrist, but Clare wrenched free and tried again. A quick instinctual punch to the stomach dropped Clare to one knee.

"Fuck, I'm sorry," I said, as I tried to help him up.

He started slapping at me as he staggered to his feet.

"Give me everything you have on you," he hissed, almost crying now. "No one touches me."

"Take it easy," I said. "I'm sorry. I didn't mean to do that."

"You fucking owe me."

"Owe you for what?"

"For everything. For all the shit I've paid for since we got here. I want my money, now."

His voice was shrill, shattery, just shy of a full-blown shriek. My back was against the wall.

"Stop," I said. "Stop it. Just relax, OK?"

Clare stuffed his hand in my pocket. I felt his fingers writhing against my thigh as he fought the fabric to pull my wallet free. He fished out fifteen pounds in cash, and flipped my wallet at the floor, where it flopped open on a bounce and landed in a split. I was braced for a hit. Instead, Clare pulled me to him. When his mouth smashed into mine, it felt like a flash grenade had detonated in my head. I was mostly gone while Clare's front teeth were grating against mine. He let me go as soon as I was all there again, as if that was something he could sense. I thought: What took so long? Clare wiped his mouth with the back of his hand and walked out the door.

I was alone in my room, doing everything but my econ reading so that, eventually, I could sit down and crack my textbook with a clear head. My laundry was half folded when Clare knocked on my door. He seemed, or pretended to seem, confused by my standoffishness. I thought: So this is how it's going to be. Two nights before, in Edinburgh, with the car gone and no money for a cab of my own, I'd slept on a bench in Waverly Station so that I could take the first train back to Leuchars. I was still sore on my right side. I figured Clare had come by to apologize, but instead he told me that his parents had sent a car for him and had extended the invitation to me. Clare didn't name a town, but his parents were apparently a short drive from St. Andrews, hiding in plain sight, or not bothering to hide anymore. I could have said that I had work to do, that I was under the weather, wiped out—all true—and I could still hear the fear in my mother's voice when she'd called to warn me about Michael Savage. But instead I went along. It was Thanksgiving, Clare said, to my complete surprise. We'd be spending the night.

"Your folks don't give much notice," I said, as the driver drifted into the fast lane on the A9, heading north. "Why are they in Scotland?"

Clare shrugged.

"Mind sharing?" he asked, touching a finger to his right nostril.

In preparation for my study session, I had dipped into Nick's gift, some of which was apparently still visible.

"Can we play the radio, sir?" I asked, hoping that the noise would mask the quick nasal intakes and the choppy dialogue that followed. I was working up a mound of powder on the end of my room key when the driver settled on an oldies station. The coke kept my eyes inside the car, and off the route we were taking. In case anybody asked me where the Savages were staying, I could tell them, honestly, that I had no idea.

The house was a broad-shouldered stone mansion, just under an hour from St. Andrews. The winding drive and oval-shaped car park looked like a river feeding off a lake of gravel. The car ground to a stop, and I found myself staring at the driver in the rearview mirror as the interior lights came on. I ducked to wipe my nose clean with my sleeve, and when I looked up, his eyes locked on mine again.

"Thanks for the lift," I said.

The driver said nothing.

The front door of the house was open and, staring into the glow of the entryway, I imagined that something terrible had happened here, that we were about to discover the bodies of Clare's parents, blood soaked, cut down in the middle of a desperate, clawing escape. And then I saw Michael Savage standing in the darkness by a head-high hedge, his arms folded across his chest. He was looking out over the roof of the sedan into the woods that bordered the lawn.

"Tom, nice to see you," he said. "Glad you could make it. Camille's a little under the weather. It's just us boys tonight. I was thinking we could head into town, find a turkey burger in the spirit of the holiday."

"What's wrong with her?" Clare asked.

Michael shot his son a look.

"Thanks for having me," I said.

"Thanks for coming. Throw your things inside and we'll get going."

In the right-hand bay of a pristine two-car garage were two ATVs parked nose to tail, the molded plastic saddlebags and rifle cases covered in a fine spray of mud. The other bay held a silver Porsche 911 that looked like it had never seen rain. Clare folded the passenger seat forward so I could climb into the cubbyhole behind it. Michael redlined the engine before he put the car in gear, and drove exactly the speed limit on the narrow, kinky country road, refusing to slow down for curves, exhibiting the kind of precision and control they teach at weekend racing schools. Clare seemed used to this, bracing his body against the padding of the passenger-side racing seat as we flew toward wherever we were headed.

"You boys hungry?" Michael asked.

I had never been less hungry.

"We ate," Clare said. "Before we left."

"There's a band playing at a pub in town. They have grub if your appetites come back. Let's go hear some music."

"That sounds great," I said, thinking of a double vodka soda and a private bathroom stall. I was coming down, and wanted another bump the way a cut will itch as it heals, begging to be torn back open.

The town, two loose strings of shops facing a narrow road, sat beside a dark unbending river, its banks covered by naked trees rooted in mud. I could see my breath in the air, and the chemical aftertaste of the coke made it seem like exhaust instead of exhalation. A bouncer sat hunched on a stool outside the bar, statuesque, a cap over his eyes. He raised his head as we approached and waved us down a flight of stairs. We ducked into a long underground room, where a band was playing on a plywood platform at the end opposite the door. They were covering "Hey, Jealousy" by the Gin Blossoms while an overweight woman, her long blond hair streaked with electric blue, danced alone in front of them, swinging her hips and her head with her hands at her sides. We sat down by the stage. Michael hung his topcoat on the back of his chair, and tossed a ring of keys into a patch of light cast by the single candle on our table. I studied the teeth cut into the blanks, wondering which locks they fit. Michael turned to me, suddenly, nodded toward the band, and asked what I thought.

"They're good," I shouted.

It was true, and he seemed eager for my approval, which I didn't understand. Michael slapped me on the shoulder. We were about the same size, I realized, picturing myself in his thin beige cashmere sweater and gingham dress shirt, which looked like something he might have worn to the office at some point. What would happen if I took his keys and walked away while he was busy talking into his son's ear? If I got into the car and drove? I knew from my valet parking days that Porsches have a heavy clutch, but I learned to drive stick on an '86 Ford Bronco, so I was used to that. I imagined Camille sitting up in bed back at the house, reading something in her native language. The sound of the garage door lurching upward as headlights swept across the bedroom wall. I climb the stairs and walk into the bedroom after letting myself in. She looks up with tired recognition, but no surprise in her expression. I'd seen enough of their life to feel fluent in it, ready to shift between situations as easily as the guitar player was changing chords on stage. I watched as he took the neck in hand and bent three strings up a full step, rising onto the balls of his feet with the sound.

By the time we piled back into the car, I had hit a patch of exhilarated clarity somewhere inside a third wind that felt like it could last for days. Michael put the windows down, and blasts of cold air wicked sweat off my face. My eyes were too dry and too tired to read the number on the mailbox as we turned down the drive, and my ears were still ringing from the music as Michael showed me to my room on the first floor. He paused in the doorway as I was unfastening my watch.

"Sleep tight," he said, and laughed to himself as he shut the door.

I lay on top of the comforter in all my clothes, and was suddenly profoundly thirsty. The first floor of the house looked like it had been furnished all at once from a single showroom; the owners had managed to take an ancient home and make it feel like no one had ever lived there. As I walked into the kitchen, I noticed an over/under shotgun leaning in a corner near the door, the oldest-looking thing in sight, the bluing on the barrel worn thin from however many pairs of hands. I wondered what trouble Michael was expecting as I sucked down water from the big chrome arch of the kitchen faucet, too high to be frightened.

"How about a glass?" Michael said from the doorway, when I came up for air.

I nodded, wiping my mouth with my sleeve. Michael filled two glasses from a filter in the fridge, and we faced each other across a marble countertop, me on a high stool, him on his feet.

"How much coke do you have left?"

I stopped midswallow.

"You boys were lit when you got here, weren't you? A father can tell. Seriously, though, what's left?"

"Some," I said. "Enough, I guess."

"Do I need an engraved invitation?" he asked. "Or do you just not want to share?"

"You want some?"

"Do you think I'm kidding? Unless you're all partied out. No? Go ahead then, do the honors."

Michael laid a prepaid phone like mine on the counter while I unfolded the paper packet and cut lines with my St. Andrews ID card. I realized he had been outside on a call.

"Do you drink with this stuff?" he asked as he rolled up a £100 note.

"It doesn't hurt."

"I'm not asking if one drinks with this stuff. I'm asking if you do."

I said I'd have a drink, and he dug into a temperature-controlled wine cabinet beneath the counter and withdrew a bottle. It was white Burgundy from Puligny-Montrachet, the faded yellow label marred by a neon orange sticker announcing that the wine had been purchased from a private collection. Michael turned his back to me and rummaged through a drawer until he found a corkscrew. Later, I looked up the bottle. The average price online was equal to a month's rent on my mother's house.

"How's school?" he asked, passing me a wineglass, and then leaning in to take a line.

"It's good. It's kind of an adjustment."

"So's everything. How's my son holding up?"

"I think he likes it."

"Do you actually believe that, or are you saying what you think I want to hear? Have people figured out who his daddy is yet?"

"A few people know."

"He tried to hide it?"

I nodded, and Michael laughed.

"Are they pissed? Righteously indignant? What?"

"I don't think anybody cares that much."

"The Brits are pretty laissez-faire about this stuff. They talk a lot of shit in the privacy of their homes, but outward moral outrage isn't their thing, from what I've seen. I think they think it's tacky."

"No one's bothering him about it, if that's what you mean."

"I'm not worried about that. That's something he needs to learn to deal with. But I am glad he has you to watch his back."

I nodded to let him know that he was welcome, for whatever that was worth. I did a line, and then another, trying and failing to think of something conversationally benign. Michael had something else in mind.

"Your old man wasn't really in the picture, from what I understand," he said.

"Not at all."

"Do you know how lucky you are?"

"Sorry?"

"You probably never thought of it that way, but it's a blessing in disguise. Could be the key to your success. You know who my dad was?"

I shook my head.

"Exactly. There's this story he used to tell me: He's driving his 1961 Mustang from Cheyenne to Minot, North Dakota. Straight shot for seven hundred miles, maybe three other cars on the road the whole way. At some point dad hits black ice and goes into a skid. There's one telephone pole a hundred yards in front of him, and he's keeping an eye on it, not too worried, just waiting for the car to lose some steam. But he's not slowing down fast enough, so he starts spinning the wheel left and right, trying to stay clear of this pole, but eventually he realizes that he's headed straight for it, that there's nothing he can do. He can't fucking believe he's about to hit the only thing for miles. Wrecks the front end of the car. You know why he hit it?"

"I don't know. God's will?"

"He hit it because that's what he was looking at. That's what he used to tell me. One time I asked my mom about the time dad wrecked his Mustang. You know what she said? 'Never happened.' It's not a story about driving. It's about hitting what you're looking at."

"I'm not sure I get it."

"Do you know how to ride a motorcycle?"

"Yes."

"So how do you turn?"

"You lean."

"Wrong. You look where you want the bike to go. Do you see what I'm getting at? When your dad's around, that's what you're looking at—whatever he is. That's why my dad told me that story. So I would stop looking at him. So I could be something bigger, something else. Then you spend your whole life building something, and your kid comes along and you realize that everything you've done is hanging over his head. When you've done a lot, it's a lot to look at. It's hard for kids to see around it when it's that big and in their faces all the time. Even if the money doesn't rot them from the inside, they need to be able to imagine something different. You want something better for your kids, but you hit what you're looking at, or something before it. Now look at you. There's nothing in your way. You aren't even thinking about what your mother does, because you've always known you're better than that. What's that look about? You've never heard that outside your head? Don't be ashamed of that. She wants that for you too. That's my point: you can do whatever you want. I was worried that I'd fucked things up for Clare, but I think this mess will be a real asset for him in a few years. It's the best thing that could have happened, actually. I'm out of the way now. He can be whatever he wants. So what are you trying to be?"

"Rich."

"Keep going. Why?"

"I don't want my mom to have to work. I want problems that aren't money problems. I want a big house down the shore. I want a boat."

"And then what?"

"What do you mean?"

"You make your money, you get all that shit, and then what? What do you think happens after that? There's not a right or a wrong answer. This won't be on the exam. I'm asking you because I don't remember what I thought when I was your age."

"I don't know. Retire early? Raise a family? Play golf on days that end in *Y,* or whatever you said?"

"It's harder than you think. I don't mean getting there. That won't be very hard for you. I mean getting out. You hit this point where you've made more money than you can reasonably spend, and you've passed four or five of your personal I'll-retire-when goals, and you keep waking up and doing it anyway. Force of habit, I guess is what it's called. My first boss at Lehman used to get really sentimental about this, which is probably why he was still herding first-year analysts at forty-five. He used to talk about retirement ad nauseum, about getting a place on the Snake River and just catching trout. He'd tell us it's not normal to hoard in abstract figures. We're supposed to want enough to get us laid, to marry the girl we couldn't fuck in high school, to get more house than we can use, but that's it. To keep going is a perversion of a natural instinct, is what he used to say. Like a cancer. The whole time I knew he was wrong."

"How's that?"

"The people who just want money never get it, or they don't get it in the quantities they imagine. Right now you think you want all the stuff you just mentioned, but it's not really about that. The stuff"—Michael held up the bottle, wagged it back and forth—"isn't the point. It's how you rationalize what you're doing. The big house is just something to look at, but what you're aiming for is something else. You, my friend, are not going to get comfortable and walk away."

"How do you know?"

"I'm looking at you and I'm telling you that you have what it takes, because I know what that looks like. Remember when you told me that story over lunch? Your mom's friend? The one who killed herself with all the pills? That was a stone-cold thing to do, and you didn't hesitate, because you had the cards. You don't really understand what you're aiming for right now, but you're definitely not the trout-fishing type. I don't even think you're as naive as you're pretending to be. Or maybe you actually believe you can just make some coin and walk away, in which case I don't know whether I want you to be right or whether I want to watch it get beaten out of you."

I had the sense that he could go on like this for days. Cocaine agreed with him in that it allowed him to agree deeply with himself, drowning out whatever doubt he may have had about his own convictions. The drugs didn't do that for me. I wanted to tell him that he was wrong about the story I had told, that I was still ashamed about the way that I had let him bait me. It hadn't felt stone-cold to me at all; the instinct and the delivery had both been white hot inside my head. I never felt like I was holding any cards. I wondered how much that mattered, given that no one else had read it that way. The wine, which I could barely taste, was almost gone.

"Should we switch to red?" Michael asked, fishing out another bottle, another Burgundy.

"Is that shotgun loaded?" I asked.

"Wouldn't be much good if it wasn't. There's another one upstairs."

"What are you worried about?"

"What do you think I'm worried about?"

"Someone who knows you went into my mom's shop and told her that I should be careful because people might be gunning for you."

Michael barely masked a flash of shock. I watched him fight the desire to ask me more, and lose.

"Who was this?"

"I don't know," I lied. "Some guy from Morgan Stanley."

"When?"

"Two weeks ago."

"Did you say anything to Clare?"

"No, of course not. Can I ask you something?"

"You can ask me whatever you want."

"Where did all that money go?"

"So you read the paper."

I nodded and tried to convey, through my expression, that I was trustworthy, that he had nothing to lose by telling me the truth, that he could look at it as a good deed, an act of mentorship, a cautionary tale.

"Two years ago, I was sitting by the pool at a hotel in Corsica next to some other balding middle-aged white guy. He was Russian, but he was speaking French to this girl who'd shown up to keep him company for the day. At one point she stops talking and says, 'You obviously weren't paying attention.' And he says, 'I'm still not paying attention.' I thought that was funny. I thought: Hey, we've got the same sense of humor. She was gone the next day, but he was back at the pool, and we started talking. I asked how long he was there for and he said a month, that he came to this hotel every year for the month of August. We spent some time together over the next few days, had a few drinks, a few meals together. We talked about our families and our kids and the things we still wanted to do with our lives. On my last day we had lunch, and he told me that he thought we could do some business together. He must have looked me up, or had someone look me up, because we barely talked about our work, which was refreshing. Anyway, he said he would hate for anything to interfere with our friendship, and that there was some risk, blah, blah, blah, and I told him I understood, and why didn't we try it out and see what happened. I knew by then that it was probably better if I didn't ask too many questions. I called my office, and we got him some money, not a huge amount, but nothing you'd want to throw away. Six weeks later, I got a call from some private banker in Anguilla who had an account in my name with double the money I had wired to this guy. Just like that. The next time we spoke, I asked how much business we could do, and he said as much as I wanted, that he couldn't promise it would always be like that, but that he knew he could make money. He put some cash into my fund, mostly as a sign of good faith."

"What was he doing with your money?"

"What do you think he was doing?"

"I don't know. Guns? Drugs?"

"I didn't know either."

"You never asked?"

"What was I going to do, run through the financials with him? Listen, the fund made money—I made money—because I knew things about companies, about industries. This engineer just came up with the next big thing; the clinical trials are fucked; they're selling the furniture; whatever. This was just instinct—someone tells me he can make money with my money and I believe him, because I've been doing this for a while, and I know a thing or two about it by now. I just let go and went with my gut. It was a whole new thing for me, but hey, evolve or die, right?"

"What if he was doing something really bad?"

"Like what? What's really bad in your mind? Look, if you have a piece of a mutual fund, then you're making money from oil, from tobacco, from big pharma, which is literally ten thousand times bigger and more evil than this," he said, pointing to the coke between us. "You want to do some real damage? Go the legal route. I knew everything about the industries I covered, and once you know everything, you realize that the distinctions between white collar and black market are pretty arbitrary. One guy has an MBA from Wharton and the other guy has a face tattoo and a gold-plated AK-47, but they're both fucking ruthless and they both live and die by the bottom line. It's true across the board. You're making money in fashion because you've got five-year-olds chained to sewing machines in El Salvador. Go to China sometime and meet the folks who made your TV and your laptop, see how they live. You want to tell me one is better than the other because it's government sanctioned, publically traded? Don't be so naive."

"That's your thesis? 'Everything is fucked so just do as much harm as you want?'"

"You don't buy that?"

"No," I said. "I don't."

"I can tell you don't really respect me," he said, finally. "But I can't tell whether it's because of what I did or because I got caught."

"I can't tell either."

"But you want what I had."

"Some version of it. With a different ending."

"Ending? What ending? Nothing's ending. I was just on the phone with someone who's trying to get me set up."

The drugs and the wine had allowed him to look past his present circumstances, but I could see that it was coming back to him in flashes as the last of my coke faded, his confidence like a radio broadcast interrupted now by bursts of ugly static. The shotgun was real; you couldn't not look at that. I was looking at him and thinking: Is this what I'm supposed to become or what I already am or something I'm never going to be? And then Michael Savage produced a vial of cocaine from his pocket, this one as big as a shotgun shell.

"Jesus," I said.

The urgency with which he tapped out a pile and nodded that I should cut it up made me think back to the day we met, and the way he had insisted that my mother's dead friend couldn't have been out of options, that there must have been something else she could have done after the cops let her attacker go. That was really about him. He was out of options, and he knew it, and it was killing him.

"You really never found out what that guy did with your money?" I asked.

"Of course I did, eventually. He was doing things you'd probably describe as 'really bad.'"

"Like what?"

"I said that you could ask me anything. I didn't say I'd answer."

"OK," I said. "Fuck, this wine is good."

"To the finer things in life," he said, raising his glass. "Now I'm going to go piss some of this out, if you'll excuse me."

I closed my eyes when he was gone and imagined I was sitting on a stool that was balanced on a radio tower on top of the tallest skyscraper in the world. I had never been that high. I could hear Michael Savage directing a stream of piss into the toilet in the powder room. The flush of a toilet, the splash of a sink. He strode back into the room.

"Here," he said, handing me another £100 note, this one unrolled. "That's for sharing earlier. Now, where were we?"

I was staring over his shoulder, and Michael, to his credit, saw in my face that his son must be standing in the doorway at his back. I snatched the vial off the counter while he did what I was probably constitutionally unable to, and swept the loose coke onto the floor.

"What are you doing?" Clare asked.

His father didn't turn around.

"We were talking," he said, looking straight at me. "Tom and I were just swapping stories."

PART III

How's it driving?" I asked my mother, slapping the center console of the BMW as we pulled away from the terminal at Newark.

"It's fine," she said. "Frances is borrowing the Celica, so I took this. The registration's about to expire. The gas mileage sucks."

"So sell it for parts," I said, putting my feet up on the dash.

"Don't be a brat. Did you sleep on the plane?"

I shook my head. We were driving south on the turnpike, past refineries and factories and oil storage tanks with "Drive Safely" printed around their midlines. It was good to be home.

"If you're not too tired, I have a surprise for you," my mother said. "I hope you're hungry."

One of her cooks had quit the year before and transformed a small Victorian house outside Princeton into a BYO restaurant—a place where she could showcase the considerable kitchen chops that had been wasted on our catering jobs. The long slab tables in the dining room had been cut from a tall black walnut that had come crashing through the attic in a storm. I had landed just in time for the friends-and-family Christmas party, which happened to coincide with their review in the New Jersey section of the *New York Times*. No one had seen the story when my mother walked into the dining room ahead of me to whoops and clapping. There was a rumor that the review would be online at 10:00 p.m., and one of the restaurant's investors, an investment banker who lived down the block, had instructed one of his first-year analysts to e-mail him the text as soon as it went up.

"He'll be there all night anyway," John said, staring down at his BlackBerry. I had never seen one before.

"Yeah, this is what you have to look forward to," he told me when I asked him how it worked. "No peace, ever. Getting fucking chewed out by a client in all caps while you're on a boat in Martinique."

Dinner was served as soon as we sat down; the kitchen had been waiting for my mother. We ate slivers of vinegar-cured tongue on toast, shards of raw fluke with Asian pear and jicama and jalapeño, short ribs slow-cooked for two days and served with grapes breaded in cornmeal and deep-fried until they were dense and sugary, like a bite of apple pie. I speared the last grape off my mother's plate and popped it in my mouth.

"Really?" she said. "I thought you ate like this all the time at school."

It was the tone she used with people who worked for her. I was stung, and too jet-lagged not to let it show.

"That was one meal, like, three months ago."

"Honey, go ask Marissa for seconds if you're still hungry," she said, overcompensating now, correcting for the lapse in maternal sensitivity. I wondered if she had forgotten how to do this. "Here, take the rest of this. I'm done."

"I'm good," I said.

The review was due up any minute, and John asked if I would mind grabbing four more bottles of champagne from the trunk of his Mercedes. I remembered what Nick had said about being the help, or not. John tossed me his keys.

I lit a cigarette in the sharp December air. Inside the trunk, the running lights revealed a case of champagne surrounded by presents in elaborate gift wrapping, loose golf balls, tools, and a baseball bat that was either for Little League or self-defense. I spun around at the sound of the restaurant's door, smoke stinging my eyes. Roger Hokenson was coming down the steps.

"Just the man I wanted to see," he said. "How's Scotland? Did you play the Old Course yet?"

"I did," I said, holding out my pack.

"How'd you shoot?"

"Three under par."

"You're shitting me," he said, popping a cigarette into his mouth.

"I'm shitting you."

Roger lit up and winked at me with his lungs full of smoke.

"Hey, I didn't realize that was Michael Savage's kid living with you guys."

"Who told you who he was?"

"Your mom mentioned it, I think."

A lie and a sign that he didn't know my mother as well as I had thought.

"How's your mom?" I asked.

"She's good, you know? She saw someone in town on a Vespa the other day and told me she should get one. It's like no one told her she's eighty goddamn years old. When do you head back?"

"Right after New Year's."

"Where's your buddy?"

"With his family."

"Have you met him?" Roger asked. "His dad, I mean."

I knew exactly what he meant.

"I never met his dad."

"Put that on your résumé. 'Never even spoke to Michael Savage.' Give yourself an edge in the job market when you graduate."

"Thanks for the tip."

"Anytime. You don't know where he is, do you?"

"Clare?"

"The whole family."

"Why are you asking me that?"

"Just curious."

"I'm serious, who wants to know?"

"A lot of people want to know. But hey, forget it. Nothing to get all riled up about, OK?"

"I've gotta get these inside for the toast," I said, slamming the trunk.

Roger watched me as I pitched my cigarette and arranged the champagne in my arms.

"See you in there," he called.

The review had just gone up when I walked in the door. John held up his hand for silence as he scrolled down through the text his analyst had e-mailed him. The antenna on his BlackBerry quivered, as if it couldn't take it anymore.

"Excellent," he said, smiling and nodding. "Highest rating."

Marissa, the chef, opened her mouth and clapped her hands to her face as everyone ripped up from the long black walnut benches to applaud.

"Tell me about the people," my mother said. She was driving us home, her hands at ten and two, her eyes fixed on the dotted line.

"Speed up," I said. "It looks worse when you go this slow."

"Don't tell me how to drive when you've been drinking. You shouldn't know a damn thing about that. I asked you a question."

"There's this girl I met at a party in New York before we went over there. You'd like her. She grew up down the shore."

"You met one girl from South Jersey in four months over there?"

"Her and a bunch of her friends," I said, laughing, realizing how that sounded. "She's the only one from Jersey. She sort of took Clare and me under her wing."

"Well, that's nice. I just hope you're meeting everyone you can while you're there. You don't know how lucky you are."

"I do know."

"Everyone keeps asking if you've seen the prince yet."

"I know him. I mean, I've met him a few times."

My mother looked over at me.

"What?" I said.

"Are you serious?"

"No, I'm lying."

"Oh."

"No, Jesus, I'm not lying. That's the truth."

"You've met the prince of England?"

"That girl I was telling you about is friends with him."

"What's he like?"

"Seems like a nice guy. He likes to party."

She looked at me again, and shook her head in disbelief.

"What?"

"Nothing."

"Hey, why would Roger care about Clare's dad?" I asked.

"What do you mean?"

"He asked if I knew where he was."

I glanced at her when she didn't answer and almost did a double take. The concern on her face made her look five years older.

"What's wrong?" I asked her.

"He asked me the same thing," she said.

"Is something going on?"

After a mile of silence, I turned on the radio, and found some classic rock to get us home.

During the day there were endless glasses to buff, garnishes to chop, deliveries to inspect, issues with the staff. Nights kicked off with the panicky pitch of a hostess's last-minute requests, followed by the din of a doorbell as the arrivals came in waves. The crush was always blinding—two hours of perpetual motion split between the heat and clatter of the kitchen and rooms thick with the smell of perfume. We caught a badly needed break in the middle of a holiday family reunion when our Friday client called to inform us of a death in the family—some ancient great aunt whom they hadn't seen in years but had to bury. This was on Wednesday. They had already paid in full.

"Should we have a dinner party?" my mother asked. "There's so much food."

"I'm going down to visit Casey if we've got tomorrow off."

"Well, bring him back with you. I've got twenty pounds of tenderloin."

Afterward, I sat in my car in the street outside the client's house, watching as the family gathered around a kitchen island to polish off a wedge of cake and some half-empty wine bottles from the bar. The mother stood behind her youngest daughter, braiding her hair between sips of Vouvray. Casey picked up right before his voice mail kicked in.

"Are you home?" I asked.

"Yeah, I'm here. Where else would I be?"

"Is it cool if I come down? We just got tomorrow off."

"Sure. Melissa went to Amy's place to help her with the baby, so I'm flying solo for a few days. Come on down."

Long Beach Island was deserted, and I rolled through a dozen flashing yellow lights before I saw another car. Casey lived above a hardware store in a small strip mall set back from the boulevard. In summer, when the streets were choked with tourists, you didn't notice the apartments that sat above the shops and bars and ice cream parlors, but now those second-story windows were the only ones with lights shining behind them. I heard a weather report on TV as I climbed the wooden stairs bolted to the building. Casey let me in, a cold draft blowing ash off the cigarette between his lips.

The decor of the two-bedroom apartment was the result of an ongoing tug-of-war between Casey and Melissa, who was ready for a shiny Philly condo with a doorman and a fitness center in the basement—a nice upper-middle-class existence on the mainland, which they could easily afford. She had picked out the black Italian leather sofa and the Lucite coffee table that was buried under one of Casey's driftwood sculptures, two old ukuleles, and a stack of *Surfer* magazines. Casey had paddled out that day, and was repairing a fresh ding in a board shaped like a blade. He surfed straight through the winter, when you can't tell a sand dune from a snowdrift, when the spray freezes in midair and rains down like hail. He offered me a beer, his face shining from a protective coat of Vaseline.

"Back from foreign lands," he said, as he fell onto the couch. "How was it?"

The room smelled faintly of epoxy as I sat on the love seat and tried to describe my life in Scotland. I wanted him to think that I was having an enriching and edifying experience overseas, but I didn't have a lot of stories to that end. I explained Raisin Sunday, and described the after party with Prince William, which didn't seem to interest Casey. I told him about Edinburgh, and how we had passed Clare off as royalty, which made him laugh, because I told him almost nothing else about that night. Before I knew it, I was describing my second encounter with Michael Savage and omitting nothing. I told Casey how badly the whole thing had shaken me, though I don't think I realized just how badly until I finished talking.

"Did you apply to Rutgers?" Casey asked when I was finished. "I can't remember."

"No," I said.

"Why not? They would have taken you with a little possession on your record. Smart motherfucker like you? In state? Good grades? No way they would have turned you down."

The derailment of my college plans was too closely tied to my afternoon at the Lawrence Township precinct for me to talk about it now. I pressed my thumb into the beveled edge of the coffee table.

"I guess I don't really get what you're doing over there," Casey said. "It seems like you were after something, some different kind of life, and instead you got this." He motioned vaguely at the space between us, as if what I had told him was still lingering there, like a smell.

"It's a good school," I said. "It's a good opportunity."

"You sound like a brochure."

"What do you want me to say? I had to go somewhere."

"I'm not talking about the school. I'm sure it's good to see another place like that. Anyway, what do I know? Don't listen to me. That shit about Clare's dad is crazy. I'd be laying a lot lower if I was him."

I told him about the warning from Marcy's cousin that my mother had delivered.

"Yeah, that sounds about right. That dude Peter Szollosi down in Wildwood deals with Russians. Those people terrify me. Peter always says they hate loose ends, and they don't think twice about anything."

Statements like that usually served as reminders of the

incomprehensible distance between our lives, but suddenly he was pulling examples from his world and applying them to mine. I didn't know whether to be frightened or excited. We watched the eleven o'clock news together, and afterward a half circle of men argued over the invasion of Iraq. "So where would you draw the line?" one of them kept asking. "Where's that line in the sand? Show me the line and we can go from there."

Casey turned off the TV and helped me make the spare bed in the second bedroom.

"There's a swell coming tomorrow, if you're up for it," he said. "Get some sleep, amigo. You look like hell."

In a dream, I walked through the empty lobby of an office building and took the elevator to the twenty-second floor. It was dark outside, but the floor was well lit and the low hum from the sleeping computers made the emptiness less ominous. I was wandering through a maze of cubicles when something floated by the window, rising slightly, spinning end over end. I tried to make out what it was and saw that the building was completely underwater. And then I heard a series of distant, muffled cracks, as if the windows on the floors below me were breaking one pane at a time. I put my hands against the glass, ready for the atmosphere to swallow me. My eyes opened then, and I realized that the sounds from my dream were real, that someone was pounding on the front door with a closed fist. The light above my head snapped on. Casey, wild-eyed and shirtless, filled the doorway.

"Get up," he said.

He was holding a short pump-action shotgun, which he pressed into my hands as I sat up and swung my legs off the bed.

"What's happening?"

"Take this and stay in here." More pounding. "You don't know what this is?"

I shook my head as hard as I could, even though I understood exactly what this was. The cops were here for Casey. They had been watching him in the months since my arrest, and now they had their warrant.

"Stay put," Casey said.

I saw his revolver in the waistband of his jeans as he turned his back to me. Casey drew the gun, cocked the hammer, and crossed the living room. Someone mashed down the mechanical bell above the peephole. I racked the slide on the shotgun, which Casey had already done, and the action belched a live red shell from the chamber. It hit the carpet, bounced once, and was still. More pounding. I wanted to tell Casey that this was all my fault, but my lungs felt like they were filled with the water that had been about to drown me in my dream. I put my finger on the trigger and moved into the doorway. It seemed better to get shot than to have to live with what I was about to see, my momentary bravery stemming from the kind of cowardice that makes death seem like the better option.

"Who is it?" Casey called.

"Casey, open up. It's Rob."

Casey uncocked the gun and unlocked the deadbolt on the door. I realized that I still needed to breathe.

"You scared the shit out of me," Casey said, as Rob strode into the room, looking around as if he had come to buy the place. "What are you breaking down my door for? It's four in the goddamn morning."

I laid the shotgun gingerly in the depression my body had left in the sheets. I could have cried at the relief. I didn't know why Rob was here; I didn't care.

"Give it to me," Rob said, for the second time, sticking out his hand.

Casey stared at him.

"Your iron. Give it to me now."

Casey drew the gun again and handed it over by the barrel. Rob emptied the cylinder into his hand and jammed the gun and the six rounds into the two front pockets of his parka. He was wearing sweatpants and black alligator loafers. It looked like he had thrown on whatever had been closest to his bed.

"What the fuck is he doing here?" Rob asked Casey as I walked into the room.

"He's visiting," Casey said. "What do you think he's doing here? Why are you here?"

"Pack," Rob said.

"What?"

"Pack a bag. You leave tonight."

"What are you talking about?"

"You want him to hear this?" Rob asked, jamming his thumb at me.

"I can leave," I said.

"Fuck that, nobody leaves. Rob, what the fuck?"

"You got about three hours before the cops show up here with a warrant. I just heard from a guy down at the precinct who was supposed to be sitting on your house all night before a raid at 6:00 a.m. They've been on you for months. The only reason you're not locked up already is you're not as stupid as you look. They don't want you around here anymore, and I can't have you bringing heat on me like this. You're gone right after they come in here and toss your place. You understand?"

"Why now?" Casey asked, after a silence. "Who talked?"

"Start packing."

"Rob, why is this happening? I pay those motherfuckers every month, just like you showed me. Whose idea was this? Who set me up?"

"Don't ask me that again."

"Then fucking tell me."

Rob took a blur of a step to close the distance between them, caught Casey by the wrist, and wrenched his arm behind his back. Casey doubled over and tried to throw him, but Rob had already snaked his right arm around Casey's neck from behind, forming a triangle-shaped vice to stop the blood flow. He straightened my friend's spine with a vicious pull that looked like it was meant to take his head off at the neck. They were the same height, and Rob was up on his toes as he gripped his left bicep with his right hand, which Casey was trying in vain to pull away from his throat. I had seen bouncers use this choke when they lost control of a room. Rob began to squeeze. Casey had five seconds of consciousness, maybe less.

"Some spic down in Wildwood set you up," Rob hissed through his teeth. "Your mother set you up. I set you up. It doesn't make a fucking bit of difference who it was. You're gonna do exactly like I tell you. I come over here in the middle of the goddamn night, and this is what I get from you? You should be down on your fucking knees."

The room and everything in it seemed to have hit that shimmering state just before combustion. Casey was slipping away.

"Rob," I said. "Jesus Christ."

Rob held on long enough to let me know he was wasn't taking orders. Casey dropped to one hand and both knees, gasping, holding his throat.

"I'm sorry," Rob said. "I lost my temper. Listen, we don't have a ton of time here, so I gotta ask some questions. Casey, sit. Sit down on the couch. Tom, get him some water. Casey, are you listening?"

Casey nodded.

"You got another piece here? Besides that duck gun?"

Casey shook his head.

"I know that's a lie."

"Then what'd you ask me for?"

"Don't fuck with me, kid. Not now. Where is it?"

"In the safe."

"Which is where?"

"Spare room. Under the bed, under the rug. The floor comes up along the wall."

"How much weight are we talking?"

"Half a key."

"What else is here that I should know about?"

"Nothing."

"Nothing? Think hard. What about the sandwich shop?"

"It's clean."

"I know you don't have anything at my restaurant. Because if you and that piece of shit Miguel are keeping one baggie there, I'll turn you in myself."

Casey looked up at him, and there was pain all over his face.

"OK," Rob said. "How much cash is here?"

"Are you kidding me?"

"You either give it to me or you give it to them. Up to you. What's here?"

"There's $20,000 in the coffee cans in the freezer."

"The safe?"

"There's $290,000 in the safe."

I stopped in the doorway with a full glass in my hand and

stared—$290,000, twenty feet away, underneath a bed I had been sleeping on.

"The rest is in the Caymans?"

Casey nodded.

I thought: The rest?

"Listen," Rob said. "Maurice is downstairs. We're gonna look the place over, get it spic and span. I need you to pop the safe, and you need to be here, in bed, in your jammies, when they show up. I promised there was no way it would look like you saw this coming down the pike."

"What happens to my money?"

"You mean how can you ever repay me for saving your life? That's nice of you to ask, so here's what you're gonna do for me: find another way to make a living. That money goes into my safe, in my home, and this"—Rob took a business card from his wallet, not his own, some chiropractor down in Margate, and wrote on it in pencil—"is the code to the safe in my home, where that money will be. If you don't fuck up again, this whole thing looks like their mistake. But listen to me, Casey, because I swear to Christ I mean this: If you ever sell anything to anybody after tonight, and I hear about it—and I will hear about it—I'll burn that money. Every dime. That's my insurance policy, because I gave my word on this. Do you understand me? You don't hand someone a roach, you don't give an aspirin to your friend here. Look at me and tell me that you understand."

"I understand."

"Because I run a business in this community, and I can never, never be associated with this."

"I know."

"Stick that money in the islands, or I can make it look like back pay at the restaurant, consulting fees, whatever. You'll pay some taxes, but that might be a good thing for you to start doing at this point. But you'll never make another cent the way you made that."

Casey nodded.

"I want you gone for a while after this gets sorted out. Take a trip, take a vacation someplace. Cool your heels."

Casey turned to me.

"Can I stay with you at school?"

"Where's school?" Rob asked.

"Scotland," I said. "St. Andrews University."

"Scotland. Perfect. Play golf, fuck sheep, do whatever they do over there. Let this blow over."

"Wait," I said, "how long are you thinking? I go to school there and they gave me shit about entering the country. You can't just up and move to the UK."

"What," Casey said, "you don't want me hanging around you over there?"

They were both looking at me now. Casey was half right—I didn't want him to see how I was living and what I was doing to myself.

"That has nothing to do with it," I said. "Fuck, why would you say that?"

"So what's the problem?" Rob asked.

"Nothing. I'll figure it out."

"Good," Rob said, looking at his watch, a gold Rolex Daytona. "Get out of here for an hour, get something to eat. You don't need to watch us digging through your shit. Tomorrow we can talk about the long term."

Casey stood up and sat back down.

"Talk to me," Rob said. "This is not the worst thing that can happen, Casey. Not by a long shot. Are you listening? This could have been a situation where my hands were tied. This could have been a situation where there was nothing I could do to help you. You know how many times I got fucked up by these guys? Be thankful that it's only this."

"Be thankful? What am I supposed to do?"

"You let me worry about that. But call Melissa. That call needs to be from you."

Casey pinched the bridge of his nose, and closed his eyes.

"I'll call her," he said. "I'll call her when we leave."

"Leave now. Tom, take your friend to breakfast. Get him fed."

Rob grabbed Casey by the shoulders as he stood up from the couch.

"You're a man, Casey," Rob said. "Take this like a man. I'm proud of you. You've got friends. Don't forget that. Be back here in an hour."

I spotted Rob's Mercedes as we took the stairs down to the frozen street. He had parked on a side street behind a pair of trash cans, invisible to the cruisers patrolling the boulevard. Maurice, a manager at the Sailfish, was sitting shotgun with the engine running and the headlights off. A cell phone lit up on the dashboard, and Maurice climbed out and started toward the house with the phone still ringing in his hand. Casey, wearing nothing but a thin gray sweatshirt, went left to avoid him. I hugged myself against the wind.

The only place open at that hour was The Chegg—shorthand for the Chicken and the Egg—an all-night turn-and-burn that specializes in atomic hot wings. It was four blocks from Casey's and lit up like a barn fire while everything around it was dark, locked up, closed for the season. At the hostess stand, a server with "Stacy" tattooed on his skinny neck was peering over the shoulder of a spray-tanned woman with bangs that looked deep-fried. They were laughing at something on her phone, both of them high as kites. The only other people inside were a man wearing headphones at a back table and another server running a vacuum around him.

"You want a table, hon?" the hostess asked as Casey walked past her. "Is he OK?" she mouthed to me.

I nodded, and she scanned the street outside, looking for whatever had shaken him, making sure it wasn't coming in behind us. I followed Casey to a booth made of unfinished wood, where he sat facing the door. The hostess reappeared with menus and ice water. Casey drained his glass without coming up for air.

"You should eat something," I said.

"I'm not gonna eat."

"Fine," I said. "I'll order something."

I flipped through the menu, absorbing nothing, imagining the next few hours of Casey's life. He would have to get undressed, kill the lights and lie in bed, waiting to hear boots on the stairs. Across the table, he looked old, drawn, exhausted. All the precautions he had taken, and for what?

"Juice?" I said. "Coffee?"

"Go," he said.

"Go where?"

"Wherever. Just don't be here in thirty seconds. I have to call Melissa."

"Are you sure?"

"Yes. Leave."

"You can come stay in Princeton if you don't want to be down here by yourself."

Casey knocked back a mouthful of ice and started chewing through the weak flat cubes. I stood up and wondered what would it take to launch into a confession right there in the dining room, in front of the hostess and the servers and the man in headphones. Casey looked up at me and I saw that he was barely in control, that it would kill him to have me there if he broke. I was terrified that something would go wrong when the cops showed up, that he would fight, that this would be last time I laid eyes on my only friend. The hostess thanked me for coming in as I walked out the door.

I had just started my car when I felt something stick in my throat. I choked twice before I realized I was crying. I let it come then, dropped my chin to my chest with both hands on the wheel, gulping down the cold stale air. Up close, the pattern pressed into the steering wheel looked like the surface of another planet, full of dry rivulets and valleys and flat planes where my hands had worn the rubber smooth. I thought back to something I had seen in the AA literature my mother's sous chef left lying around when he was in recovery—a bolded line that encouraged the reader to admit that their life had become unmanageable. I had wondered what that might feel like. When my breathing had returned to normal, I sang a few verses of Neil Young's "Out on the Weekend" to get the kinks out of my voice. Once I was certain that I wouldn't choke up again, I called my mother.

"What's wrong?" she said, hushing her voice. "What's the matter? Where are you?"

"I'm in Beach Haven. Casey's in trouble."

My mother took a long breath.

"Let me guess," she said. "Is he in jail?"

"No," I said. "Not yet. I'm coming home. I just wanted to let you know."

"Tom? I need to talk to you."

"I'm driving. Can we talk tomorrow?"

"No, you'll blow me off tomorrow, and I'm awake now."

I heard her stand up and cross her bedroom. I wondered if someone was there with her.

"I keep thinking about this thing you said to me one night when I was running out the door, when you were a baby. I had Anna from the diner coming over to watch you. You were three, three and a half, running around in these overalls that you made me put you in every day. I told you that Anna was going to take care of you while mommy went out for a little while, and you looked up at me with this frown on your chubby little face, and you said: 'I take care of me.' And I know how important that is to you, sweetheart, but you're not doing a very good job right now. And I'm not talking about the thing at Lawrenceville. It's not hard for me to imagine why you were doing that. I'm disappointed, but I'm more upset with myself than I am with you. It's what you saw growing up, which is my fault. I'm not wringing my hands and asking why, you know? Does that make sense?"

I heard her close and lock the bathroom door, and I was sure now that someone else was there. A guest from the party, maybe, someone I had laid eyes on at the house, someone I had served. I started my car.

"What's worrying me now, because I'm not understanding it, I guess, is how you're picking the people in your life. It's like you can't relate to anyone unless they're running from something. What are you looking for, sweetheart? It's not something I need you to tell me right now. I just want you to think about it. Is something upsetting you?"

"I don't think so," I said.

"Is there anything you want to ask me? Anything about your dad?"

"Not really," I said, realizing, as I said it, that it wasn't true.

"OK. Are you on 539?"

"Almost."

"Watch out for deer," she said. "And cops."

She was up and dressed when I walked into the kitchen at 5:30 a.m., grinding fresh black pepper over a skillet of scrambled eggs with parsley and fresh pecorino. If someone had been there with her, he was gone now. She wiped her hands clean as I came through the door, opened her arms, and told me to come here. We ate together while the sun rose in another time zone and turned our sky blue with a slow leak of light.

I woke up to the buzz of my UK phone vibrating in the pile of loose change on my bedside table. I had been back in St. Andrews for five days, and it had been exactly that long since I'd spoken to anyone besides the deliverymen from Balaka who brought me an aluminum tub of Chicken Tikka Masala once a day. I had shut myself in to do four months of reading in the week before exams. It was dark outside when I woke up on the floor, but by then it was only light for a few hours each day. My bed was covered in textbooks and notebooks, reams of paper soaked in liters of ink, and I was devouring everything from post-Keynesian economics to the poetry of Robert Burns while Clare's Adderall suppressed my appetite. I checked my watch as I grabbed blindly for my phone. 4:25 p.m.

"Hello?"

It was Casey. He had sent me an e-mail to confirm that he was coming over, but this was the first time I had heard his voice since we'd parted ways on LBI.

"Hey, Mike called me this morning and asked if he could come over with me. But if you can't take two guests, or if you can't take Mike, just say so. No hard feelings."

"Of course Mike can come," I said. Mike was a scratch golfer; I had been expecting this call. "Ask him if he wants to play the Old Course."

"I'm sure he does. He was on this crazy run in Atlantic City, playing like thirty-six hours at a stretch, eating speed all day, just killing it at the tables. He wants to cool off and get healthy again. Needs a vacation worse than anyone I've seen. What's the weather like?"

"All over the place. The rain comes out of nowhere, but it doesn't snow or anything. It gets dark right after lunch right now. It's that far north."

"You're kidding me."

"No, it's pitch black outside," I said, walking to the window. "We're only five hours ahead."

"You don't get depressed?"

"You do."

"You don't sound so hot."

"I just woke up. I've got exams until you get here and then we've got a week off."

"Well, keep your head out of the oven until then. I'm stoked to come over. It's a big trip for me. Thanks for doing this."

"Get here safe," I said.

There was a hum in my ears when I hung up, but the Adderall had a way of making words on a page feel like company, which made this isolation almost bearable. I pressed one hot cheek against the windowpane. A young couple was standing under a streetlight in the parking lot, the girl walking slow circles around the boy. He had a thin ponytail and wore combat boots that looked like buckets at the bottom of his skinny legs. She was heavy, pretty. They looked like they spent a lot of time on multiplayer video games and science fiction. As they started back toward the hall together, and I realized they must live in the building, that we were practically neighbors, possibly classmates, and yet I had never laid eyes on them before. There were so many people here I would never know.

When my exams were finished, when I had written my last frantic essay in the pages of a flimsy sky-blue notebook, I took the long way back to Andrew Melville, walking by the water, smoking and massaging the back of my neck where it felt like my vertebrae had been glued together. I checked my watch, hoping there would be time to strip my filthy sheets and clean my room, but there was no time for that now. Mike and Casey had landed in Edinburgh two hours earlier, and taken the train to Leuchars, where I had told them I would meet them with a cab.

It was misty enough that the taxi driver had to use his wipers to get us to the station. The train had just pulled out when we arrived, and Mike and Casey were making their way across the elevated walkway that crossed the tracks from the northbound side. They had never left America before. I was starting to think that people should just stay where they were from.

"What the fuck is this weather?" Mike asked as he bounded down the stairs.

"Par for the course," I said. "Hey, Case."

"Hey, bro," he said. "Thanks for having us."

"Can you believe that fucking hunk of metal just flew across an ocean?" Mike asked.

"He asked everyone sitting around us that," Casey said, laughing. "You should have seen the looks on their faces."

"Do you know what those things weigh?" Mike asked. "How do they not just fall out of the sky?"

"I've wondered that myself," the cab driver said.

"Right?" Mike said. "Fucking miracle if you ask me."

Mike sat up front and peppered the driver with questions about the food, the weather, the venereal cleanliness of the local females, turning to me to repeat anything he thought to be of note, as if I didn't live here, or didn't speak the language.

"Bro, what's the name of the hotel?" Mike asked Casey.

"The St. Andrews Bay," Casey said.

"You heard of that spot?" Mike asked the driver. "Nice place? Dive?"

"Best in town," the driver said.

I turned to Casey.

"Why did you get a hotel?"

"The three of us in your dorm room? I'm on vacation, buddy. Don't worry about me."

I could see the town in the distance as we turned into the circular drive of the St. Andrews Bay Hotel, a solitary, U-shaped fortress that stood guard over a private golf course. I had never heard of this place. A helicopter dropped out of the sky and alighted somewhere behind the building, delivering guests.

Under the soaring ceiling of the lobby, Casey put down Mike's Am Ex for incidentals, and explained that he'd be paying cash. The hotel was newer and more luxurious than the one on the Old Course, with thicker carpeting and modern furniture upholstered in plaid. I lay on a queen-sized bed in their two-bedroom suite, watching a National Geographic special on a Russian supermax prison where the convicts were forced to walk bent over at the waist anytime they left their cells. Mike walked out of the bathroom, soaking wet and stark naked.

"Son of a bitch," he said to Casey, who was counting British pounds from a teller's envelope and laying them in stacks on the bedside table. "I left my entire fucking Dopp kit in New Jersey. Do you have any Old Spice?"

"Just stay out of my vitamins," Casey said, pointing to his open duffel without looking up.

An hour later, we were polishing off a round of beers and sandwiches at the North Point Café, two tables from where I had eaten lunch with Clare's parents. Mike sat facing the big front window, and glanced up from his plate to examine every passerby. He turned to me suddenly, arugula hanging from the corner of his mouth.

"You never said they had waves here."

"There's nothing rideable," I said. "It's a bay."

"So guys just walk around like that for kicks?"

I turned in time to see a pedestrian on Market Street wearing a fleece vest over a full wetsuit and carrying a battered surfboard under his arm. We stared at each other and stood up as one man. Casey glanced down at the bill and tossed cash on the table as Mike and I scrambled for the door. The surfer was waiting for a traffic light as we spilled into the street.

"You've never seen this?" Casey asked as we jogged east.

I shook my head. Mike slowed as we caught our mark, and fell into step beside him.

"Hey, man," he said. "We saw you walk by the restaurant back there. Are there waves here?"

"Not always," the man said in a Welsh accent. "It's breaking today, though."

"Where?" I asked.

"East Sands. Just up the way. Are you on holiday?"

"He goes to school here," Mike said. "At least he says he does. We're his boys from back home."

We were passing the crumbling ruins of St. Andrews Cathedral and the graveyard that had been swallowing the dead since the 1100s—places I had seen in pictures but never bothered to seek out. I heard the surf as we started up a short, steep hill at the east end of town, and I was telling myself that this was impossible even as we crested the hill and found ourselves looking down at a crescent-shaped beach. I counted three peaks in fifteen seconds, three sandbars that were causing the waist-high swell to break.

"How the fuck did you miss this one?" Mike asked.

I could think of several reasons, none of them good. We followed our guide to a cluster of surfers, one of whom had just come in.

"How was it?" Mike asked him.

"Really nice, mate. Best it's been in months. The tide's just pushing in."

Mike introduced us all by name.

"We've met before," the surfer said to me, unstrapping his ankle leash. He had bright blue eyes, a deep cleft in his chin, and a nose that was jagged on the bridge from a bad break, the kind of face that stays with you.

"You're mates with Damien and Jules," he said in response to my blank look, as if this were the logical explanation for my forgetting. It was such an obvious dismissal that Casey laughed to break the tension. The surfer turned to Mike.

"I'm Wells," he said.

The two of them began discussing tides and takeoff spots.

"How did you not hear about this?" Casey asked as we watched someone pull into a closeout and disappear in the whitewater. Mike was taking off his clothes.

"Bro, really?" Casey asked.

"My boy Wells here is loaning me his suit," Mike said. "I'm getting out there."

"For fuck's sake," Casey said. "Don't take the man's suit."

"It's no trouble," Wells said. "I'm ready for dry clothes. I'd like to watch my mates a bit."

"One ride, bro," Mike said. "One good ride. 'Yeah, I surfed in Scotland.' Who's gonna believe that back home? Where's a fucking camera when you need one."

Mike dropped his jeans, and stood there, in the January air, wearing only his white boxer briefs and the ink under his skin. Wells tossed him the suit, and once Mike had wrestled into it, he strapped on the leash—something that he never did in Jersey—and jogged into the shore break with the board under his arm. Casey and I sat down in the sand.

"What happened with the cops?" I asked, unable to contain myself any longer.

"I was outta there by noon. Fucking Rob. I don't know how he does it. This guy I used to cut lawns with was in for a DUI. We made a night of it."

"How's Melissa?"

"She's taking the whole thing like a fucking champ. It was really hard for her, the stuff I was doing. She never cared about the money. She said that before, I just wasn't hearing her. I was waiting til I got here to tell you this, but Rob set me up with something."

"At the restaurants?"

"No," Casey said. "Not this time. It's a job in Mexico. We're moving in a month."

"Are you joking?"

"This guy Rob knows is investing in some new hotel in Playa del Carmen, like an hour south of Cancún. They got this roof deck with a club they want me to manage. They're giving me a little piece of equity to make sure I stick around."

"Mexico?"

"What, you're the only person who can set up in another country for a while? Melissa's gonna do some PR and events for the hotel, that kind of thing."

The blithe conversion of a career in cocaine to a management gig in an emerging market, a partnership, a piece of equity. It felt like my whole life up to that point had been a series of miscalculations. Casey smacked my shoulder with the back of his hand, and pointed toward the water.

"Here he goes," he said.

Mike was scratching for a wave that had slipped by everyone sitting on the biggest peak. He caught it, popped up, and walked down the length of the board. With the toes of his left foot wrapped around the nose, he did a quick half pirouette and brought his feet together, riding backward with his ankles hanging off the board in midair and his arms extended. People on the beach were pointing at him, telling friends to watch. The wave closed out and Mike dove behind the rumbling whitewater, which swallowed him and then the board. His hand surfaced before his head, and he was holding up a finger as he spit out salt water to speak.

"One more!" he yelled to us.

We were back at the hotel when Casey finally asked how Clare was holding up. Mike was in the shower again, "defrosting," as he put it, with the bathroom door open so that he could still hear us and be heard. I said I hadn't seen Clare in a while.

"Really?" Casey said. "Why not?"

"Get him over here!" Mike called.

I shot Clare a text with the invitation and the room number, hoping that he wouldn't answer. Casey called Melissa while I stretched out on the bed again and wondered how everyone would feel about staying here tonight, ordering room service and pay-per-view. I had told Casey about Kelsey before I knew she had a boyfriend. There would be that to explain, and putting Jules and Damien and Mike in one room seemed like a terrible idea. The front desk called to say we had a visitor.

"Hey, buddy," Casey said as he opened the door. "Good to see you."

Mike stepped out of the bathroom with a towel around his waist this time.

"Dude, tell me you knew that there's a break here. Is Tom just asleep at the wheel?"

Clare looked at me.

"Jesus Christ, put the straw down once in a while. People surf here. You didn't know that either?"

"Did you guys go surfing?" Clare asked.

"I did," Mike said. "I dropped in on Prince what's his face."

"You're kidding me," I said.

I had seen someone in the lineup who looked vaguely like William, but William didn't strike me as a surfer, and lookalikes were obviously not out of the question.

"Oh shit. Did I forget to tell you that?" Mike said. "He's not bad, actually. He was pretty cool about me stealing his wave."

"His bodyguards should be here any minute to cavity search you before they throw you out of the country."

"Bro, sign me up," Mike said. "I've paid good money to have someone put a finger in my ass, and they didn't even have a sexy accent."

"Hey," Clare said, "Damien wanted me to tell you that he's having a dinner party at that flat he bought."

"Tonight? He knows I've got friends here, right?"

"He knows," Clare said. "He wants to meet them."

The dishes had just been cleared from a farmhouse table long enough to be a runway. It was unclear how the previous owners had gotten it up to the airy third-story flat on Queen's Gardens, and the movers couldn't get it out, so the table had come with the place. The table and chairs were the only furniture so far; the blank white walls and the echo from the pressed tin ceiling seemed to amplify the emptiness. A dinner of mostly takeout had devolved into a drunken game of "Never have I ever . . ." and a girl with an Essex accent—which I learned to distinguish after hearing that Essex was the New Jersey of England—was asking if anyone had ever let themselves be tied up by a stranger. One last dinner plate was making its way around the table, covered in cocaine. I had promised myself that I would abstain while Casey was around, but that resolution had dissolved in champagne.

Casey seemed to be enjoying himself, and Mary had taken a shine to Mike as soon as we walked in the door. They had disappeared into the powder room together after two drinks, and emerged twenty minutes later in each other's clothes. She wore his striped dress shirt unbuttoned to reveal a black satin bra, while Mike had her sky-blue blazer stretched over his bare torso, the sleeves ending halfway down his forearms, tight as leggings. Jules was ignoring them. Kelsey was still in her studio, working on her collection for the fashion show, which was all anyone could talk about by then.

"I can't drink any more champagne," Mary yelled, one hand pressed against Mike's stomach as if she was feeling for the kick of a baby. I had never seen her this loose or involved. "Is there any still white wine?"

"Did you hear what Christopher Hitchens told Piers Morgan about champagne over lunch?" one of the English twins asked. "He reckons the four most overrated things in life are champagne, lobster, anal sex, and picnics."

"There's at least one thing on that list that you can't live without," Mike said to Mary.

Mary slapped his bare chest in mock horror.

"She loves picnics, bro," Mike said to Damien. "It's like the third thing she told me."

Mary dipped her fingers in Mike's vodka and flicked them in his face.

"Do you have a tee time yet?" Damien asked him. They had been discussing golf.

"Nah, man. Tom said he could set that up."

"Your friend Tom picked up golf pretty quickly."

"He's a good learner," Mike said. "That's why we're so proud of him back home."

"What else do you have planned?"

"Not a damn thing. I'd paddle out again if that swell sticks around. You know they have waves here, right?"

"I did know that. Do you hunt? That's worth looking into."

"What's in season?"

"Pheasant, grouse, deer. Jules, am I missing anything? Maybe we should go up to your place in the Highlands."

"Don't see why not," Jules said. "There's a driven shoot tomorrow on our neighbor's land."

Jules stood up to answer the door before I could ask what a driven shoot was. He came back with Kelsey, who was complaining about the fashion show's executive producer until she saw a stranger sitting next to Mary, wearing Mary's clothes.

"Kelsey, these are my friends from home," I said. "Kelsey's from New Jersey too."

"All right," Mike said as she kissed him on both cheeks. "Good to meet you. Where you from?"

"Ocean City," Kelsey said, stepping back and regarding Mike with her hands on her hips. "Can I ask you something? Do you know how to walk?"

Mike shot me a look, asking me to translate. I had no idea what Kelsey meant.

"Jesus," she said, reading our confusion. "I'm sorry, I've been in my head all day. I meant have you modeled before. Have you walked a runway?"

"Nah, but I always thought I should be a model," Mike said. "I mean, I'm fucking gorgeous, right?"

"Right," Kelsey said. "That's why I asked."

Mike looked like an actor who had forgotten his line. Sincere compliments were apparently a kind of social kryptonite for him. The plate of coke landed in front of Casey then. I could barely hide my shock when he rerolled the bill and took a line and then another.

"You did that flyer for Kmart that one time," Casey said to Mike, before touching his ring finger to the plate and rubbing it across his gums. "Those gay yellow shorts? Remember that?"

"Yeah, that's right." Mike said, regaining his footing, turning back to Kelsey. "So yeah, I am a model. What do you want me to do?"

"Walk to me," she said.

My heart jumped as she backed up and beckoned to him. Instead of following her lead, Mike boosted up onto one end of the table, steadied himself, and strutted straight down its length, his eyes burning a hole into a spot on the far wall. He walked right to the edge, paused, thrust one hip forward like a weapon, spun on his heel, and walked back, kicking over an empty wineglass that Damien caught before it hit the floor. Kelsey looked to Jules as Mike jumped down to applause. Jules was nodding his head, his mouth turned down in a deep frown of approval.

"Right?" Kelsey said. "You need a little coaching, but my God. How long are you in town?"

Mike looked at Casey.

"Unclear," Casey said.

"Well, if you stick around until next week, I want you in my show."

"I'm game to stick around," Mike said. "I dig this place."

She asked him for his suit size, which he didn't know, but Kelsey told him not to worry about that. She fell into the empty chair next to Jules, and pulled her hair back.

"Let's go have a smoke outside," Casey said to me.

You could just hear the ocean from the balcony off the living room.

"This is them, right?" Casey said. "The guys Wells said you knew?"

"Yeah, this is them. Hey, I thought you said you didn't fuck with coke?"

"I did, didn't I? I guess that's just something that you say."

We listened to the surf in silence until Jules stuck his head through the door.

"Do you two need to pack?" he asked.

"Pack for what?"

"We're heading up to my family's shooting estate. Damien's just gone to get his car."

"Who's we?"

"Damien, myself, Clare, you, your mates, if you're interested. And Mary. Mary likes to watch men kill things. And this way we won't be distracting Kelsey."

It was the first time I had heard him say her name aloud.

"We'll be ready in a few," I said to Jules, who nodded and ducked back inside.

"You wanna see a castle?" I asked Casey.

"When in Rome," he said.

I woke up to hazy daylight and lay in bed, staring at a ceiling painted like the sky. Someone had left a pitcher of hard well water on my bedside table, and I swallowed three glasses before I peeled back the linen sheets and stepped onto the cool stone floor. I walked to the window and stared out at the manicured piece of Scottish countryside through leaded glass. An actual castle. It was like coming to in a Jane Austin adaptation. I wondered how many times Kelsey had come up here with Jules, how many mornings she had come to in a four-poster bed upstairs. I was glad she wasn't here now.

I followed the sound of voices and silverware on china down a long hall lined with high-backed chairs and oil portraits of stern-faced men in high, frilly collars. The hall opened into a cavernous dining area with a kitchen that looked out on a murky pond. The ruins of a proper English breakfast—sausage, poached eggs, grilled tomato slices—were being cleared from the table to make way for the guns being laid out by a stocky man with grease-stained hands. Casey was applying oil to the action of a 12-gauge shotgun.

"Morning, sunshine," he said.

"Bro, check these threads out," Mike said, turning in place so I could admire his borrowed herringbone trousers and a hunter-green shooting vest with a suede patch sewn into the shoulder. He stuffed his hands into the pockets to strike a pose. Something surprised him, and he pulled a prescription pill bottle from deep inside the vest. He read the label, rattled the contents, and tossed the bottle to Jules, whistling in awe.

"Shall we?" Jules said, pocketing the pills.

We piled into Damien's Land Rover, the guns broken down and packed in leather-wrapped cases stacked like a layer cake in the trunk. Jules drove us off his estate and, after a few miles of country road and a gate that I jumped out to unhitch, onto another. I wondered whose property this was as we headed toward a line of Range Rovers parked just off the dirt track that ran through a hilly piece of countryside. There were at least a dozen people gathered under a cluster of trees, men and women—mostly men, I saw as we drew near—all of them in tweed and houndstooth, Barbour jackets, riding boots. A stocked bar cart sat between two large rectangular tables covered in white tablecloths. One table held tea sandwiches, fresh fruit, and carafes of coffee, while the other was covered in shotguns, all of them broken open and unloaded. Mary recognized two of the women, who kissed her hello and asked after her mother. A pair of supercharged adolescent black labs ran circles around the shooting party, restless, ready for work.

I had been hoping to play the knowledgeable host with Mike and Casey, but I had no idea what was supposed to happen next. Jules rejoined us with a heavy whiskey on the rocks, and explained the workings of a driven shoot. We were after duck, he said. A large flock was fed every morning on the far side of the low hill in front of us. They were fed again at sundown on the pond behind us, imprinting them with a single flight path between their daily meals. This was how they spent their lives: feeding, fattening, flying back and forth. And when you wanted to shoot them, you called your gamekeeper, who assembled a team of "beaters" armed with sticks and arranged them on the far side of the hill, where they were waiting now, invisible to us. Their job was to flush the birds from their morning feeding ground, forcing them to take off for the pond, the only other place they knew. That flight path took them straight over five shooting stations built into the base of the hill, each of them designed to hold a shooter and a loader for the guns. The gamekeeper was talking into a two-way radio, telling the beaters that we would be getting started shortly.

"So ducks are gonna come flying over this hill whenever that dude says so?" Mike asked.

Jules nodded over the rim of his glass.

"That's the craziest shit I've ever heard. Whose idea was this?"

Jules explained that this was usually done with pheasant, grouse, and partridge, but that these American mallards had been imported from Texas by the estate's new owner, who ran the real estate group for a big U.S. private equity shop, and who was talking to the gamekeeper in the watered-down southern accent I had heard on kids at Lawrenceville who came from Memphis, Nashville, and Houston suburbs. He had made a fortune over the last few years, and this property was his eight-figure bid to become an English country gentleman while he was working out of his firm's London office. He came over to introduce himself and thank us all for coming, clearly disappointed that we were Americans, or northerners, or some combination of the two. Jules said he was a damn good shot, and that the royal family's gamekeeper designed this shoot himself. This was how you got to know your neighbors here.

Mike and Casey both shot skeet in the Pine Barrens and hunted when they could, but the smiles they were trading told me they had never seen or heard of anything like this. I hadn't either, and yet it was exactly the kind of thing I wanted to show them. When people down the shore asked about their trip to Scotland, this was the story they would hear. The gamekeeper called for everyone to man their stations; five loaders were already in place with two guns apiece. It was decided that the Jersey boys would sit out the first round to watch how this worked. Clare had disappeared.

When everyone was ready, the gamekeeper called into his radio for the first flight. Nothing happened for what felt like a long time. Then the first pair of birds appeared over the hilltop, two painterly little double arches against the sunless sky. They were closest to the owner, who took the first two shots, dropping one and then the other. I looked back to the hill and saw six, seven, ten ducks coming at us, and soon they were raining down out of the sky. The clean kills were breathtaking: a bird, wings pounding, would turn off in midflight and crash into the wet ground like something filled with sand. A less-clean hit sent the duck into a death spiral or resulted in a bad landing, a tumble, and a broken neck. One mallard kept trying to walk off with his neck bent like the top arch of a pretzel, his head nearly buried in the feathers of his chest, as if he had been trying to look behind himself and had gotten stuck that way. The gamekeeper caught me staring at the bird, and dispatched it with two quick whacks of his stick. He turned his back to me and called into his radio for another flight.

There was a lull, finally, and the first squad left their stations. I shook my head when the gamekeeper asked if I wanted a spot in the next round. This was more death than I had ever seen. The air smelled like wet dirt and gunpowder. A few clumps of iridescent plumage floated down out of the sky.

Mike took the fourth position in the second squad; Jules took the fifth. Another flight of ducks appeared above the hilltop. Mike was shooting well, but there was something wrong with Jules. He was missing wildly, upsetting his balance as he swung the gun. He must have dipped into the pills, and washed one down with Scotch. I had watched him pile coke and Molly on top of ten drinks with no discernible effect, but whatever Mike had found inside that vest had fucked Jules up. A loaded shotgun slipped out of his hands as the loader passed it to him. I watched the loader leap back and then attempt to cover both the error and his reaction to it, scooping up the gun with his back turned to the crowd for cover. You didn't call attention to mistakes in public here; Michael Savage wasn't wrong about that. Mike dropped a bird with his bottom barrel, and then swung for a bird that Jules missed. Another clean kill, another duck crashing into the ground.

"Where the fuck is Clare?" I asked.

"Pretending to be on the phone," Casey said, nodding toward the cars, a shotgun broken open on his forearm. "He took off like he was on fire when the owner came over to talk. You think that guy knows Clare's dad?"

I didn't know what to think about Clare anymore. The second squad was done. Mike and Jules were coming toward us, guns on their shoulders.

"Don't shoot down my line again," Jules said to Mike.

Mike stopped to let him pass and then winked at me, unconcerned.

Damien took the wheel for the ride home. The sun was dropping fast as we drove back through a cold north wind that seemed to be blowing darkness in with it.

"Stop the car," Jules said, suddenly.

Damien looked to him for an explanation.

"Stop," Jules said, and Damien did.

I saw the pecking order that existed between them, the chain of command that was normally invisible to me. And then I saw what Jules was stopping for: a deer, grazing at the edge of the field, just outside the tree line.

"You can't shoot them from the car, homeboy," Mike said. "We're not on safari."

But Jules was already out of the car, walking around to what he called the boot, which he opened. I turned to find him digging through the field bag packed with ammunition, tossing boxes of birdshot aside until he found the slugs buried at the bottom. He put a gun together, stuck his head into the car, and whispered: "They're in season."

The deer raised her head and froze as Jules stepped down off the road. I was praying she would make a run for it, but Jules had frozen too, and soon the deer went back to grazing. Her body shuddered with the first report, but Jules had missed completely. The air around us seemed to freeze with the echo of the second shot, and the doe's hind leg buckled underneath her. She started limping for the line of trees at the edge of the clearing, dragging her back left hoof under a shattered joint. Jules started for the car where he had left the shells and then slipped on the rise that led up to the road.

"Motherfucker," Mike said. He jumped out, grabbed the box of slugs, and then scooped the shotgun off the slope where Jules was struggling to his feet. Mike set off at a jog across the field, gun in one hand, ammo in the other.

We watched Mike disappear into the trees, and waited. Jules sat down on the shoulder of the road and lit a cigarette. There was a report, a pause, another. I tried to judge how far the deer had made it, but the gunshots seemed to come from all around us.

"What's he doing?" I asked Casey.

"You know what he's doing."

"There he is," Damien said, pointing as Mike came out of the woods a hundred yards from the spot where he had disappeared. Mary gasped. The dead doe was draped across his shoulders like he was Errol Flynn in *Robin Hood,* on his way to confront the king. Mike's knees buckled as he struggled to find his footing on the damp grass, the weight of the carcass threatening to topple him as he came on. As he drew closer I saw that the side of his face and the front of his shirt were dark with blood, not shadow. The clean side of his jaw was brilliant with sweat in the glow of the headlights as he ran up the rise and into the road. He stood directly in front of the car, staring down the high beams and breathing so hard through flared nostrils that each inhalation contorted his face into a snarl. He dropped to a squat, and heaved the animal onto the hood. There was a dull thud and a metallic snap as the dead weight depressed the ridge in the metal. The doe slid slowly across the smooth finish like something moving on ice, and stopped as one leg tangled in the top half of the headlight cage. It looked like a different animal, some primitive breed of deer with a smaller cranial structure and exposed teeth. Half its head was missing where the slugs had torn away the flesh and bone.

"Hey, learn how to shoot before you shoot at things," Mike said, staring into the windshield, squinting against the lights, assuming Jules was in the car.

He was wrong about that. I watched Mike stumble backward, raise his hands, and drop his stare. He cocked his head as if he had just misheard something, his eyes trained on the ground in front of him. Jules was standing just outside the glow of the high beams with a shotgun pointed at Mike's chest.

"It's unloaded," Jules said.

"What the fuck, man," Casey said.

"It's unloaded," Jules said again.

"So put it down."

"Why? It's unloaded. Everybody just relax."

"Jules," Mary said. "Put it down, please. Before someone gets hurt."

No heat or panic in her voice. She had seen much worse from him.

"It's unloaded," Jules said. "What's there to be afraid of?"

I would have shattered his skull with the tire iron, but I also saw how hard this was for him. On most days he could have it all: Kelsey, Mary if he felt like it, the pills, the Scotch on top of them, the birds, the deer. This was how he had lived up to now, which made it a matter of life for him, and also a matter of death. You can't deny someone the only existence they've ever known and expect them to take it lying down. Of course, you also can't point guns at people. I could see the headline and the grainy photos in the London tabloids: DRUG-FUELED HIGHLANDS WEEKEND ENDS IN FATAL SHOOTING. A story about absent parents and kids left to their own devices in a house full of unused prescription medication and expensive firearms. This, I thought, is exactly how people end up dead.

I held my breath as Casey stepped into the space between Mike and Jules, the twin barrels inches from his sternum. He said something that I couldn't hear, and lifted the gun very gently, pointing it up at the sky. Jules kept his eyes locked on Mike as Casey eased the gun out of his hands, hurled it like a javelin, and then wrapped Jules in the same choke that Rob had used on him. He let up only after Jules lost consciousness, then dropped him face first onto the road, kicked him hard enough to roll him over, and pressed a foot down on his throat.

"Stop that," Mary said. "It's done, there's no need for that."

She took a step toward Casey, who looked up at her and stopped her in her tracks. Mike stood there with his fists clenched and his eyes closed, breathing deeply through his nose. He turned his back to us and started down the road.

"I'm going to pull up," Damien said. "It's miles to the house. Can someone tell him to get in?"

"I wouldn't do that," Casey said. "He likes walking. I'd let him walk if I were you."

It was a long walk to the St. Andrews Bay hotel from Andrew Melville Hall, with a busy stretch of highway in between. I stood on the shoulder, waiting for traffic to clear. Damien had driven us back to St. Andrews the night before with Jules passed out in the front seat next to him. No one spoke the whole way home. I passed out after midnight, slept for fifteen hours, and woke up to a text from Casey, telling me to come over whenever I was up. The sun was dropping fast when I finally left my room and it was dark out by the time I hit the hotel drive.

I heard female voices behind the door to Mike and Casey's suite. Kelsey answered. Behind her, Mike was pulling on a pair of gym shorts, and I tried to imagine what this meant through a flash of panic, which Kelsey read in my face.

"We were just doing a little fitting," she said, opening the door to reveal Mary sitting Indian style on the floor in front of the TV. "And now I have a shitload of tailoring to do if your friend here is gonna walk tomorrow. We took bets on how long you'd sleep. What time did you get up?"

"Three o'clock."

"Casey wins, right?" she said, as Casey came out of the bathroom.

"Sleeping beauty," Casey said. "You want something to drink?"

"Sure," I said, taking a step toward the whiskey, ice, and soda laid out on the dresser. Kelsey matched my move, blocked my path, and placed her hands on my hips.

"Are these the jeans you had on in Spring Lake?"

I nodded.

"That's funny," she said, smiling.

"Why?" I asked, craning my neck to see the clothes spread out on the bed. Kelsey skipped over, stuffed them all inside the plastic cover, zipped it shut.

"Let me see," I said.

"Not now. You'll see soon enough. I put you boys at a table. Best seats in the house."

Mike had rejoined Mary on the floor, where they resumed a game of Mario Kart. He held a hand in front of Mary's eyes as they rounded the final turn on a racecourse that ran through the treetops of a prehistoric forest. Mary screamed and slapped his forearm as her go kart–driving princess tumbled into the canopy below the track and disappeared.

"Bro, they have Nintendo," Mike said over his shoulder, as the turtle driving his cart took an automated victory lap on screen. "This place is Cristal sippin', right?"

Mike was setting up another game, scrolling through the avatars. I was trying to understand how this had come together so effortlessly while I had been struggling to find my place here since I'd disembarked. Kelsey was policing the room, tucking an errant compact back into her purse, draping the garment bag over her arm. Her brisk, directed air reminded me of the way my mother left the house when I was young, calling out instructions to the babysitter as she put her earrings in. At the last minute she would put her hands on my shoulders and tell me to be good while she was gone, to be asleep when she got home. A goodnight kiss, a quick exit, perfume in her wake. I was remembering her tone and the rhythm of her movements, and then it was real. Kelsey kissed me on the cheek, and moved a lock of hair off my forehead with her finger.

"Back to work," she said. "I'll see you tomorrow, kids. Don't be late."

The St. Andrews Charity Fashion Show was held at the St. Andrews Bay Hotel, having outgrown the Student Union and the ballroom at the Old Course. Mike had been in rehearsals since 9:00 a.m., and Casey was staying upstairs, so I split a cab to the hotel with Clare. Time alone with him meant long tense silences since the night we'd spent with his father. I was texting Kelsey to wish her luck when the cab driver hit the brakes and Clare said:

"Holy shit."

Traffic on the thin shoulderless road was backed up for a quarter mile, and the St. Andrews Bay was unrecognizable as the stately, empty hotel that Mike and Casey had checked into. The circular drive was choked with cabs and chauffeured cars, and the entrance was blotted out by floodlights and flashbulbs, the light reflected and amplified by the wall of towering high-sheen screens covered in the logos of a champagne house, my mobile phone provider, and a Scottish bank. People had talked about the fashion show like it was a big deal, but nothing had prepared me for this. I let Clare pay, and we cut across the lawn. There was a red carpet and a maze of velvet ropes leading to the doors, which were barricaded by a mix of bouncer types in black tie and women clutching clipboards. We made our way between idling cars until a bouncer appeared in our path, halting us with a massive hand.

"Would you mind joining the queue?"

"We're on the designer's guest list," I said, following Kelsey's instructions. "We're VIP."

The bouncer looked me up and down, incredulous. He gave our names to a haughty and exasperated woman with a clipboard and an earpiece. After some dramatic flipping back and forth, she found our names and waved us in.

The crowd in the lobby was a mix of dressed-up academics, high-fashion Londoners, and corporate guests in business suits and black ties. There was a family checking in at the front desk, the two young children clinging to their mother's legs while she and her husband looked around in mild shock. I wondered how the hotel explained this to its guests, how anyone could explain this—a student fashion show where no one looked like a student. From across the room, I spotted Kelsey giving an on-camera interview while a group of older men in suits and ties stood silently at her side, their hands clasped, their eyes wandering to the crowd and back to Kelsey as she took another question from a local access news reporter. One of the men was the president of St. Andrews, and the others looked like executives from the corporate sponsors, all of them stiff and smiling. Kelsey's dress was simple and black, with sleeves that ended just below her elbows. She looked nervous and happy in a way I hadn't seen before, and she kept tucking a few strands of hair behind her left ear and letting her fingers slip down her neck while she talked. I tried to remember who I thought she was the first second I laid eyes on her in Kildare's, when she was sketching in her notebook, preparing for this.

Kelsey shook hands with the president and then motioned for

the cameraman to follow her across the lobby and backstage. I didn't see Casey until he was standing right in front of us, in a dark suit and slim tie he had borrowed from one of Kelsey's friends. We laughed at the room around us.

"Right?" Casey said. "It's a circus in here. Your girl got us great seats."

Clare and I followed him into the grand ballroom—a sea of white tables, white flowers, and enough champagne to drown the crowd. A black spot-lit runway split the room in two.

"Drinks," Casey said, pointing to a packed bar in the corner. While we waded through the crowd, I picked up a program and discovered that the event had raised more than £200,000 for cancer research the year before, and that the cost of our table was £4,000. I flipped to Kelsey's bio while Casey placed an order. Born in Bordentown, New Jersey; Wildwood Catholic High School; a Young Designer Award from the New Jersey Fashion Council. Her collection was titled "Day Two." Casey handed me a highball with a lime wedge, something with tonic, I didn't care what. We touched glasses. It was gin.

"To ending world hunger," he said.

Two men were already seated at the table Casey led us to. Kelsey had mentioned that a few suits would be joining us, employees from the Royal Bank of Scotland who got prime seats in exchange for their firm's donation. Clare and Casey introduced themselves while I watched Jules cross the room to a table where Prince William was sitting with the woman he would later marry. She stood up to kiss Jules, and recoiled in mock horror at the scratches and the swelling on the side of his face, the road rash Casey had inflicted. Jules said something that made her laugh, and then they all sat down. The whole thing was a joke to him.

Casey was talking to one of the bankers, explaining that

our friend from home was in the show. The only thing left in my glass by then was ice and lime. I excused myself and made my way to the bar, but the line was longer than before, and after half a minute of rattling the ice in my glass, I found the bathroom instead.

I waited in a locked stall for someone to open a faucet, and then took three quick bumps from Michael Savage's industrial-sized vial. The men at the sink were talking about football and how they hoped they'd see some tits like last year's. I leaned back against the white partition with my arms folded and my eyes closed, willing the coke to come up a little faster. The painted metal was cool against my shoulders, and I tried to concentrate on that, and not on the ache created by the distance between Kelsey and me. I wished that nothing had ever happened between us, that the memory of all my time with her could be packed into a box and taken off my hands. Here, you carry this, I can't hold it anymore. Clare sent a text asking me to come back to the table, which seemed odd because we had ten minutes until the show unless my watch was running slow. Back in the ballroom, I spotted Casey coming toward me, shaking his head. The lights flashed three times, and a booming voice asked people to find their seats.

"What's wrong?" I asked.

"You missed it," Casey said. "Clare was pouring champagne and one of those bankers made a crack about him taking the bottle and leaving the country."

"What?"

"They know who his dad is. Those little cards by everyone's seat? The school used his real name. I guess they put two and two together. Clare asked me if he should leave."

"That's crazy."

"Is it? It's pretty tense over there. I'm getting drinks. Go sit down. Clare needs company."

The look on Clare's face as I approached the table reminded me of a rabbit I saw as a kid, right after it was dropped into a terrarium with an eight-foot albino python that my mother's boyfriend owned. There were two empty seats between Clare and the two men who were ignoring him now, talking to a pair of women who had materialized behind their chairs. I sat down between them and Clare, leaving a seat for Casey as a buffer.

"Hey," I said. "Everything cool?"

Clare ignored me, so I turned my attention to our tablemates. The one next to Casey's empty chair was either drunk or sunburned on his nose, thick necked, with a razor-shaved haircut that didn't quite hide his receding hairline. I spotted suspenders under his pinstriped suit jacket as he reached for his drink. His friend was handsome, Indian, and hawkish, his face long and severe. His black hair was swept straight back, the tracks from the comb like grooves in a record. Both of them were men in the sense that I felt eleven years old in comparison, and I dropped my eyes to the table when they caught me staring, which they somehow did at the same time. It was easy to forget your place in the world at St. Andrews, to forget that we were all just kids.

The women behind the bankers' chairs were laughing and looking uncomfortably at each other, trying and failing not to look at Clare. Then I caught the words *criminal royalty* and saw that Suspenders had turned his back to us so that he could stab his thumb at his own chest to indicate Clare without Clare seeing. I wondered what was taking Casey so long as the lights went down, and the president of the university walked to the end of the runway, microphone in hand. He was proud, he said, of the creativity the students had demonstrated, and grateful for the generosity displayed by the sponsors and our hosts at the hotel. He talked about how humbling it was to be a part of this, which I understood. The music came up as he exited stage left—a spare track by a Swedish electronic music group with the patter of a steel drum behind the pulsing bass.

The opening collection was Kelsey's, and the look on the first model seemed a little plain at first. It was Damien, in slim tuxedo. His hair looked windswept or slept on, and he had a cigarette tucked behind one ear. He walked to the end of the runway and, after a gaping yawn, stripped off his jacket and tossed it to someone sitting at his feet. Then he pulled his bow tie loose and ripped his white shirt wide open, the buttons from the button strip flying into the crowd. When he was down to a white V-neck undershirt, he bent from the waist to retrieve the jacket, which he slung over his shoulder before he turned on his heel and walked away. The next model, a blond boy I had never seen before, wore no shirt, slim gray sweatpants, and a short tuxedo jacket with the sleeves pushed up to his elbows. I didn't get what she was doing until I saw the black rubber sandals on his feet, which stopped my breath. I understood what "Day Two" meant now. She was riffing on the clothes you wound up in after partying all night in a tux, the clothes Clare and I had worn on the morning that I met her. Casey slid into the seat beside me.

"Everything cool?" he mouthed.

I shook my head as Mike started down the runway. He was barefoot, with dark makeup around his eyes in artful imitation of dark circles, his black pants rolled up as if he were walking on the beach. The sleeves of his white tuxedo shirt had been torn off so that his tattoos gave the look some color. He had a bottle of a sponsor's champagne in his hand, and he knocked back a swig at the end of the runway. A pair of women came after him, one in a beautiful embroidered skirt and a Supremes T-shirt, the other in a gown that had been chopped to a jagged edge above her knees. It went on like that—beat-up formal wear mixed with cheap basics and party scraps. I was willing the coke to stop working now, trying hard to slow my thoughts and take this in, asking myself if Kelsey was talking to me, telling me that our first day together had been on her mind ever since.

"Wake up," Casey said, slapping my thigh under the table.

Something was happening, but whatever it was could wait. Mike came down the runway in what I knew would be the last look of her collection: a pair of dark jeans with a white T-shirt and black lace-ups. The runway stood empty after he disappeared, and I sat there craning my neck, waiting for her to emerge to applause.

"Mate, I asked you a question," Suspenders said to Clare. "Who bought your ticket? Because these seats weren't cheap."

"This girl I know did that collection," I said. "She got us these seats."

No one seemed to hear me.

"So this isn't someone else's hard-earned cash you're spending?" Suspenders said, ignoring me. "That's good. That's good to know."

The Indian man had a hand on his friend's arm, and was telling him to chill out, to save it.

"Let me ask you—" Suspenders started to say, slapping his friend's hand away, but Clare stood up from the table so abruptly that the man jerked back, his torso bouncing off his chair as Clare stalked through the crowd.

"Guilty conscience," he said, nervously. "Good riddance."

He rocked back in his seat, pretending to enjoy the show, ignoring all the eyes on him. I stood up and headed for the bathroom to touch up my high.

I was on my way back to the table when everything—the roaming spotlights, the models they were trained on, the tempo of the music—seemed to slow down all at once. It was something I'd experienced just before both car accidents I've been involved in: a slide into slow motion when a threat announces itself in your peripheral vision. The threat, in this case, was a bottle of lager about to be smashed over the head of Suspenders, who was still leaning back in his chair, looking entertained and comfortable. Clare hadn't left. He'd done a loop around the room or gone back to the bar or wandered out into the lobby and spotted a bottle on a windowsill—I couldn't say for sure. His nostrils were flared and he had his bottom lip between his teeth, which made him look as if he were in pain instead of ready to inflict it. I saw Suspenders recognize terror in the expression of the woman across from him, and spin around in his chair, which was the worst thing he could have done. The glass didn't shatter, but its first point of contact was the top of his eye socket, where it split the skin like a razor blade through rubber. Everyone but Casey ripped up from their seats, which seemed to bring the world back up to speed. The man had fallen back against the table, blood already coating half his face. Clare stumbled back as Suspenders stood up to charge him, but then Casey turned his body, dropped his head and tackled Suspenders at the waist, taking him to the floor without standing up.

I stood there, three tables away, frozen between fight and flight. Three models had stalled on the runway, and Mike, in his hurry to hit the floor from backstage, decked the nearest one from behind as the other two jumped down to get out of his way. I watched him take a flying leap off the edge of the runway and disappear from sight. His momentum made up my mind, and I threw myself at the perimeter formed by the banker's friends, grabbed two handfuls of someone's suit jacket and hurled him aside as hard as I could. I was just getting my balance back when someone caught my wrist, wrenched my hand behind my back, and took me to the floor. My face bounced against the sharp artificial fibers of the carpet, and I squirmed under the knee in my back, trying to see who this was, and why I had been singled out now that the fight had stalled and everyone was being held at bay and calmed down. I turned just far enough to recognize the driver who had taken Clare and me to visit Michael Savage, who was evidently not a driver. He was signaling to someone, and then a uniformed policeman took his place. I felt the cuffs go on.

Through the frosted windows of the interrogation room, the shadows of planes swept across the flecked linoleum floor tiles, vanishing like water stains, the roar of the engines deadened to a crackling static. It was a clear day at sunrise, judging from the glow behind the glass. Leuchars air base was just across the street. The room contained a table and a pair of chairs—the rickety, bowlegged furnishings of a high school cafeteria—and a poster that explained the rights of government employees under Scottish law. The smell of cheap vinegar was coming from the chilled patches of sweat in the armpits of my shirt. I rolled up my sleeves, trying to look ready for whatever came next. The officer leaning on the far wall shifted his weight from one foot to the other. I touched my tongue to the fresh cut on my bottom lip.

The two of us had been alone for over an hour without speaking a word. Just above the collar of the officer's blue uniform shirt was a wisp of tattoo—some gothic script, maybe, or a tendril of some flora or fauna—inked into his pale neck. We couldn't be that far apart in age.

"Hey," I said. "What happens now?"

He wouldn't meet my eyes.

"Really? Come on, man. No one's here. Can you please just tell me what the hell is going on?"

He gave no sign that he had heard me, but just then the door opened, and both our bodies jerked. Standing in the doorway was a woman with dyed red hair and green eyes. She looked like someone who worked in the cosmetics section of a drug store.

"They're ready," she said to the officer.

There were forty-two missed calls on my phone when the woman behind the station's booking desk handed it back to me along with my Rolex, which had stopped at 6:20 a.m., and some paperwork explaining when and where to face the charges against me. I called Casey's room while I waited for a cab, and was about to leave a message when I heard the call-waiting tone, and realized he was calling me.

"Where the fuck are you?" he asked.

"At the police station. I've been here all night."

"Did you hit a cop or something? How are you the only person who got nailed? Did you just get out?"

"Yeah, with a court date, and a possession charge. What happened to Clare?"

There was a pause. I felt him shifting gears.

"I think Clare's still in the hospital," Casey said. "I don't know for sure. That Indian guy knew how to fight. Smashed Clare's head into the table and got some hard shots in after that. Clare was still out when they took him away."

"How bad is it?"

"I just told you how bad it is. Clear shit coming out his nose. Awful. Plus assault charges whenever he comes to. Don't worry about him now, just get your ass to Kelsey's."

Damien's Land Rover was parked across the street from Kelsey's flat when I climbed out of the cab. Someone tapped a horn; the car was full of people. I crossed the street as Damien rolled down the window. Mike was riding shotgun in tuxedo pants and a hooded sweatshirt, the dark makeup he'd worn for the show still smudged around his eyes. Casey sat behind him, holding a bag of frozen corn over his eye.

"Did you hear anything about Clare?" I asked.

"Get in or get out of the way," Damien said.

I climbed into the backseat and got my first good look at Casey. A blood vessel had broken in his eye, and the blue of the iris was suspended in a sea of red, surrounded by swollen tissue that was already turning purple. A pair of Kelsey's oversized sunglasses was hanging from his collar. As we pulled away from the curb, I stared up at Kelsey's window. Her light was on. I watched for movement, shadows, anything, but there was only a cool glow from inside.

"Where are we going?" I asked.

"Back," Casey said. "We'll swing by your hall and help you pack. I'll get you a ticket. Time to go home."

"I have to be in court next week."

"Not in Jersey you don't," Mike said.

The week before my spring semester exams at Rutgers, I was sitting in a diner on the ground floor of a new hotel in Atlantic City. The building was a gutted and remodeled Howard Johnson's, and investors from around the state had poured money into the project, anticipating a revival of the historic, dilapidated beach town. A Philadelphia restaurateur was responsible for the restaurants and the diner was supposed to be a re-creation of the places where he'd spent late nights and early mornings in his twenties. He must have had good drugs back then, because his remembrance—waitresses whose short skirts matched the shiny plaid of the upholstered stools, a Kobe beef burger, a champagne cocktail list—had nothing to do with the chrome boxes along Route 18. It was a stylized vision of New Jersey that looked out on the real thing: the hourly motels and cash-for-gold shops that flanked Atlantic Avenue.

Casey sat across from me, the remnants of his eggs Benedict pushed to the center of our table, a section of the *New York Times* covering his face. He was in town for a hotel management conference that he'd asked to attend so he could pick up the last of his things on LBI and put his affairs in order. I had been thinking about Clare since we'd driven past the exit that lead to the causeway, remembering the first time I'd brought him down the shore, wondering if it was 85 degrees and sunny where he was too. I hadn't spoken to him since St. Andrews, but Mike heard from Mary that he had come through fine, and withdrawn from school to take time off, which was what he should have done in the first place. I went back to my waffles and when I looked up again, Casey was staring at me with the paper on his lap.

"What?" I said. "What's going on?"

Casey handed me the *Times* and pointed to the middle column. Michael Savage had been found dead in his hotel room in Qatar. I looked up at Casey, then back down at the page, trying to make out what was written there.

"No cause of death yet," Casey said, looking at me.

I stood up and walked outside, feeling like my insides had evaporated. A shitty Oldsmobile rolled past, the glare of the sunlight on the windshield blinding me for an instant. I tried three matches on a cigarette and then gave up.

"You OK?" Casey called to me, holding the door for an elderly couple.

I didn't answer.

"You wanna tell me what's going on?"

I was looking out over the boardwalk to the beach, which was full of adults in beach chairs, and kids streaking along the edge of the water with buckets and boogie boards. Three children were burying a man up to his neck in sand.

"They didn't pick me up for fighting at the fashion show," I said. "They picked me up because they figured I was holding, and they wanted something on me."

I told Casey about the second room I had been led to, the one populated by my arresting officer, the agent who had been masquerading as a limo driver, and Professor Watkins, who apparently had long-standing ties to British intelligence and who had clearly been woken up for this. The authorities had been all over Michael Savage while he was in Scotland, but he had disappeared just before they planned to pick him up. They wanted anything that I could get them: numbers from Clare's phone, e-mails from his laptop, any information I could dig up as to his father's whereabouts without arousing his suspicion. They had offered me a free ride at St. Andrews, a clean record in the States, an introduction at whatever financial services firm I saw myself at. They told me they were trying to protect Michael Savage because he seemed to think that he could handle the people who were after him. I remembered the cop with the ponytail in Lawrenceville, the one who told me I was helping Casey by giving him up. I thought: I've heard this before.

"They told me this might happen," I said. "I thought they just wanted me to rat him out."

"Good," Casey said.

"Good?"

"Good that you didn't help them. Fuck them. What were you gonna do, anyway? You're not exactly James Bond. God, they must have been desperate if they were coming to you for help. A kid who couldn't sell fucking weed in high school without getting busted? And honestly? Fuck Clare's dad. What was he thinking, messing with those people? If you don't see how that's gonna end, you're too stupid to be alive. That's natural selection."

"He's dead," I said, trying to understand where this hostility was coming from.

"That's what happens. That was his choice. Let's go back in and settle up."

It must have been his last two words, because until then all I wanted was to go back inside, finish our coffee, and kill the rest of the morning watching TV in the room and pretending that none of this had ever happened. Instead, I told Casey that I had given his name to the cops.

"What?" he said.

"I told the cops about you when I got arrested. I told them that I got my stuff from you. I gave them your name. It's my fault that your house got searched and that you had to move to Mexico."

"And you're telling me this why?"

"Because I just told you how I didn't sell Clare's dad out, but it wasn't always like that. I wanted you to know."

"I already knew."

"What do you mean you already knew?"

"It took me about five minutes after you left the Chegg, but I put two and two together. I didn't want to believe it, but it was a hard thing not to see. You looked more fucked up than me when Rob showed up that night."

"How did you not slit my throat?"

"Because I would have done the same thing. I should never have helped you get set up in the first place. I knew you couldn't hack it if things went wrong. But that's not even the point. Do you honestly think I got popped because you squealed to some cops in another county about an ounce of weed? Get your head out of your ass. That's like saying a plane crashed because you had your cell phone on. Who knows why they came down on me like that. Anyway, it doesn't matter. Look how it all worked out."

"What if it hadn't?"

"Who gives a fuck about what didn't happen? You're still here. I'm still here. Leave it alone. Don't ever bring it up again. You hear me?"

This was the moment I had prayed for, certain it would never come: to have Casey absolve me and tell me it was not my fault. He was saying that now, and I felt no different. It was clear to me that I would need to look somewhere besides the people I knew if I was going to figure out how to live the rest of my life.

"Our waitress thinks we dined and ditched," Casey said. "Let's go back inside, unless you want to explain this to the cops."

There was construction all over southbound U.S. 1 the next week and the drive from Rutgers down to Princeton took me twice as long as usual. I parked behind my mother's house and pitched my cigarette into the neighbor's yard. I was stopping by to pick up my surfboard and hit the beach for a few hours after a long morning in the library. A dean in the Rutgers English department was a regular at my mother's shop, and she had talked the school into letting me enroll halfway through the first week of January classes after I showed up at Newark airport unannounced. My mother was waiting on a long line of customers when I banged through the screen door.

"Hey," she called to me. "You back for good?"

"Just grabbing a board. I'll be back for dinner. You need anything?"

"No," she said, drying her hands. "I'm fine. I've got everything I need."

I drove down the shore, sticking to the back roads, obeying the various speed limits. A strong south wind was keeping people off the beach, and I found a parking spot along the boardwalk. The house on Howell and Ocean was for sale.

Back at the shop, I had gone to the fridge to make a sandwich for the road and there, between my Dean's List certificates from Lawrenceville and my acceptance letter from St. Andrews, was the article announcing that Clare's father had been found dead in his hotel room, held in place by a magnet from Conte's Pizzeria. My mother had put it there as a kind of memorial, not realizing that it belonged on our fridge alongside the records of my various accomplishments. I wondered if Kelsey was right about everyone having a fixed amount of luck and if I had used up mine in coming through this. I stripped down in the driver's seat and then sat in my car with the top half of my wetsuit bunched up around my waist, looking out over the boardwalk at the water. The ocean was a mess, a long field of crumbling slate-gray slabs. I was watching for a makeable wave, a clean line, a section that would hold up, however briefly, before crashing down. No one else was out.

On the beach, the wind kicked up a fine mist of sand that stung the tops of my bare feet. I walked as far into the shore break as I could, but then a set came through, and I started duck diving, pushing the nose of my board just under the rumbling walls of whitewater, kicking down, gasping on the other side from the cold and the force of the swell. I finally made it past the inside sandbars, and sat on my board, catching my breath. The current was sucking me south fast enough that I could track my movement against the clouds on the horizon. I turned my head and looked back at the beach to find a marker, to see where I was.

ACKNOWLEDGMENTS

To Julie Barer for keeping the faith and making all things possible. To Allison Lorentzen for her vision and commitment, and to everyone at Viking, especially Nicholas Bromley and Shannon Twomey. To Alexander Chee for everything, but especially for helping me believe that this was something I could do. To Matthew Sharpe for strong and crucial guidance. To Jim Nelson for making my mid-twenties awesome and for teaching me to ask hard questions about my work. To Mike and Greg Hokenson for decades of unwavering support and friendship. To Nancy Hokenson for giving me a place to write time and again. To Jim Salant, friend, editor, artistic conscience. To William Boggess for stepping up and stepping in. To Eric Sullivan and Noah Kistler for company at the kitchen table. To Greg Greenberg and Daniel del Valle for those early reads. To the teachers who mattered: Elan Leibner, Mark Schoeffel, Bill Williams, Jim Adams, Martha Gracey, Paul Watkins, Aaron Kunin. To the editors who gave me a shot: Tyler Cabot, Aimee Bell, Matt Tyrnauer, Heather Halberstadt. To Jessica Agnessens for reading the cards. To the Piltin family, especially my cousin Chris, for giving me a window on the shore. To Deborah Castel for being right about so many things. To Nonna for all the love and all the food. To Philip and Margaret Parish for keeping me honest. And to Herman and Rosemary, my parents, for all of it.